WEEKEND
ON
SULLIVAN'S
ISLAND

ASHLEY FARLEY

also by ashley farley

After the Storm

Scent of Magnolia

Virginia Vineyards

Love Child

Blind Love

Forbidden Love

Love and War

Palmetto Island

Muddy Bottom

Change of Tides

Lowcountry on My Mind

Sail Away

Hope Springs Series

Dream Big, Stella!

Show Me the Way

Mistletoe and Wedding Bells

Matters of the Heart

Road to New Beginnings

Stand Alone

On My Terms

Tangled in Ivy

Lies that Bind

one
cooper

Cooper spotted her in the crowd of art enthusiasts at his inaugural gallery opening. He monitored her as he spoke with his other guests. She moved from painting to painting, pausing for a moment in front of each one. As she studied the bald eagle composition, she twirled a strand of honey-colored hair around her index finger and gnawed on her lower lip, mannerisms Cooper knew all too well.

When she turned away from the painting, her eyes met his, and a smile crept across her bow lips. She had changed in the years since he'd last seen her. How long had it been? Three years. Maybe four. She was no longer the tomboyish teenager who had stolen his heart. She was now a sophisticated young woman.

Annie strode confidently toward him with shoulders back and head held high. But she greeted him with a playful slap on the shoulder, yet another reminiscent gesture.

"Cooper! I'm so impressed. Who knew you had such talent?"

"It came as a surprise to me as well," he said with a chuckle, a sound foreign to his ears. He'd been unhappy for so long. Was he finally coming out of his funk?

"How did you discover this talent?"

"Totally by chance. I walked past an art store during my lunch hour one day, and the display of supplies in the window inspired me to go inside. I decided to give it a try. I bought a canvas and a few tubes of paint, and here we are."

Her doe brown eyes widened. "Are you serious? You just went home and created your first masterpiece?"

Heat radiated up his neck. "Not exactly. My first attempt was a disaster. I took a couple of painting workshops at the fine arts museum to develop my techniques."

Annie looked around the room at the paintings, her gaze landing on the bald eagle. "The eagle is by far my favorite. The scenery looks like Moss Creek. Is that where you spotted the eagle?"

"Good eye." A faraway expression washed over Cooper's face as he remembered the experience. "It was one of the most magnificent things I've ever witnessed. He came outta nowhere, gliding over the lawn before careening back toward the marsh. I'm lucky I had my camera with me. I snapped dozens of photographs, which I used later when working on the painting."

"Have you seen him again since that day?" she asked, her eyes still on the painting.

"No, but I've been on the lookout for him."

A server approached with a tray of white wine in plastic cups, which they both refused. "Is this your catering gig?" Cooper asked.

She dipped her chin and glared at him from beneath furrowed brows. "Um . . . no. Tasty Provisions doesn't serve cheap wine and store-bought cubed cheese."

"My bad! Sean is the foodie in the family," he said about his twin brother, the restaurant owner. "Thanks for stopping by. Are you here alone?"

"Actually, I'm with my boyfriend." Annie glanced around the room. "He's here somewhere."

Cooper's heart sank at the mention of a boyfriend. "Is he an art collector?"

"He has a few impressive pieces, but I wouldn't call him a collector. No offense, but I don't think Tyler came for the art. He's very social. He doesn't like to miss a party. When he suggested we attend the opening, I didn't realize you were the artist. I'm impressed, Cooper. Your work is inspirational."

"Thank you, Annie. That really means a lot." Cooper's spirits lifted. Until now, he'd only shared his art with a few people, mostly family members who felt obligated to praise his talent.

Annie gave him a once-over. "I almost didn't recognize you with the long hair. The new look fits your artist persona."

"I'm trying to distinguish myself from my twin," he said, tucking a stray strand of auburn hair into his man bun.

"Well, I think it's very boho," she said, her appreciative tone contradicting the hint of distaste on her lips.

A guy with sandy wavy hair and a face too pretty to be handsome placed a possessive hand on Annie's back. "Come on, babe. Let's get outta here. This artist sucks."

Annie cast Cooper an apologetic look as her boyfriend led her into the crowd.

Wealth clung to the guy like his custom-made navy sport coat. Cooper knew the type well. Old Charleston money, home on the Battery, membership at the yacht club, multiple generations of ancestors buried in St. Philip's graveyard. What was Annie doing with someone like that?

Cooper turned in the opposite direction and came face to face with Brooke Horne. They had family in common—Brooke's little sister, Lizbet, was married to Cooper's cousin Jamie—but he didn't consider her a friend. She was a hot little firecracker, petite and feminine despite her boy-short, white-blonde hair. And off limits to him because she was gay.

Brooke offered her tiny hand. "Congratulations on your opening, Cooper. Your talent is outstanding. I love the sunrise composition. I've been to Moss Creek several times with Lizbet and Jamie. When I look at the painting, I envision myself sitting on the dock with a steaming mug of coffee in hand, watching those first pink rays of dawn break the horizon."

Her words touched Cooper deeply. Until now, his painting had been an outlet to satisfy a burning need to create. His day job as a web designer failed to offer such fulfillment. Perhaps he could make a living painting full time. He would become a hermit and live out his days in solitude at Moss Creek.

Brooke shook her head, returning both to the present. "I wish I could afford one of your paintings."

"Stick around. If none of them sell, I'll give you the fire-sale price."

Brooke's smile reached her dazzling blue eyes. "You have nothing to worry about. I've been eavesdropping on the crowd. Everyone loves your work. I predict every one of your paintings will sell."

"Are you always so optimistic?"

"Trust me, it's a curse." A faint blush creeped up her neck, letting him know he'd touched a sore spot. Was her cheerfulness a cover-up? But for what? She seemed so put-together.

Brooke stood on her tiptoes and kissed his cheek. "It was great seeing you, Cooper. Congrats again, and if you run into my sister, give her a hug for me," she said and wandered off toward the exit.

Cooper spent the next ninety minutes mingling with the crowd and answering their many questions about his work. To his surprise, after living reclusively these past months, he found he enjoyed talking to these strangers about his art.

The crowd had dwindled to only a few when Lia, the gallery owner, threw her arms around his neck from behind. "You're an overnight success, Cooper. I've spoken to a couple of critics. They love you. Their social media posts alone will make your career."

Excitement fluttered across his chest. "Seriously? Have you sold any paintings?"

"All but two." She held up two fingers with pale pink manicured nails.

"Did someone buy the bald eagle?"

"I currently have three people bidding on it. The eagle is your crowning glory." She took him by the hand. "Come on. My assistant is closing the gallery. You and I are going to celebrate." She dragged him outside into the sultry night air.

"Wait a minute, Lia." He stopped walking, wrenching his hand free. "Where are we going?"

"Bourbon N' Bubbles. A group of my friends are there." She teetered on her wedges, and Cooper wondered how much she'd had to drink.

"I can't tonight. But thanks anyway."

Lia placed her hands on her hips. "Don't be such a bore. When's the last time you had any fun?"

He knew exactly when his fun had ended. On a late September night nearly a year ago. Besides, he doubted her idea of fun was the same as his. "But I have to drive home to Prospect."

"Whatevs." She dismissed him with a wave of her hand. "You can crash on my couch."

Lia had made it known she was interested in him, and Cooper suspected she meant for him to sleep in her bed. But he wasn't ready for casual sex. Especially in his current state of brokenness. He needed a sweet Southern girl like Annie or Brooke. Lia may be Southern, but there didn't appear to be anything sweet about her.

"Sorry, Cooper, but I'm not taking no for an answer. As the Lowcountry's most promising up-and-coming artist, you now have a reputation to uphold." Flicking her dark hair over her shoulder, Lia fished her phone out of her purse. "I'll order an Uber."

Cooper let out a reluctant breath. She would not give up. He suspected Lia was the type who always got her way. "I'll drive. We can Uber home, if necessary," he said, although he had no intention of staying long at Bourbon N' Bubbles.

Lia babbled nonstop during the short drive, going on about all the prominent Charlestonians who'd attended the gallery opening. By the time they reached their destination on Upper King, his head had begun to throb. When they entered the upscale bar, the occupants cheered. Not for the Lowcountry's most promising up-and-coming artist, but for Lia. She was their queen, and as Cooper stood near the door watching the scene unfold, he was very much the peasant. He clearly didn't belong here. But where did he belong? His twin brother had a new girlfriend, and most of his childhood friends had moved to cities up north like Washington or New York. He no longer fit in anywhere. He was a loner, destined to live out his days painting pretty pictures.

When he could no longer see Lia in the crowd, he slipped out of the door. She would never even miss him.

two
annie

Annie knew the crowd was watching them as she and Tyler exited the art gallery. They weren't interested in her. They were curious about the eye candy, her boyfriend, Charleston's most eligible bachelor. Part of her hated the feeling of always being on show, while another part enjoyed the luxuries that dating a wealthy guy offered—boats and sports cars and dinners at upscale restaurants. Dating him was like being on vacation at a five-star resort. Unfortunately, all vacations eventually came to an end.

They waited for the light to change at the intersection of Broad and Meeting Streets. "Where to now?" Tyler asked. "I'm starving. Wanna get some dinner?"

Annie rolled her eyes. "You're always hungry."

He winked at her. "That's why I'm dating Charleston's premier caterer? I've got a hankering for your shrimp and grits. What say we go to my place? We can pick up some shrimp at Harris Teeter on the way."

"Let's go out instead. I've been cooking all day. Sorelle is nearby. If we wait a few minutes, the crowd will die down and we can get a table." Truth be told, they almost never had to wait for a table. Restaurant owners were always eager to serve Tyler. Social media posts featuring a member of the Gerry family were the best advertisement money could buy.

"I'm not in the mood for Italian. Now that I started thinking about your shrimp and grits, I'm craving them."

Tyler was used to getting his way. His mother lived to indulge him. Annie tried hard not to give in to his every whim.

"I'll make shrimp and grits for you tomorrow night. I have something I want to show you." The light turned green, and Annie motioned for him to follow her. "Come on! I promise it won't take long."

Tyler had to work hard to keep up with her. He was tall but his body was long and his leg short. "Seriously, Annie. I'm hungry. This better be important."

"It's important to me. I need your opinion on something. Then we'll eat." Annie pulled out her phone, and as they strolled toward their destination, she interpreted Sorelle's Italian menu for him. "Since you're craving shrimp, you should get the Shrimp Oreganata, which is scampi-style shrimp."

"I think I'll have the tuna, so I can work up an appetite for tomorrow night when you cook shrimp and grits for me."

"You're relentless," Annie said, dropping her phone in her bag.

"I am when I want something," he said, draping an arm around her shoulders.

Annie stopped in front of a gray single house with double-decker porches extending the length of one side. "Well? What do you think?"

Tyler seemed unimpressed. "I think it's a gray single house, like a million other gray single houses in Charleston. Who lives here?"

"Me. Maybe. Heidi owns the house. Her upstairs tenant just moved out. But I'm not sure I can afford the rent. Wait until you see it." Annie dangled the keys and darted up the stairs to the second floor.

He hurried up the stairs after her. "Why would you pay rent if your mom owns the place?"

"Because she has to pay the mortgage. We're not wealthy like your family, Tyler."

Unlocking the bolt, she swung open the door, and they stepped inside. The interior featured worn oak floors and walls painted in high-gloss white. The living room occupied the center of the apartment with an updated kitchen at one end and two bedrooms at the other. Annie circled the living room, pausing at the floor-to-ceiling windows to look out over the twinkling lights of downtown Charleston. "Isn't it fabulous?"

Tyler joined her at the window. "Pedestrian is the word that comes to mind. It's too white. Maybe if you painted the walls."

"White is fresh. White feels like a clean slate for a new beginning." Annie turned her back to the window and admired the space. Cooper's bald eagle painting would look fabulous over the mantel on the old Charleston brick fireplace. She checked her phone for messages. She was in a bidding war with two other people for the painting. Annie had an advantage over the other interested parties. Lia was Tyler's sister.

Tyler hugged her from behind. "So, babe . . . if you're looking to make a change, why don't you move in with me?"

She laughed. "Yeah, right. Why would I do that when we've only been dating for a few weeks?"

"We've been together for two months, actually."

She craned her neck to see his serious expression. "You're not joking?"

He spun her around into his arms. "My feelings for you are real, Annie. Two months is too soon to get engaged, but not to move in together."

Engaged? To be married? She often daydreamed about marrying Tyler. But she was nowhere near ready for such a major commitment. He was the first serious boyfriend she'd had since . . . since high school. "I don't know, Tyler. I'm not sure I'm ready to live together."

He fingered a lock of her hair. "Why not? You already spend most nights at my apartment."

Tyler never shied away from a challenge, and Annie had kept his attention by playing hard to get. Living with him would be a bad move. She suspected he'd quickly tire of her and move on to someone else.

Annie freed herself from his embrace and turned to face him. "I'm twenty-eight years old and still living with my mom. I need to be on my own for a while."

"That's ridiculous. You're an adult. It's not like you have a curfew or anything. Besides, Heidi is never there. She's basically living with Hugh."

"Still, it's her house and her furniture. I don't own so much as a coffee maker. I need my own space."

"But why now? Why wait until you're twenty-eight years old?" The lawyer in him was coming out. He was arguing for the sake of arguing.

Annie let out an exasperated breath. "Because Hugh is selling his house and moving in with Heidi so they can save money to buy waterfront property. And I work a lot. Our business took off so fast, I haven't had time to even think about looking for my own place until now."

"You don't work a lot, Annie. You work *all* the time." Tyler constantly complained about her long hours. Most evenings and weekends, she was busy catering cocktail parties and weddings.

"I'm a caterer, Tyler. It's the nature of our business." Hard work was all Annie had ever known. With a deadbeat for a father and an absent mother, from the time she was old enough, she'd had to work part-time jobs to help put food on the table.

Tyler took her in his arms again. "At least think about moving in with me before you commit to renting this place. We could have our own little love nest."

His converted warehouse studio apartment was not her idea of a love nest. The handsome decor was more suited for a bachelor. Tyler was an exercise fanatic, and his apartment had an underlying stench of sweat. If they decided to live together, she would insist they find something together. Not hers or his, but theirs.

"I don't need to think about it, Tyler," Annie snapped. "I'm not moving in with you. At least not now. We haven't been together long enough."

"Do you know how many girls I've dated who would kill for the chance to live with me?"

"I'm not most girls, Tyler."

"Suit yourself. It's your loss," he said, and shoved her away.

She stumbled backward, catching herself before she fell. "Hey! That was uncalled for."

He rushed over to her. "I'm sorry, Annie. I didn't mean to push you so hard. I'm upset and I got carried away. Why don't you feel for me the way I feel for you?"

Here we go, Annie thought. *Everything is always about Tyler.*

"You know I have feelings for you. I just don't like you very much when you're behaving like a jerk." She spun around and crossed the room to the door.

He followed on her heels to the street. "Can we get dinner now?" he asked, as though nothing had happened between them.

She looked past him into the house's quaint side yard. "I'm tired. I think I'll just head home."

"You do that," he said through clenched teeth and strode off, retracing their steps from earlier.

Annie shivered at the memory of him shoving her. She replayed the scene in slow motion. He'd seemed genuinely sorry, and she was partially to blame. She'd insulted him, and he'd overreacted.

As Annie headed off in the opposite direction, she thought

back to the first time they'd met. They're *meet-cute* was back in early June. She'd been on a spy mission for Heidi, tasting new menu items at 167 Raw, and he'd been grabbing a quick lunch. He'd sat down next to her at the bar and struck up a conversation.

"Those look good," he'd said, peering over at her platter of raw oysters. "Are they local?"

"From the Chesapeake Bay, actually. They are my favorites."

He'd reached over and grabbed an oyster shell off her platter and slurped down the oyster. "Yum! They are good."

She'd been appalled at first, but then charmed by his naughty boy grin, she'd burst into laughter. By the time they'd finished lunch, he'd asked her out on a date.

Guys like Tyler weren't attracted to girls like Annie. She catered to them. She didn't date them. This was her one and only chance to get the lifestyle she'd always dreamed of, and she had no intention of blowing it.

Annie arrived home to find her mom and boyfriend, Hugh, on the swing on the upstairs porch. They made a striking couple for two people in their late fifties. They were both fit and attractive and fun to be around. She would miss hanging out with them when she moved.

Annie had been a troubled sixteen-year-old when Heidi reentered her life. She'd been furious to learn her mom had spent most of Annie's life catering to the stars in Hollywood while Annie and her poor fisher father had been struggling to make ends meet. But Heidi had endeared herself to Annie by offering the motherly advice she'd needed. As a result, Annie had given her a second chance. Shortly thereafter, Heidi had signed over a portion of her catering business, Tasty Provisions, to Annie. They'd been working together ever since.

"How was the gallery opening?" Heidi asked. "Did you see Cooper?"

Annie pulled up a chair and plopped down. "How'd you know he was the featured artist?"

"His mama told me," Heidi said with a sheepish grin.

"Well, you could've told *me*. You knew I was going to that opening. Why did you keep that tidbit from me?"

Heidi studied her pink fingernails. "Must have slipped my mind. Did you speak to him?"

Her mom was the hardest working woman Annie had ever met. Nothing ever slipped Heidi's mind. "Briefly. He's very talented. The gallery was mobbed. I made an offer on one of his paintings. I'm waiting to find out if I got it."

Hugh smiled. "Good for you! We have a budding art collector in the family."

"That's a stretch. But his paintings are hard to resist. You would appreciate his work, Hugh, as much as you love wildlife. The painting I'm bidding on is of a bald eagle. It's so realistic I want to reach out and touch the majestic bird."

"I'm intrigued," Hugh said. "I'll check out his work."

"Did you look at the apartment?" Heidi asked.

"I did." Annie fished the keys out of her pocket and tossed them to her mom. "I'll take it. Do you need a security deposit?"

Heidi threw the keys back. "You keep them. And the first month's rent will do just fine. Unless you get a pet, and then I'll need a deposit."

"A pet is the last thing I need. I don't even have a bed. Or a couch. Heck, I don't even own a lamp." Feeling overwhelmed, Annie propped her arm on the chair and rested her head in her hand. "Where does one go to buy furniture?"

"Any number of places," Heidi said. "I would start with Jackie. She has a warehouse full of cast-off furniture."

Annie groaned at the mention of Cooper's mom. "I'll pass."

"You need to let go of the past, Annie. What happened was years ago. Ancient history. Not only is Jackie my friend, but she's also one of our most valuable clients. You can't avoid her forever."

Annie wasn't sure she would ever forgive Jackie for the way

she'd treated her when she and Cooper had dated. "Why not? I've avoided her this long."

"Your mom is right about Jackie," Hugh chimed in. "I've worked with her on several projects over the years. She has a wonderful sense of humor and impeccable taste. I see where Cooper gets his creative talent."

Annie sat back in her chair. "So, she's a rock star. That doesn't mean she likes me."

"She asks about you all the time," Heidi said. "If you put your feelings aside, you and Jackie might become friends. Who knows? Maybe you and Cooper will get back together."

Annie rolled her eyes. "Stop already! You know I'm with Tyler now."

"And why is that? Because you're in love with him? Or because you want his money?"

"Honey!" Hugh said in a warning tone. "That's uncalled for."

Annie laughed. "I'm used to it. She says stuff like that all the time. She's convinced I belong with Cooper, even though we haven't seen each other in years." Her phone pinged with an incoming text, and she shot up out of her chair when she read it. "I won the bidding war. The bald eagle painting is mine. I bought my first artwork."

Heidi smiled. "Congratulations, sweetheart."

Annie was suddenly eager to move into her new apartment and hang her first painting over the mantel. "Maybe I *will* call Jackie. Do you think she has a bed in her warehouse?"

Heidi nodded, her messy bleached-blonde bun dancing on top of her head. "I'm sure she does. She has furniture and accessories she's bought *from* clients and things she's ordered *for* clients that didn't work."

"Then I guess I have nothing to lose." She said goodnight and went inside to the kitchen. She made herself a ham sandwich, brewed a cup of Tasty Provision's specially blended lavender tea, and took her dinner to her bedroom.

After eating her sandwich, she pulled out her laptop and created a Pinterest board with photographs of ideas for her apartment. She wasn't sure which she was more excited about, her apartment or the painting. She'd felt a special connection to the artwork when she'd studied it at the gallery. The same special connection she'd once experienced with the artist.

three
brooke

B rooke stood in front of the art gallery, debating whether to go straight home or take the long way. There was nothing waiting for her at home but family heirlooms and horrible memories. She headed on foot toward East Bay Street. She would walk down to the seawall and then work her way back over to Tradd Street.

Brooke loved her advertising job. Her clients were boutique hotels, trendy restaurants, and upscale retail establishments. But nothing else in her life was going her way. She had no new love interests, and after breaking up with her partner at the beginning of the summer, she wasn't looking for any. Her home, which she had neither the energy nor the money to maintain, had been in her family for generations. She absently rubbed her stomach. There was this one thing . . . But it was such a long shot, she refused to get her hopes up. She thought about what Cooper had said. *Are you always this optimistic?* Lately, her optimistic tank had been running on empty.

Brooke removed her phone from her purse and typed out a brief text to her sister, checking to see how her day went. She was reading Lizbet's response, not paying attention to where she was walking, when she stepped out in front of an oncoming rickshaw. The driver of the three-wheeled bicycle swerved to miss her as someone grabbed her around the waist from behind, pulling her out of harm's way.

"Hey! Watch where you're going!" screamed the driver of the bike buggy.

"I'm sorry!" Brooke cried. "I didn't see you coming."

"Put down the phone, you crazy bitch," the driver yelled over his shoulder as he pedaled his passengers up East Bay.

Brooke looked up at her rescuer, the man who was still holding her in his muscular arms. Her breath hitched, and his name was soft on her lips. "Grady?"

He loosened his grip on her. "Brooke? Wow! Look at you. You're all grown up."

"I was thinking the same about you. I almost didn't recognize you." Grady had shed his boyish good looks and grown into a man with toned muscles, chiseled facial features, and a scruffy beard. Soft rays from the setting sun cast a glow on his sexy golden eyes. If she were into men, this guy would be in trouble.

Grady guided her back to the safety of the sidewalk. "You almost got yourself killed just now. Must have been an important text you were reading. Was it from your boyfriend?"

Brooke glanced down at the phone, still gripped in her hand. "No, my sister."

"Right. And how is Lizbet?" he asked, in that deep honeyed voice she'd once known so well.

"She's great, married and living in Prospect. I'll tell her you asked about her."

Brooke's eyes filled with tears as the enormity of the near miss hit her. If anything had happened to the egg, Lizbet would never forgive her. Brooke would never forgive herself if she let her sister down.

Grady noticed her tears and handed her a blue checkered handkerchief. "Here. This might help."

"Thanks," she said, blotting her eyes. Of all the guys she knew, Grady would be the one to carry a handkerchief. He'd always had an old-school way about him that reminded her of her father. "Do you encounter crying women often?"

"You're the first today," he said with a chuckle. "To be honest, I can't stand the humidity. I'm in and out of air-conditioning all day, and my sunglasses are constantly fogging up." He grinned, revealing sparkling white teeth. "But don't worry. That one is clean."

Brooke's shoulders heaved with the onslaught of more tears. "I'm so sorry," she sobbed into the handkerchief. "I don't know what's wrong with me."

He pulled her in for a half hug. "You almost got run over. Naturally, you're shaken up. I'll walk you home. Do you live nearby?"

"I'm living at home, on Tradd Street," she said with a hiccup. "I don't want to be a burden."

"Not a burden at all. I'm staying with my parents. But I have nothing else going on tonight." His parents' stately home was on South Battery, a block away from where they stood.

She pulled the handkerchief away from her face. "Are you sure?"

"Positive. It'll give us a chance to catch up," he said, extending an elbow for her.

As they strolled through the downtown streets, the years slipped away, and they were back in high school, walking home from school or sports practice. Their senior class had voted Brooke and Grady the Cutest Couple that Never Was. Despite being joined at the hip, nothing romantic ever transpired between them. Not even an innocent kiss. They'd been in love with the same girl, the class heartbreaker, Annabelle Butler, a beautiful blonde with a perfect figure and an outgoing personality.

Brooke had composed herself by the time they reached her front porch.

Grady shoved his hands into his pockets. "My mom has kept me up to date on your family. I'm sorry about Lula and Phillip. I can't imagine losing both my parents, especially within a couple of years of each other."

Brooke nodded. "These past few years have been difficult. Thank goodness I have Lizbet."

He shifted his weight as though hesitant to leave. "Well . . . I . . ."

"Can I offer you a drink? It's the least I can do after I've caused you so much trouble."

"Sure! A beer would be great if you have one."

She fumbled in her bag for her keys and unlocked the door. "Wanna come inside?"

"I'll wait out here." He gestured at the swing. "In our spot."

Brooke smiled at the memory. They'd shared so many secrets on that swing, all their hopes and dreams for the future.

In the kitchen, she retrieved a craft beer and lime Perrier from the refrigerator and returned to the porch, joining him on the swing. She unscrewed the Perrier cap and sipped the sparkling water. She would much prefer a glass of wine, especially after her near miss with the rickshaw. But the sacrifice was a small price to pay compared to the enormity of the gift she would hopefully give her sister. She would turn thirty in September. The time had come for Brooke to step out of her party-girl shoes and grow up.

She kicked off her sneakers and tucked her legs beneath her. "So . . . last I heard, you were living in Atlanta. Are you in town for an event? Or just visiting your folks?"

"I actually live in Charleston now. I moved back a few months ago. I tired of the crime in Atlanta." Grady's lips turned downward as his expression turned serious. "I've thought about you a lot over the years. I hated we lost touch when we went away to college."

She settled back in the corner of the swing. "That's my fault. When I went to school in California to start a new life, I cut ties with all my old friends. Some of which I regret. Others, not so much."

"I understood you needed space to explore your sexuality. But it shocked me when you boycotted the holidays," Grady said, taking a swig of beer and smacking his lips.

"I came out of the closet my freshman year, but I couldn't bring myself to tell my bigoted mother about it. I felt like a fraud every time I spoke to her on the phone. I certainly didn't have the courage to face her in person."

Grady's brow pinched as he considered this. "Lula was old-fashioned, but I never thought of her as a bigot. I assume you eventually told her you're gay?"

"Yep. She nearly lost her mind when I brought Sawyer home to meet her. But she eventually came around and ended up loving her."

Grady had been the first person Brooke had ever confided in about being gay. She'd been so confused, and he'd been patient and nonjudgmental. They'd been each other's dates to all the important events—proms and homecoming dances. "I wonder whatever happened to Annabelle Butler."

Grady laughed out loud. "She got married, had three kids, and gained fifty pounds."

Brooke's mouth dropped open. "No way! How do you know this?"

"She lives in Atlanta. I used to see her all the time when I lived there. She married a great guy."

"Good for Annabelle. I'm glad she got her happily ever after." Brooke wondered why the kids voted the Most Popular and Best Looking in high school always got their happily ever afters.

Grady rested an arm on the back of the swing. "We spent a lot of time on this porch back in the day. We were sitting on this swing, just like we are now, when we first confessed our love for Annabelle."

Brooke's face warmed. "I remember."

"Do you live here alone?"

"Now I do. Lizbet was staying here during the winter months, while she was working out some issues in her marriage, and my partner moved out at the beginning of the summer."

His eyes narrowed. "I'm sorry. Was it a nasty breakup?"

"You could say that. Our relationship had become toxic. Breakups are never easy. Especially if you'd been together for a long time."

"Is she still in Charleston?"

"No, she moved to Boston." While Brooke missed Sawyer's presence, she didn't miss her overbearing personality. She nudged Grady's arm. "What about you? Are you still single?"

"I am. I've had my share of girlfriends over the years, but . . ."

"But what? None of them measured up to Annabelle?"

Grady chuckled. "Nah, I took her on a date once in college. Turns out, we had zero chemistry."

Brooke's blue eyes widened. "No! After all that time you spent crushing her?"

"Right?" His smile faded, and he set his golden eyes on her. "Truth is, I never found a girl who felt right for me."

Brooke squirmed beneath his intense gaze. As teenagers, she'd always been able to read his thoughts, but she had no idea what was on this man's mind now. In some ways, he was the same old Grady. In others, he was a total stranger.

When the silence grew uncomfortable, she said, "I'm in advertising. What do you do?"

"Real estate." He gestured at the house next door. "I work for your old neighbor, Midge, at her firm."

Brooke brightened. "How is Midge? I bet she's fun to work with."

"She's doing well. But she's demanding. She runs a tight ship. Have you given any thought to selling this place? An old home like this must require a lot of upkeep."

"I've thought about it. But this house has been in my family for generations. I feel obligated to hold on to it."

"That obligation comes at a high price of maintenance," he said, draining the last of his beer.

"No kidding. The kitchen and baths need renovating, but I can barely afford the taxes on my salary."

"You should downsize to something more fitting your spunky little self," he said with mischief in his eyes.

"I'll think about it," she said with a sad smile. When was the last time she felt spunky?

Grady stood to go. "I've enjoyed catching up. Let's grab lunch soon." He fiddled with his phone. "I have your old number. Is it still the same?"

"It is. How about yours?" she asked, checking her phone to make sure she still had his number.

"Yep." He bent over and kissed the top of her head. "Good night, Brooke. Now that we've reconnected, don't you dare disappear on me again."

"Don't worry. I'm not going anywhere. And thanks again for saving my life." Her smile faded as he walked down the short sidewalk. She was usually so careful when she crossed the city streets.

Brooke stared down at the chipped pink polish on her fingernails. She'd let her nails go since Sawyer left. One Saturday a month, they'd treated themselves to manis and pedis. What was the point of indulging herself when there was no special someone to impress?

She looked up from her nails to the house, admiring its cheerful yellow siding and green front door. The housing market was hot right now. Someone would snatch up this charming home in an instant. But selling would mean severing the remaining ties to her mother. She worked hard to keep everything as it was before Lula died. She hadn't dared change a thing for fear of erasing her mama's memory. Traces of Lula were in every room. In the kitchen, which had served as the hub of activity for their family life. But mostly in the living room where Lula's portrait hung above an antique French settee.

Brooke collected their empty bottles and took them inside to the recycling bin in the kitchen. She was on her way up the stairs when the sight of her mother's portrait drew her back down to the living room. A beautiful young Lula, dressed in her white debutant gown, stared out at her.

"Tell me what I should do, Mama. I'm stuck in a rut, and I don't know how to get out of it. I need to make a change, but I don't know what change. I've never felt this scared or alone before. If only I had an ounce of your strength. Give me a sign, Mama. Tell me what to do."

Brooke turned her back on her mama and continued up the stairs to her bedroom.

She changed into her nightgown and crossed the hall to her bathroom, where she brushed her teeth and washed her face. Returning to her bedroom, she stubbed her toe on one of her pink ten-pound dumbbells in the doorway. *Ouch! How did that get there?* She'd worked out with her dumbbells yesterday, but she was certain she'd put them away. She definitely hadn't left one in the middle of the doorway. Could this be the sign of strength she'd asked for from her mother? *Come on, Brooke. You don't believe in ghosts.* But what other explanation was there? The dumbbell had not been on the floor when she went into her bedroom to change into her gown or when she'd exited her bedroom for the bathroom.

Brooke returned the dumbbell to the closet, setting it down beside its mate, and crawled into bed. She turned out the lamp on the nightstand and stared into the darkness. Hypothetically speaking, if she *did* actually believe in ghosts, what was her mother trying to tell her? That she needed to get stronger? Or that she was already strong enough to get out of the rut? Assuming she was ready to start a new life, where would she even begin?

four
cooper

C ooper tumbled out of bed when his alarm sounded a few minutes before daybreak on Friday morning. Without wasting valuable time to dress, he attached his superzoom lens to his camera, inserted a memory card, and left the cottage, walking across the gravel driveway to the main house. He let himself into the game room and tiptoed, so as not to wake his brother, up the stairs to the main floor of the house. Through french doors, he exited onto the veranda and stood near the railing, blinking several times as his eyes adjusted to the dim early morning light.

His heart skipped a beat when he spotted the bald eagle perched on a dock piling fifty yards away, staring back at him but not moving as though unafraid of the human who had invaded his silent natural habitat.

Cooper slowly raised the camera and manually focused the lens. He pressed and held down the shutter button while the camera recorded a continuous stream of images of the eagle spreading its magnificent wings and swooping away over the marsh into the pink rays of dawn.

Waving the camera in the air, he let out a loud whoop. He'd been waiting months for the eagle to return. He didn't bother checking the images on the camera's LCD display. He knew they were good.

Cooper stretched out on the chaise lounge with the heavy camera resting on his gut. He thought about Annie as he watched the sun rise. Their encounter at the gallery opening last night had set him on edge. It had taken him years to get over Annie. Was it possible he still had feelings for her? She was with someone else now anyway—the douche in the blue sport coat with the pretty face and salon styled hair who thought Cooper's art sucked.

Cooper warned himself not to trust his emotions. He'd been in therapy for months. Big Moses, the family shrink, assured him he was ready to resume his social life and encouraged him to try dating. But the thought of falling for someone again, the risk of losing another person he cared about, terrified him.

What Cooper needed was a rebound girlfriend, a distraction to take his mind off Maggie's death. He hadn't been in love with Maggie. They hadn't been dating long enough. But he'd had strong feelings for her that might have eventually led to love.

Cooper returned to the guest cottage, stopping in his kitchen for a cup of coffee before continuing upstairs to his office. He sipped coffee and drummed his fingers on the desk while he waited for the images to upload to his desktop computer. He could hardly believe his eyes as he scrolled through them. The images of the eagle with its glorious wingspan flying off into the rising sun were phenomenal.

Cooper settled into his chair and focused his attention on his latest web design project. He was still at work, four hours and three coffees later, when he heard the crunch of gravel in the driveway. He assumed his brother was leaving for work, but when he checked the time on his computer, it shocked him to see it was nearly eleven o'clock. Sean would have left hours ago.

The sound of a car door slamming followed by a loud knocking drove him from his desk to the window. Across the driveway, Lia was standing in the carport, at the back door of the main house, looking around as though unsure where to go. Her dark hair was pulled back in a high ponytail, and she wore white shorts and a yellow cotton shirt with her bikini straps tied around her neck.

Cooper dashed down the stairs and out into the driveway. "Lia! What're you doing here?"

Lia's face lit up. "There you are." She closed the distance between them. "I was on my way to Folly Beach for the day, and since I was so close, I decided to give you the good news in person. And I'm glad I did. It gives me the opportunity to see your sanctuary. This place is impressive." She spread her arms wide at the two-story lowcountry-style house and the moss-draped live oaks dotting the expansive lawn. "I see why you call it Moss Creek. Who owns this estate?"

"I grew up here. This is my family's home. But my parents just deeded the property over to my brother and me. They have busy lives in Charleston and don't have time to handle the upkeep."

She pointed past him at the guest cottage. "Who lives there?"

Cooper patted his chest. "Me."

She threw a thumb over her shoulder. "Then who lives in the big house?"

"My twin brother, Sean."

Lia slid her sunglasses down her nose. "I hate to tell you, Cooper, but you got the short end of the stick."

He laughed. "I volunteered to live over here. It's a long story."

"Ooh! Do tell."

Cooper chuckled. "It's not the juicy drama you're hoping for. I was living with my brother in the main house until a few months ago. Sean, who owns a restaurant, invited his chef and her four-year-old son to live here. The chef was having money and child-care problems. The kid was a handful, and I needed a quiet place to work, so I moved into the guesthouse."

"Do the chef and her son still live here?"

"Nope. She no longer works for Sean. Turns out she had more

than financial problems. But by the time she moved out, I was already settled in the guest cottage. To be honest, I like the smaller space. It's cozy."

Lia pushed her sunglasses back into place. "Cozy is overrated, Cooper. You should restake your claim on the big house."

Cooper shrugged off his irritation. "You mentioned you had good news?"

"Right. Guess what? All your paintings have officially sold. The bald eagle went for an astronomical amount."

Cooper's eyes bugged out when she told him how much the winner paid for the painting. "That's incredible. Speaking of the bald eagle, she paid me a visit this morning."

Lia shielded her eyes as she stared up at the sky, as though expecting to see the eagle. "How do you know it's a she?"

"I don't, for sure. But the bird is massive. Male eagles are about two-thirds the size of females."

She looked from the sky to him. "Interesting. I didn't know that."

"Fortunately, I had my camera with me. I took a bunch of photographs. I've uploaded them to my computer. Wanna see them?"

"Sure!" She nodded her head, her ponytail bobbing up and down.

They walked toward the guesthouse. "Are you playing hooky from work today?" Cooper asked.

"Maybe. But I deserve it! I worked extra hard getting ready for your exhibit. Besides, it's Friday."

He opened the cottage door for her, and she waltzed right in, circling the small downstairs as she inspected the decor. Sniffing, she turned up her pert nose. "It smells musty in here." She stared down at the green shag carpet. "Must be the carpet. I bet there's mold growing in there. Avocado green dates this carpet back to the 1970s."

He laughed. "Sounds about right."

"And your mother calls herself an interior designer. Shame on her." Cooper's mother, Jackie, who was a decorator for Lia's mother, had introduced Cooper to Lia.

"We've rarely used the cottage. There's been no need for her to redecorate it."

Lia continued to the kitchen. "What's that?" she asked, pointing to a wire dog crate.

"What does it look like? A dog crate. I have a red lab puppy. She's away at training. I take it you don't like dogs."

The mention of training brought relief to Lia's face. "I'm fine with them as long as they sit and stay and don't get dog hair on my clothes."

"Then you don't like dogs. Otherwise, you wouldn't mind the hair." He motioned her to the stairs. "My office is on the second floor."

Following her up the stairs, he admired her fine bottom and long, tanned legs. She had a hot body. Maybe she was a dating prospect after all.

When they reached his office, she threw open the french doors and stepped out onto the balcony. "You have a marvelous view from up here, and I agree the cottage is cozy. Give it a mini face-lift and it would be way more charming."

"I don't have time for home improvement projects." He sat down at his desk. "Do you wanna see these pics or not?"

"Of course." Lia came to stand behind him, peering over his shoulder as he scrolled through the best of the images. "Wow, Cooper! The photographs themselves are art."

"Thanks. But I don't aspire to be a photographer. I'll pick one or two and use them as inspiration for paintings."

"Great idea! We can offer them to the two losing bidders from last night."

Cooper pushed back from the desk and stood to face Lia. She was near enough for him to smell her floral perfume.

Lia inched closer to him. "I should go," she said, but made no move to leave.

Cooper had a sudden urge to kiss her pouty lips. Their personalities were too different for them to make a good match. But she might be a suitable candidate for his rebound relationship. Bottom line, he saw no harm in getting to know her better. And no time like the present. While he was behind on his web design work, he wasn't in the mood to sit at a computer today. And he needed more time to contemplate the bald eagle composition before starting to paint.

"Why don't you stay? We could go out on the boat. Maybe ride over to the ocean and then grab some lunch at my brother's restaurant on the way back."

"That sounds nice. Much better than sitting on the beach alone all day," Lia said without hesitation, as though she'd been hoping for an invitation all along.

"Perfect! Give me a minute to change, and I'll meet you downstairs."

Retreating to his bedroom, Cooper slipped on a pair of board shorts, sprayed on sunscreen, and tied his hair back out of his face.

Lia looped her arm through his on the way out to the dock. "What happened to you last night? You bailed on me. You could've at least told me you were leaving Bourbon N Bubbles."

"I lost you in the crowd. You didn't even notice I was gone, did you?"

She rested her head on his shoulder. "I did when it was time to go home."

Lia knew her way around a boat like most Lowcountry girls who grew up on the water. She helped him untie from the dock, and on the way out to the mouth of the ocean, she perched next to him on the leaning post, talking nonstop about her wealthy friends and their shenanigans. Cooper enjoyed the company, if not the conversation. She was too snarky and judgmental for his liking. But even if she wasn't his future wife, she was a step in the right direction. Moses would be proud.

When they stopped in at The Lighthouse for lunch, his brother gave him a thumbs-up of approval. After the difficult past few months, Sean would approve of Cooper dating a female Shrek.

When they returned home to Moss Creek, Lia sunbathed in a lounge chair on the dock while Cooper fished for flounder. The tide was too high to catch anything, but he enjoyed the warm sun on his face and their companionable silence. Cooper was relieved to see she was capable of going long stretches of time without talking.

When he walked her to her car late afternoon, Lia asked if he had any other paintings she could hang in the gallery until he finished the bald eagle.

"You might be interested in some of my earlier work. I'll show you what I have, and you can decide if it's worthy of your gallery." He led her to the garage where he'd stored a dozen more paintings.

Lia flipped through the unframed canvases. "Some of these are quite good. If you don't mind, I'll take a few with me."

"Mind? I'm flattered you like them," he said and then helped her choose six paintings and load them into her SUV.

She slammed the rear door closed and turned toward him. Pinching his chin, she pressed her luscious lips against his.

Cooper's body reacted to the kiss, startling him, and he pushed her away.

Lia ran her thumb across his lower lip, rubbing off her lipstick. "Don't worry, Cooper. You're safe with me. I don't do relationships."

He shook his head, puzzled by her honesty. "Why not?"

"I enjoy my freedom too much. I made a vow to never marry. Having a husband and children doesn't fit into my dream of becoming the East Coast's most distinguished art broker."

"But aren't you worried about growing old alone?"

"I won't be alone. I'll have a string of kept men. When I grow tired of one, I'll replace him with someone new."

Cooper laughed out loud. "You're something else, Lia Gerry. I never know what'll come out of your mouth next."

"Good! I like to keep my guys on their toes." She tapped his cheek. "Bye now, Cooper Hart. Thanks for the fun day. Let me know if you're in Charleston, and we can grab a drink."

Cooper shook his head. "I'm afraid of where a drink with you might end."

Lia leaned in close and whispered in his ear, "I know where the drink will end. In my bed with no strings attached. Consider yourself warned."

"Duly noted," Cooper said with a smile as he opened her car door for her.

She climbed in, started the engine, and sped off down the tree-lined driveway, leaving a stunned Cooper staring at her tail-lights. He suspected Lia was too much of a handful for him, even for a casual fling.

After storing his fishing gear in the utility shed, Cooper returned to his cottage. He chuckled to himself at the sight of the green shag carpet. The decor was feminine and outdated. Since he planned to stay at Moss Creek for the foreseeable future, he might as well fix up the cottage to his taste.

Grabbing a hammer out of the junk drawer, he peeled back the carpet from one corner of the room to find beautifully stained oak floors underneath. He would refinish the floors, paint the walls, and replace some of the older furniture.

He pulled out his phone and clicked on his mom's number. Jackie answered on the first ring.

"Cooper! You must have telepathy. I was going to call you later. I'm sorry I didn't get a chance to speak to you at the opening last night. Everyone was raving about your work. You're a tremendous success. As I knew you would be."

"Thanks, Mom. I owe you one for introducing me to Lia."

"Lia is very good at her job, but she's a barracuda in designer clothes. You do not want to get romantically involved with her."

Cooper could hardly believe his ears. His mother was a mind reader. "So the reason I'm calling . . . I'm thinking of giving the cottage a mini face-lift, and I was wondering if you have any leftover living room furniture."

"Do I ever! A whole warehouse full. Your father and I are visiting friends in Beaufort this weekend. Can you come to Charleston on Monday?"

Cooper thought about his web design work piling up. If he worked overtime this weekend, he could afford to take the day off on Monday. "I can make that work. What time?"

"Around eleven. We can grab a quick lunch afterward."

He hesitated. He knew why his mother wanted to have lunch. She'd been hounding him for details about what had happened in Richmond. Moses assured him that talking about it was part of the healing process. He would have to tell her, eventually. "Lunch sounds good," he said finally. "Have a good weekend and tell Dad hello."

Cooper stuffed his phone back in his pocket and set about moving the furniture and pulling up the carpet. Now that he'd committed to the renovation, he was eager to get started.

five
annie

Annie was carrying an armload of hanging clothes to her car early on Saturday morning when her mom emerged from her bedroom.

"What're you doing?" Heidi asked, tying the sash of her silky pink bathrobe.

"What does it look like? I'm moving. You're finally getting rid of me," Annie said in a tone more sarcastic than she'd intended.

"Oh, honey. You don't have to move out. Just because I suggested you rent the apartment, doesn't mean you're obligated to do so. We're all adults. We can live together in this house just fine." Heidi gestured toward the bedroom. Through the cracked door, Annie saw the soft mound under the bedcovers that was Hugh's body.

"So you're okay with Tyler and me shacking up under your roof?"

"Not at all. Let me get the door for you," Heidi teased, and they both burst into laughter.

Annie dropped the bundle of clothes on the dining table and wrapped her arms around Heidi. "I will miss you though."

Heidi's lips turned downward into a pout. "I will miss you too. But we'll see each other every day at work. At least for now."

Annie drew away from her. "What does that mean?"

"Hugh is determined for us to retire to one of the beaches to live out our days in the surf and sand. And the grueling hours will be a challenge when you start your family. At some point, we may decide to sell the business."

Annie gawked at her. She wasn't sure where her mother was going with this conversation. "But you and I already have our plan. When you retire, I'm going to run Tasty Provisions. No way will I ever sell the company we worked so hard to build."

"Then you'd better find yourself a supportive husband," Heidi said, brushing a strand of hair out of Annie's face.

Annie smacked her hand away. "Why would I marry someone who isn't supportive?"

"There are varying degrees of support, sweetheart. It takes a special man to provide the support you will need to run a thriving catering company. I'm not sure Tyler is that kind of man."

"Ugh! I should've known this was about Tyler." Annie would never dare admit to her mom that Tyler already complained about her long work hours.

"You could always hire a nanny." Heidi turned her back on her. "Would you like some coffee for the road?" she asked on her way to the kitchen.

"Sure," Annie said, following her.

Heidi poured her expensive Columbian coffee beans into her grinder. "Anyway, we don't need to talk about my retirement now. It's way down the road."

"As is marriage for me," Annie said above the noise of the grinder.

"That may be sooner than you think." Heidi measured out the ground coffee into the filter and turned on the coffeemaker.

Maybe, Annie thought. Tyler had asked her to move in with

him. If she played her cards right, a marriage proposal could be on the horizon.

Annie retrieved a to-go cup from the overhead cabinet. "I hope you don't mind, but I may be a little late getting to work. I'm going to drop these clothes off at the apartment and then run out to Target."

"Take your time. We're in good shape for the wedding this afternoon." Heidi filled her ceramic mug and Annie's to-go cup with coffee. "Have you contacted Jackie about the furniture yet?"

"That's on my list for today," Annie said, securing the lid on her cup.

"What will you sleep on?"

"An air mattress, until I can get something better."

Heidi walked with Annie to the living room, holding Annie's coffee while she gathered up the clothes in one arm.

"I have some things in the attic you can use."

"Like what?" Annie asked, taking back her coffee.

"Hmm. Let's see. There's a nice set of pots and pans up there. A couple of throw rugs. A small chest of drawers. And some other miscellaneous odds and ends." Heidi opened the door for Annie. "We'll look on Sunday. Hugh can move everything over to the apartment in his truck."

"That sounds great. I'll see you at the office soon." Annie blew her mom a kiss as she squeezed past her with her armload.

After stowing her clothes in the back of her Mini Cooper, Annie then climbed into the driver's seat. She rummaged through her bag for her phone and sent Jackie a text. *Hi Jackie. This is Annie. I'm moving into a new apartment, and Heidi says you might have some furniture for sale. Any chance I can take a look?*

Jackie responded immediately. *Lovely to hear from you, Annie. Let's meet at my warehouse on Monday at eleven. I'll send you the address.*

Giving the text a thumbs-up, she dropped the phone into the cup holder, started the engine, and sped off.

Annie spent ninety minutes at Target, filling three shopping carts with household items. Sheets and towels and accessories for the bathroom. A wide assortment of utensils and gadgets for the kitchen, including a Keurig and an Instant Pot. And from the electronics department, a large screen television that was entirely too big for her living room and required assistance from an employee to carry it out to the parking lot. She rarely watched TV, but Tyler loved sporting events. Why not splurge a little? For the past few years, she'd been saving the money she would've spent on rent if she hadn't been living with Heidi.

The television barely fit in the back of the Mini, and with her other purchases organized on top, she couldn't see anything out of the rearview mirror. She was headed out of the parking lot when she spotted a sign in the mattress warehouse window advertising a summer sale. She whipped into a vacant parking space and went inside the store.

An older gentleman with plump rosy cheeks and a bulbous nose greeted her at the door.

"I saw your sign in the window. Is everything on sale?" she asked.

"Almost everything. Are you looking for anything specifically?"

"Not really. I'm a first-time buyer. I want something comfortable, obviously. And supportive. And I need to have it delivered within the week, if possible."

"I believe we can find you something." He walked Annie around the store, showing her the options. She tested and retested several mattresses before finally deciding.

The sales agent sat Annie down at his desk and began typing on his keyboard. "You're in luck. That model is available in our warehouse. And we can deliver it . . ."—he paused while the computer processed her order—"as early as tomorrow." He smiled at her and stuck his hand out for her credit card.

On the drive back to downtown, she called Lia about her painting. "Any chance I can have it delivered today? And I'll need someone to help hang it."

"Our gallery doesn't provide white-glove service," Lia said in a snippy tone.

"Well, you should, as much money as I paid for the painting."

"You could always get Tyler to help you," Lia suggested. "Oh wait. I forgot. My brother is the least handy person I know. He pays an electrician to change his lightbulbs."

"Just send your assistant to hang it," Annie said and hung up on her. She could only take her boyfriend's sister in small doses.

Annie was unloading her things from the car when her phone pinged with a text from Tyler. *Where are you?*

She thumbed off a response. *Moving stuff into my apartment.*

Cool. I'm bringing you lunch.

How typical of Tyler not to ask if she even wanted lunch. What if she'd already eaten or if she wasn't hungry? But she was hungry, and she didn't have time to pick up food and still make it to work by two.

Annie had just finished unloading her Mini when Tyler and Lia's assistant, Benny, arrived at the same time.

"I don't understand the hype," Tyler said as they watched Benny drill a hole in the brick fireplace. "I could paint better than this guy."

Irritation crawled up Annie's neck. "I'd like to see you try."

"I would if I were interested in that sort of thing. I hate to say it, Annie, but you wasted your money. There are artists with way more talent than this Cooper dude."

"Your sister doesn't think so. And she's the art expert."

Annie coached Benny as he adjusted the painting to the right height. He gathered his tools, and she walked him to the door, slipping him a small tip for his trouble.

"Let's eat. I'm starving," Tyler said, rubbing his belly.

Annie would rather stare at her painting, but she'd had only coffee for breakfast, and her stomach had begun to rumble.

Tyler looked around the empty apartment. Seeing there was no place to sit, he set the bag of sandwiches he'd brought on the kitchen counter. "One Reuben for you," he said, handing her a paper-wrapped sandwich.

"Did you remember to tell them no kraut?" Unwrapping the sandwich, she peeled back the bread and curled up her nose at the sight of the slimy sauerkraut. "Nope. You forgot."

"A Reuben isn't a Reuben without the sauerkraut, Annie."

Annie glared at him. "I know that, Tyler. It's a pastrami and Swiss on rye with thousand island dressing. The way I always order it."

"What's the big deal? Just scrape it off," he said, taking a bite of his Italian hoagie.

Realizing she'd forgotten to buy a trash can at Target, Annie used her finger to scrape the kraut off the sandwich into the disposal.

Tyler picked a wilted piece of lettuce off his hoagie and dropped it onto his paper wrapper. "Wanna go sailing later? The wind is supposed to pick up, and the conditions will be ideal this afternoon."

"I can't. I have to work. We're catering a wedding." Annie bit into the sandwich, but the lingering taste of kraut almost made her gag.

"When is this going to end, Annie?"

She set down the sandwich and wiped her mouth with a napkin. "When is what going to end?"

"The constant round of parties."

"Um . . . never. This isn't my social life, Tyler. This is my career."

"I get that, but why do you have to be at every single event?"

"I don't. Heidi and I take turns working the smaller events. Disasters happen when one of us isn't there to supervise."

"Why not hire a capable person to cover for you? Then you and Heidi wouldn't have to work so hard."

"Our profit margins are already thin without paying that capable person's big fat salary. Besides, neither of us is complaining about the hard work. We're used to it."

Tyler was the one complaining. Annie remembered her conversation with Heidi from that morning. The long hours weren't just a problem for *her* boyfriend. Even Hugh, the most understanding man in the world, got tired of Heidi working all the time. Annie's demanding career would always be an issue, regardless of who she was in a relationship with.

Tyler finished his hoagie and balled up his wrapper. In the absence of a trash can, he tossed it into the sink. "Eliza Irwin's wedding is next weekend. It's the largest social event of the summer."

"I'm aware. Her parents hired a fancy wedding planner out of Atlanta. It's one of the largest and most elaborate weddings we've ever catered."

Tyler pulled her into his arms. "I'm counting on you to go as my date."

"Heidi is counting on me. Maybe I can dress as a guest and still work the event." Annie expected him to argue, but when he kissed her, she realized he had other things on his mind.

"Why don't we christen your bedroom?" he said in a husky voice as he walked her backward across the living room. He stopped short in the doorway. "Where's your bed?"

"Obviously, I don't have one. My new mattress is coming tomorrow."

He glanced around. "We could do it on the kitchen counter?"

Annie pushed him away. "Gross, Tyler. That's unsanitary. Besides, I'm due at work soon, and I want to put all this away before I go," she said, gesturing at her mountain of Target purchases.

Tyler eyed the pile with a quizzical expression, as though considering whether to offer to help.

"You'd better get a move on if you're going sailing." She walked him to the door and kissed his cheek. "Tonight's wedding is early. If I finish in time, we can meet for drinks afterward," she said to appease him. She had no intention of going out after work. She would come home, set up her air mattress in the living room in front of the fireplace, and admire her new painting until she fell asleep.

brooke

Brooke met her sister at their father's waterfront condo on Sunday to begin the emotional process of cleaning out his things. They started in the bedroom. While Lizbet emptied his underwear drawer, Brooke removed his starched white shirts from the hangers in the closet and neatly folded them into a stack on the bed. As she worked, Brooke tried to imagine herself living in the drab condo. The one-bedroom unit offered too few windows. With so little sunlight, she doubted painting the walls stark white would help.

"Have you experienced any symptoms yet?" Lizbet asked, closing the underwear drawer and moving on to socks.

Brooke smiled at her sister's eagerness. "It's too soon. The procedure was only a couple of weeks ago."

"It'll be three weeks on Tuesday. The fertility specialist says we should get a positive result by now." A playful grin spread across Lizbet's lips. "Should we do a home pregnancy test?"

"Why disappoint ourselves with a false negative? We'll wait until we go for the blood test on Wednesday like we planned."

Lizbet dropped a handful of black sock balls into a box and slammed the drawer shut. "You don't sound very hopeful."

"Why would you say that? Because I don't want to rush out and buy a pregnancy test?" Brooke yanked the last shirt off the hanger and closed the closet door. "I'm cautiously optimistic that at least one of your two eggs will take. But if it doesn't work this time, we'll try again in a couple of months."

"But in vitro is so expensive, and I don't have an endless supply of frozen eggs. What if none of them take and I run out of eggs?" Lizbet asked, her voice quivering.

"Oh, honey." Brooke went around to Lizbet's side of the bed. "I know this is difficult for you. But be patient. You only have to wait three more days. I'm sure both eggs will take, and then I'll be pregnant with twins." She pulled her sister in for a half hug. "I'm giving up my girlish figure for you. I'll have morning sickness, swollen feet, and hemorrhoids. In exchange, I expect a lot of pampering."

This brought a smile to Lizbet's face. "Don't worry. Jamie and I plan to smother you with attention."

"Good. I'm glad that's settled." She dropped her arm from around her sister's waist. "Now, back to work. I'll take the bathroom, and you do the linen closet."

Brooke grabbed a trash bag and emptied the contents of the bathroom cabinets and drawers. Catching her reflection in the mirror, she tried to imagine what she would look like in nine months with two babies growing in her belly. According to her internet research, a woman of normal weight carrying twins should gain between 37 and 54 pounds. She wondered how much of that would appear on her face.

A serious case of endometriosis had rendered her sister infertile and nearly cost Lizbet her marriage. Brooke was grateful for the chance to give Lizbet and Jamie the baby they so desperately wanted. But she was praying for twins, a boy and a girl, because she was only willing to be a surrogate once. At some point, Brooke hoped to start her own family. When she found the right partner.

The sisters saved the kitchen for last. While Brooke sorted through the meager contents of her father's drawers, Lizbet made grilled pesto chicken sandwiches for their lunch with ingredients she'd brought from home. When the food was ready, they went out onto the small balcony to eat.

Brooke took a bite of her sandwich and moaned in delight. "This is delicious."

"I made extra if you want seconds." Lizbet's gray eyes twinkled. "Since you might be eating for two. Or three."

Brooke let out a groan at the thought of how much food she would have to consume if she was pregnant. "Are you going to monitor my every bite?"

Lizbet bobbed her head, her ponytail swinging. "You know it. To make sure my baby gets the proper nutrition. Your every move too. We'll put you on a strict exercise program."

"Oh yeah? And how do you plan to monitor this exercise program when you live in a different town thirty minutes away?"

"By installing video cameras in the house," Lizbet teased.

"I wouldn't do that if I were you. You might see something you aren't prepared for." *Like our mother's ghost,* Brooke thought. She popped a potato chip into her mouth. "By the way, I ran into Grady Ellington the other night after Cooper's art show. He's moved back to town from Atlanta." She leaves out the part about Grady saving her life. Lizbet didn't need to know Brooke almost got her egg, or eggs, killed by a rickshaw.

"Aww, I love Grady. How's he doing? Is he still adorable?"

"I would not describe the man version of Grady as adorable." Brooke took another bite of the sandwich. Suddenly ravenous, she gobbled down the first half and reached for the second. "Wait until you see him, Liz. He's drop-dead gorgeous. He would be perfect for you if you weren't married to Jamie."

"But I *am* married to Jamie. *Happily* married."

Brooke felt her sister's eyes on her. "What're you looking at?"

"You! You literally have stars in your eyes. If I didn't know better, I'd think you were the one crushing Grady."

"But you *do* know better. Because I'm gay. And potentially pregnant." Brooke ate the last of the sandwich and wiped her mouth. "Anyway, there's a reason I brought him up. Grady is a real estate agent. He works for Midge. What do you think about listing the condo with him? If we're sure we want to sell."

Lizbet appeared surprised. "What do you mean? I thought we'd already decided to sell. The other option would be to rent it. But then we'd be responsible for the maintenance. Knowing our luck, we'd get stuck with a rowdy tenant who causes trouble for the building's other occupants."

"I research the possibility, and renting isn't an option. At least not right now. The homeowners' association only allows a certain number of units to be rented at a time. And they are currently at their maximum. I thought about moving in here."

Lizbet stopped chewing. "Seriously?"

"I thought about it. For about a second. It's not really my style, although the view is nice." Brooke watched a boat gliding across the harbor, its white sail billowing in the wind. "So, you're okay with Grady listing the condo."

"Of course! I would've suggested Midge anyway."

"Then I'll set up an appointment with him right away," Brooke said, more excited than she should be about the prospect of seeing Grady again. "We should talk about Tradd Street. Mom was the quintessential caretaker of that house. I spend every weekend cleaning and maintaining the yard. But the silver and brass needs polishing. The carpets need steam cleaning. There's an endless to-do list. I can't keep up, and I can't meet her high standards."

"No one expects you to," Lizbet said. "She was a stay-at-home mom. You have a full-time career. You're doing your best. That's all anyone can ask."

Brooke took a deep breath. "Do you think maybe it's time to

let it go? The house hasn't been the same since Mom died. And it's too big for just little old me."

Lizbet's face tightened. "I know it's a lot to manage, and the burden has mostly fallen on you. But one day you'll find someone new, and you'll have kids of your own. Don't you want them to grow up there?"

"Honestly, I'm not sure anymore. I could use a fresh start, and I like the idea of having my own place."

"But the house is filled with so many wonderful memories from our childhood."

"And plenty of terrible memories of everything that happened with Sawyer." Brooke got up and walked over to the railing. "Selling the house would be bittersweet. But all good things eventually come to an end."

"I suggest we think about this before we rush into anything."

Brooke spun around. "Why the pushback, Liz? We've talked about selling the house before, and you seemed on board with the idea. If we sold both properties, we could split the money and divvy up the furniture. You and Jamie could finally get your dream house on the water."

"That's true. Jamie and I have been talking about looking for a bigger house. We're waiting to find out . . . "

"How many babies you're having," Brooke finished with a smile. "I get it. Your adorable little house will be too small with twins running around."

Lizbet held up her hands to show her index and third fingers crossed. "Where would you live if we sell the house?"

"I haven't really thought about it," Brooke lied. She'd thought about little else since Grady mentioned it on Thursday night. "I'd probably look for a small house. Although I could see myself in a funky studio apartment somewhere."

Lizbet gave her the hairy eyeball. "In some sketchy part of town? Not while you're carrying my baby, you won't."

"Your baby is safe with me," Brooke said and thought, *If there is a baby*.

"I understand what you're saying about the house, Brooke. But can you give me some time to think about it?"

"Of course." Brooke pulled her sister to her feet. "Come on. We still have a lot of work left to do."

The sisters returned to the kitchen and boxed up their father's cookware and dinnerware. When they finished, they stood looking at the assortment of boxes in the living room.

"I'm surprised at how few possessions Dad had." Lizbet removed a black-and-white framed photograph of their parents on their wedding day from one of the boxes. "Aside from his clothes, this is his only personal effect."

"Dad lost his will to live when Mom died. Surviving with the bare necessities is all he's been doing these past few years."

Lizbet hugged the photograph to her chest. "Do you mind if I take this?"

"Of course not. Take anything you want. There are a dozen more like that one at home," Brooke groaned. "When the time comes, cleaning out Tradd Street will be a major chore. Our grandparents bought that house in the 1950s. Decades' worth of junk has accumulated in the attic."

Lizbet cut her eyes at Brooke. "All the more reason not to sell."

"Regardless of whether we put it on the market, we still need to clean out the attic."

Lizbet wagged her finger at Brooke. "Don't you dare go up in that hot attic while you're carrying my baby. If cleaning out the attic is that important to you, I'll take some time off work and help you."

"I'll take you up on that offer." Aside from tending their mother's perennial garden, Lizbet had done little to help with the chores during her recent extended visit. She needed to see what was involved in maintaining such a complex house. Brooke could force the issue and win the debate. But for her sister to be at peace with selling the house, she needed to decide on her own.

cooper

Cooper spent Sunday morning ripping out carpet in the living room, kitchen, and the runner on the stairs. He even got rid of the stained rugs in the bedrooms upstairs. By the time he'd finished, carpet fibers and dust clung to his sweat-dampened clothes and skin. When he hauled the last scraps out of the cottage, he found his brother inspecting his growing mountain of debris in the driveway.

"What's going on, Coop? If I didn't know better, I'd think you were working on a project."

"What's that supposed to mean?" Cooper wiped sweat out of his eyes with the back of his hand. "Are you saying I'm not capable of taking on a project?"

"Not at all. The old Cooper was handy and resourceful and skilled with power tools. But I have my doubts about the new Cooper. He has shown no interests in projects since he moved back home."

"Okay, wise guy, since we're talking about me in the third person, the old Cooper is emerging from the quicksand of depression. He's sprucing up the cottage, giving it a much-needed makeover. Wanna help?"

"I wish I could, but I have to be at the restaurant soon." Sean gestured at the pile of trash. "I hope you're planning to get rid of all this."

"Nah, bro. I thought I'd leave it for the new Cooper."

"Aren't you funny?" Sean said, punching him in the arm.

"Seriously," Cooper said. "Do you know anyone with a truck and access to the dump?"

"Not off the top of my head, but I'll ask around. Are you doing other renovations besides the carpet?" Sean toed a remnant with his shoe. "This stuff is disgusting."

"Tell me about it." Cooper pulled the sweat-sodden blue bandana off his head and stuffed it in his back pocket. "I'm going to clean the floors and paint the walls. And I might get some furniture from Mom's warehouse if she has any items that aren't too girly."

Sean checked his phone for the time. "We're always busy at the restaurant on Sundays, but I can help paint later in the week."

"That'd be great! I'll buy extra rollers and brushes when I go to the hardware store."

After Sean left for work, Cooper went back inside the cottage to admire his handiwork. The rooms already felt bigger and smelled less musty without the carpet. He was too inspired by his progress to quit now. If he hustled, he could get the floors cleaned today. Why not procrastinate his paying job a little longer?

He took a quick shower and headed off to the local hardware store. He chose several products to use on the floors before venturing to the paint department, where he encountered hundreds of color swatches. He selected several neutral-colored swatches, but they all looked the same to him. Feeling overwhelmed, he sought the assistance of a sales associate, a plain-looking young woman with hazel eyes.

He explained to her, "I'm renovating my cottage, and I'm looking for a tried-and-true neutral paint color. I'd like to use the same color in all the rooms. I don't want white. I'm looking for something with depth, not too yellow or too gray, that will contrast with white trim." Feeling flustered, he handed her the swatches. "Here. You pick. I'm an artist. I don't know why I'm finding this so difficult."

The sales associate laughed. "Because there are so many options, and they are all pretty much the same." She glanced at the swatches he'd chosen. "I don't particularly care for any of these. My favorite neutrals are from Benjamin Moore's line of paints." She moved down the aisle to another display and picked out several swatches. "Ballet White or Soft Chamois would be my first choices. Cloud White is nice too, although it may not be enough color for you. If you still want more depth, I'd consider Tapestry Beige."

She showed him several others, but the first three appealed to him the most.

"As an artist, you already know paint changes color in different lighting," she said. "I would suggest buying two sample sizes of each of your top two choices and trying them in your different rooms."

"That's a great idea. I like the Tapestry Beige and Ballet White the best. Can you mix them up for me?"

"Of course." She removed two sample size containers of eggshell paint from the shelf and took them behind the counter.

"Do you have all these different colors memorized?" Cooper asked as she tinted and mixed the paints.

"I know the most popular colors of each brand. But I studied graphic design, so color is kinda my thing."

"Really? I'm a graphic designer as well. How did you end up working in a hardware store?" Cooper's hand shot up. "I'm sorry. I'm being nosy. You don't have to answer that."

"I don't mind. I got pregnant and married my senior year in college. I work here part-time on the weekends when my husband can watch the baby."

The mention of pregnancy got his attention, and he studied

the young woman more closely. She appeared a few years younger than him. And while she wasn't striking, something about her reminded him of Annie. Maybe it was her upturned nose. Or maybe it was because he couldn't seem to get Annie off his mind these days.

Cooper wondered if the sales associate had ever considered abortion. And if she would've eventually married the baby's father if she hadn't gotten pregnant.

"Were you able to finish college?" he asked her.

She nodded as she printed labels for his paint samples. "I've been searching for a job in graphic design, but I need to work remotely, and I haven't found the right situation yet." She stuck the labels on the samples and handed them to him. "You can pay for these up front."

Cooper placed the paint in his cart. "So what area of graphic design are you interested in?"

"Web design is my first choice. I've created a few websites for friends. I'm considering starting my own gig, but with the baby, I haven't gotten around to it yet."

"I just started my own firm, and I'm already swamped with new business. Sooner than later, I will need to hire another designer to help with the workload. I can take your business card if you think you might be interested."

"I absolutely would be interested. My cards are in my purse in the back room. But here." She scrawled her name and number on a sticky note and handed it to him. "I'm Nicole Simon."

"Nice to meet you, Nicole. I'm Cooper Hart. I'll keep this handy in case I decide to expand." He folded the note and slipped it into his pocket.

"By the way, if you need help with your renovation, my husband is a project manager for a local contractor, and he's always looking for part-time work."

"Does he have a truck and access to the dump? I removed all

the old carpet from the cottage this morning, and I need someone to haul it off."

"Kevin can do that. He's also skilled at both plumbing and electrical." Nicole's hazel eyes were aglow as she talked about her husband.

"He sounds like someone I should know. My brother and I own a house together. We are always looking for someone reliable to help with odd jobs." Cooper took her pad and pen and wrote his name and number. "Please have him reach out."

"For sure," Nicole said with an enthusiastic nod.

Cooper said goodbye and went to the main checkout to pay for his supplies.

Back at Moss Creek, he spent the afternoon cleaning floors, storing the furniture he no longer wanted in the garage, and rolling samples of the two paint colors on the walls in every room. He wanted to see the paint in the morning light, but so far, the Ballet White was winning the contest.

It was seven o'clock by the time he sat down at his computer with a chicken Caesar salad and a glass of sweet tea. His client's website redesign loomed ahead of him. He was way behind on schedule and would have to pull a late night to get caught up. But instead of diving into his work, he opened the Word document that housed his waiting list of clients. He read down the list. The names of a local romance writer and women's boutique owner jumped out at him. These projects would be ideal for Nicole. *If* she had any talent.

He removed her number from his wallet and sent her a quick text. *I've been thinking about our conversation. I'd like to see your work. Will you send over a couple of your projects?*

Cooper propped an arm on his desk as he shoveled his salad into his mouth. While he'd never met Nicole's husband, the couple's seemingly stringent work ethic impressed Cooper. Life had thrown them a curve ball, but they were making the most of their unplanned pregnancy. He remembered how Nicole's face had lit up when she'd talked about her husband. They were fighting the odds against them. And winning.

Cooper wondered how his life might have turned out if things had worked out differently for Annie and him. He wouldn't have gone to college in Virginia, wouldn't have studied graphics. If they'd gotten married, instead of becoming a web designer, Cooper might have become a project manager with a local construction group. Which sounded cool to him. But fate had taken each of them down a different path. He'd gone off to college and Annie to culinary school in New York. And he'd made the mistake of letting their relationship slip away.

eight
annie

Jackie's warehouse was a large metal building in an industrial complex just west of the Ashley River. When she arrived, Annie was shocked to see Cooper waiting with his mom out front. Cooper and Annie being here at the same time was not a coincidence. There were no coincidences where Jackie was concerned. What was Cooper's mother up to?

"Annie, darling." Jackie held her at arm's length. "Look at you! I haven't laid eyes on you in ages. Love the shorter hair. You look so grown up. So professional." She cut her eyes at her son. "I keep telling Cooper to cut his rat's nest of hair so we can see his face."

Cooper blushed as he fastened his hair into a messy bun with an elastic. "My hair is the same length as Annie's boyfriend's. Isn't it, Annie?"

"Hmm." Annie tapped her chin. "I'm not sure about that. Maybe just a little. Like three inches. Your hair is past your shoulders. Tyler's is just long on the back of his neck. But your man bun fits the image of a budding artist."

"See!" Cooper glared at his mother. "I'm trying to look the part. I want people to recognize me as an artist, not as my brother's twin."

Jackie patted her son's cheek. "It's a mother's responsibility to make sure her son is presentable. Clean cut is a much better look for you." She motioned them to the warehouse door. "Now, let's see if we can find some goodies for your new homes."

Cooper and Annie stepped in line behind Jackie. "Do you think it's ironic we're both here at the same time?" she asked out of the side of her mouth.

"Not really. We're both in the market for furniture. And from what I hear, she has plenty of it."

They entered the building, a massive warehouse jam-packed with furniture and accessories. A blue sectional caught Annie's eye, and she ventured off to investigate. The pale woven fabric was scrumptious, soft yet durable looking. It would be the center showpiece of her apartment.

Jackie hustled back and forth between Annie and Cooper as she helped them locate the items on their wish lists. Annie sneaked frequent peeks at Cooper, who appeared interested in a handsome caramel leather sofa, a pair of burnt-orange velvet chairs, a bed with chunky turned posts, and various masculine-looking accessories.

To go with the blue sectional, Annie chose rattan side tables, a pair of white ceramic table lamps, and a coffee table with a gold base and marble top. For her bedroom, she selected a wicker headboard with matching nightstands and a white chinoiserie mirror to go above the chest of drawers from Heidi's attic.

"I need to arrange delivery," Annie said, handing Jackie her credit card.

Jackie swiped the card through her Square card reader. "You can take the smaller items with you today, and I'll have Carlos, my delivery man, arrange a time this afternoon or tomorrow to bring over your sectional."

"I drive a Mini Cooper," Annie said. "I'll be lucky to fit the lamps."

Jackie peered at her over the top of her reading glasses. "That surprises me with you being a caterer. I would think you'd need something bigger to haul food around."

"I usually drive one of our vans when I'm at work. The Mini makes for easy parking in downtown Charleston."

"That's a valid point." Jackie handed Annie her credit card. "In that case, Cooper can take a load in his SUV."

Annie felt a flush creep up her neck. What would Cooper think when he saw the bald eagle painting hanging above her mantel? "That's okay. I'll figure something else out. If Hugh will loan me his truck, my boyfriend can help me," she said, even though she had a difficult time imagining Tyler moving furniture.

Jackie pursed her lips at the mention of Annie's boyfriend. "I'd hate to inconvenience Hugh. Cooper has plenty of time, don't you, son?"

Cooper gave Annie an apologetic smile. Jackie wasn't taking no for an answer. "I don't mind, Annie. We can knock this out in no time, and you can enjoy your new furniture today."

Annie let out a reluctant sigh. "If you're sure. I'll send you the address."

After loading everything into Cooper's SUV, they headed in separate cars across the Ashley River toward downtown. When they reached her apartment, Annie grabbed a lamp out of the back of her Mini and hurried up the stairs. Cooper followed with one of the sofa end tables.

Setting the table down in the living room, he stuck his head in the bedroom and walked through the small kitchen. "This place suits you, Annie. It has a good vibe with all this natural light." He stopped short when he caught sight of the painting above the mantel. "You bought my painting."

Annie made light of the situation. "Why wouldn't I? It's an excellent investment. I figure it'll be worth a lot of money one day when you're rich and famous. I will brag to my friends that I knew you a long time ago," she said, the words sounding bitter-sweet on her lips.

"Do you ever think about what might have been?"

Annie felt his eyes on her, but she didn't dare meet his gaze. "You mean if you hadn't ditched me when you went away to college?"

"That's not fair, Annie. You can't put all the blame on me. You were in culinary school in New York, and we *agreed* to see other people."

"Whatever, Cooper. I try not to dwell on the past. It was twelve years ago, nearly half my lifetime." Truth be told, she thought about what *might have been* all the time. Annie had been so certain they would one day get married. It had crushed her when he told her he wanted to date other people. He'd promised they would see each other over holidays and during the summers. But she knew they wouldn't. And they hadn't.

Cooper moved over to the fireplace, staring up at the painting. "I saw the bald eagle again the other day. I took a bunch of photographs. I can hardly wait to start a new painting."

Annie softened as she joined him in front of the fireplace. "To be honest, the painting is more than an investment. I'm deeply moved by it. Maybe it's because I once knew you so well, because I know how much the natural habitat of the inlet means to you." She extended a hand toward the painting. "Your love of the marsh and the ocean and the wildlife is right there on the canvas." She dropped her hand to her side. "Maybe I'm reading too much into it."

When Cooper didn't respond, Annie sneaked a glance at him. His eyes were wet, and his expression pained. "I'm sorry, Coop. I didn't mean to upset you. I heard you were going through a rough patch. If you ever need to talk, I'm a good listener."

"I remember that about you. And thanks. I'm much better now. Moses is helping me work through my issues."

"I'm just glad you're getting help." Annie didn't press for details, even though she was curious about the awful thing that had happened to him in Richmond. Did a girl break his heart?

What Cooper and Annie went through in high school had devastated them. But not enough to cause him to have a breakdown.

Cooper swiped at his eyes as he turned away from the painting. "Thanks for sharing your thoughts about my work. I'm glad to know the painting means something to you." He started toward the door. "Let's get the rest of your stuff. Mom's waiting to take me to lunch."

Fifteen minutes later, the rest of the furniture was in place in her apartment. Cooper even helped her hang the white chinoiserie mirror above her chest of drawers in her bedroom.

Cooper fiddled with his man bun as he looked at his reflection in the mirror. "Do you really hate my hair?"

"I never said that. Your hair is fine," Annie lied. She much preferred the way his sun-streaked auburn waves used to sweep over his forehead. "What's up with your mom anyway? She was being so nice. I thought she hated me."

Cooper turned away from the mirror. "Why would you say that?"

"You know why. She blames me for everything that happened. She thought I was trying to trap you into marrying me."

"She never thought that, Annie. Mom has always loved you. She was just upset because we were so young. We were all emotional basket cases."

"I guess," Annie said and walked with Cooper to the door.

With his hand on the knob, Cooper asked, "How serious are you with your boyfriend? Any chance you'd like to have dinner sometime?"

"I'm sorry, Cooper. Tyler and I are exclusive. But I would very much like to be friends. I meant what I said. If you ever need to talk. We can meet for coffee or lunch sometime."

"I already have a therapist, Annie. But thanks anyway." He hurried down the stairs and sped off in his SUV.

There was a time, Annie would've taken Cooper back with no questions asked. He'd broken her heart, and it had taken several tough years to get over him. She couldn't endure that kind of hurt again. Her relationship with Tyler was safe. She didn't care for him the way she'd once cared about Cooper. There was some truth to what Heidi claimed. Annie wasn't after his money, per se. Just everything the kind of money he had could buy. Power and social status and security.

nine
cooper

Jackie was waiting for Cooper in front of the warehouse when he returned. He rolled down his window. "What's up?"

"We need to go. I made a lunch reservation at Cru for one o'clock." She motioned for him to come with her. "You can ride with me."

Cooper rolled up his window and got out of his SUV. "I don't understand," he said, stepping in line beside her as she hurried toward her convertible. "I just came from downtown. I could've just met you there."

She cast him an apologetic smile. "Sorry. I wasn't thinking."

"Because you were too busy playing matchmaker.

"So what if I was? You and Annie needed time alone together. To rekindle your feelings for each other."

Cooper's face burned as he remembered asking Annie for a date. "I hate to tell you, Mom, but Annie has a serious boyfriend."

"Heidi predicts that won't last. Then you'll be waiting in the wings." Jackie opened her passenger door. "Get in."

Cooper checked his watch. "I really need to get back to work. Isn't there somewhere closer we can eat?"

"Nowhere I'd want to eat. The service at Cru is quick. Come on, son. It'll be fun. We haven't had lunch together in ages."

"Fine," Cooper said and folded his tall frame into her tiny front seat.

Jackie started the engine and they sped off.

Cooper gripped the seat. "Slow down, Mom. You're driving like a maniac. You're gonna kill us."

She grinned over at him, a smudge of red lipstick on her front tooth. "I thought you were in a hurry."

"I'm not in a hurry to die. Please, slow down."

"Fine," she said, letting up on the gas pedal. "By the way, I picked out a few accessories to go with your furniture for the guest cottage. Carlos can deliver everything this afternoon if you'd like."

"I'd rather wait until after I paint." If he didn't get caught up on his work, he would never find the time to paint, either the cottage walls *or* the bald eagle he couldn't stop thinking about. "I'll let you know when I'm ready. I may finish by Friday, but it'll probably be early next week."

Cru Cafe was crowded and noisy, and Cooper felt the beginning of a headache as the hostess showed them to their table. The waitress appeared right away, and with only a quick look at the menu, he ordered a Shrimp B.L.T. and sweet tea.

Jackie smiled up at the waitress, her lipstick smudge now gone. "I'll have the Chinese Chicken Salad with grilled shrimp, and a glass of your house chardonnay. Please," she said, handing the waitress her menu.

Cooper swore under his breath. His mother was having wine. She was summoning the courage to grill him about what had happened in Richmond. He figured the direct approach was best. Otherwise, she'd beat around the bush all afternoon long. "I'm not in the mood to talk about Richmond, Mom."

She folded her hands on the table. "Talking about it will help."

"I *am* talking about it. With Moses."

The waitress delivered their drinks and scurried off to help another customer. "Good!" She sipped her wine. "He must be helping, because you seem better."

Cooper stared down at his sweet tea. "Moses has been great."

"I'm here for you too, son."

"Why does everyone want to be my therapist today? First Annie and now you."

"Because we care about you, son." Jackie reached for his hand. "I've respected your privacy since you moved home so suddenly in September. But I'm your mom, and I can tell something is drastically wrong, and I have a right to know what it is."

"I guess you're right." Withdrawing his hand from hers, Cooper sat back in his chair with his tea. "So, I met this girl. Maggie. Charles introduced us. She was his best childhood friend."

"Charles?" Jackie asked with a furrowed brow.

"My roommate, Mom. Geez."

Recognition registered on Jackie's face. "Of course. Adorable Charles from Nashville," she said, sipping more wine.

He ran a thumb around his glass. "Anyway, Maggie and I really connected. I hadn't met a girl I liked so much since Annie. Then one night last September, I came home from playing pickup basketball to find both Maggie and Charles dead."

Jackie's breath hitched as her hand flew to her mouth. "Oh my word. What happened?"

"Drugs. Neither of them was into that kind of thing. At least as far as I knew. I wanna believe it was an isolated incident. Apparently, Maggie snorted some cocaine laced with fentanyl. According to the medical examiner, she died instantly." Cooper swallowed past the lump in his throat, willing himself to continue. "Charles shot himself in the head. The police think it was a knee-jerk reaction to Maggie's death. He really loved her. It's the only thing that makes sense."

"Why on earth did he have a handgun in his possession?"

Cooper glared at his mother. She had never understood an outdoorsman's obsession with guns. "The same reason I have a handgun in my possession. I have a permit to carry, and I use it responsibly."

She gave him a sharp look. "I do not approve of you owning a pistol. I suggest you hand it over to your father for safekeeping until you're feeling better."

Cooper lowered his voice to a loud whisper. "I would never shoot myself, Mom. Anyway, if I was going to kill myself, I would've done it months ago."

"I'm sorry about your friends, Cooper. I understand why you are so devastated. I wish you'd told me sooner. I might have been able to help. Did you attend their funerals?"

Cooper shook his head. "I'll forever regret not going. Their parents had a joint funeral and buried them side by side in the cemetery."

The waitress arrived with their food, saving him from having to say anything more. Tears blurred his vision as he stared down at his plate, and not trusting his voice to speak, he ate his sandwich in silence.

Out of the corner of his eye, he saw Lia and her assistant enter the restaurant and sit down at the community table. Cooper didn't think Lia had noticed him, but when he and his mom got up to leave twenty minutes later, she hurried out of the restaurant behind him.

Lia flashed his mom a kilowatt smile. "Hey, Jackie. You're looking as fabulous as ever." She placed a possessive hand on Cooper's arm. "I have a favor to ask your son. Do you mind if I borrow him for a minute?"

"Not at all. You two chat. I'll wait for you in the car, Cooper."

When his mom was out of earshot, Cooper said, "I don't mean to be rude, Lia, but I'm in a hurry. I have a ton of work waiting for me in my office."

"In that case, I'll make it quick. I'm going to a wedding this weekend. The bride's parents are my parents' best friends. And I was wondering if you would be my plus-one. You'll know a ton of people there. They've invited half the state of South Carolina." She bounced on her toes with hands pressed together under her chin. "Please, Cooper. I promise it will be super fun."

Cooper doubted he would know anyone at this wedding, let alone a ton of people. But he had no plans for the weekend. Or any weekend for the rest of the summer. "Can I let you know tomorrow? I'm bogged down with work, and I need to see how much I can crank out tonight."

"Of course. Tomorrow's fine. The wedding and reception are being held at Magnolia Plantation, and they've booked a killer band." She kissed his cheek and hurried back inside.

Cooper didn't mention the wedding to his mom on the drive back to the warehouse, but when he started toward Prospect in his own car, he felt panic setting in as the day's events converged on him. Seeing Annie again. Confiding in his mom about Maggie and Charles. Lia inviting him to a wedding he didn't want to attend but knew he should.

He reached for his phone and called Moses, who answered on the first ring. "I'm glad I caught you. Several things have happened today. Some good. Some bad. All confusing. I'm having trouble processing."

"Calm down, son, and take some deep breaths. Everything will be all right."

Even Moses's smooth voice failed to set Cooper at ease. "I'm not so sure about that," he mumbled.

"Tell me what happened," Moses said.

"I took your advice and told Mom about Charles and Maggie. Instead of feeling better, I feel crummy. I want to go home, crawl into my bed, and never get out."

"I'm sorry, bud. But you must trust the process. Telling your mom is probably the most difficult. And now you've got that behind you. Next time will be easier."

"I'm not sure there will be a next time. I'm considering moving to a remote part of Alaska, hundreds of miles away from other humans."

Moses chuckled. "As tempting as that sounds right now, the loneliness will eventually eat you alive. Where are you?"

"I just left Charleston heading home."

"My three o'clock canceled on me. Do you wanna swing by my office on your way into town?"

Cooper realized he was driving over the speed limit and slowed down. "I don't have time. I have a ton of work to do, which is part of the problem. I have a long waiting list of clients, but I lack the bandwidth and the inspiration to design all their websites. Painting is all I feel like doing."

"Can you afford to paint full time?" Moses asked.

"I can now. But who knows how long that success will last? The web design business is my safety net if my talent dries up or the economy goes bust."

"You're wise to be thinking along those lines."

After discussing Cooper's options for alleviating some of his work stress, they concluded that hiring another designer was his best bet.

"I've already created an LLC. I just need to hire an accountant and figure out healthcare." Cooper let out a deep breath as some of the tension left his body.

"You need the health-care coverage for yourself anyway. Now, tell me the good thing that happened today."

"In hindsight, I'm not sure it's a good thing. I saw Annie. I still have feelings for her, but she's in a serious relationship with someone else. Then there's this other girl, my art dealer. Lia asked me to be her date for a wedding this weekend. She's not really my type, and I'm not in the mood to go to a wedding, but I feel like I should go."

"You absolutely should go. You deserve to have some fun for a change, Cooper. It's a good thing she's not your type, because you're not ready for a serious relationship. But a word of warning. If you break her heart, you could ruin your professional relationship."

Cooper chuckled. "Got it. What do I do about Annie?"

"Avoid her at all costs. The last thing you wanna do is fall for someone who's taken."

"I'll try," Cooper said, although he wasn't sure he could follow Moses's advice. He had no intention of causing trouble for Annie with her boyfriend, but he wouldn't avoid her either. As he ended the call with Moses, he found himself hoping to see Annie at the wedding.

Cooper arrived home to find an email from Nicole Simon in his inbox. He carefully perused her portfolio. The websites she'd created had good flow and were aesthetically appealing with a solid choice of images.

Cooper responded to the email, setting up a Zoom interview with Nicole for later that afternoon. If he hired a team of designers to do the grunt work, his time would be freed up to manage the big picture elements of the business—communicating with clients, keeping his designers on schedule, and putting finishing touches on the websites. Then, he could turn his attention to his true passion. His art.

ten
brooke

Brooke took Wednesday afternoon off from work to spend with her sister. They had a doctor's appointment for the pregnancy test, and then they would meet with Grady about putting their father's condo on the market. She'd spoken to Grady at length on the phone yesterday, asking him to help her convince Lizbet to sell the Tradd Street house. Surely, between the two of them, they could talk some sense into her sister.

Lizbet squirmed in her chair as they waited in the doctor's office for the results of her pregnancy test.

Brooke looked up from the office copy of *Motherhood* magazine. "Will you please sit still? You're making me nervous."

"I can't help it," Lizbet snapped. "This waiting is driving me insane."

"Get used to it. If we're pregnant, you have nine long months of waiting ahead of you."

When Brooke returned her attention to the magazine, Lizbet snatched it away. "Stop reading that stupid magazine and talk to me. I'm freaking out here. It's your job to support me."

Brooke gave her the stink eye. "Excuse me? It's your job to support me. I'm the one who might be carrying your baby."

"*Might?* What do you know that I don't know?" Lizbet asked in a suspicious tone. "Are you keeping something from me? Did you sneak and do a store-bought test? Was it negative?"

"Chill, Liz. I would never do something like that behind your back. If it makes you feel better, I have a hunch we'll get the results we want."

"Seriously?" Lizbet sat up straight in her chair. "What makes you say that? Are you having symptoms?"

Mischief tugged at Brooke's lips. "Does rushing to the store in the middle of the night to buy beets count as a craving?"

"Yes! Because you hate beets. If you're craving them, you *must* be pregnant." Lizbet's gray eyes narrowed as she studied Brooke's face. "You're joking."

"I am. I'm trying to get you to relax." Brooke hadn't mentioned to her sister about the breast tenderness and the queasiness for fear the symptoms were a figment of her imagination.

A nurse wearing a uniform top covered in hearts and carrying a file folder called Brooke's name. Their smiles faded as they got up and followed her to the examining room.

"Dr. Carroll will be with you momentarily," the nurse said and closed the door behind her when she exited the room.

Brooke hopped onto the examining bed. When Lizbet appeared confused, as though uncertain where to sit, she patted the paper bed covering beside her. "Sit here. Next to me. We're in this together."

Lizbet sat down gingerly, as though afraid to wrinkle the paper. "I'm terrified, Brooke. I don't think I can take more disappointment. Month after month of hoping, only to have negative pregnancy tests. And then the hysterectomy, the realization that I would never carry my own child. What if I never have a baby?"

Brooke stroked her sister's thigh. "Don't be scared, Liz. I have a good feeling about this." But when Dr. Carroll entered the room wearing a grim face, the bottom dropped out of her stomach.

Lizbet shivered beside her, and Brooke placed an arm around her shoulders.

"Good morning, ladies." The obstetrician studied the chart and looked up at them, a wide smile now spread across her face. "I have good news. You're pregnant."

Lizbet slumped against Brooke in relief. "Thank goodness. You scared me. You looked so serious when you came in."

"Did I? I'm sorry. Hectic morning. But you're definitely pregnant." Dr. Carroll consulted the chart again. "In fact, your hCG levels are very high."

"What does that mean?" Brooke asked.

"It's too early to know for sure, but you could be carrying twins."

"Yes!" Lizbet said, her butt coming off the examining table. "When will we know for sure?"

"We'll do an ultrasound in a few weeks." Dr. Carroll set the file down on the counter. "I have a special fondness for you two. I believe someone up there is looking out for you," she said, an index finger aimed at the ceiling.

"Our parents," the sisters said at the same time.

The doctor's eyes widened. "Both of them?"

The sisters nodded in unison.

"I was referring to God, but you're in excellent hands with your own special guardian angels. Your baby or babies are due mid-April." The doctor scribbled something on the back of a business card and handed it to Brooke. "Here's my contact information, including my cell number. If you have any concerns at all, call me. Don't drink alcohol and don't smoke anything. Monitor caffeine consumption, although it's best to avoid it if possible. Eat healthy, exercise, and continue taking your prenatal vitamins."

"Yes, ma'am," Brooke said.

Lizbet slid off the bed to her feet and gave the doctor a hug. "Thank you, Dr. Carroll. For everything. You've been so good to me."

The doctor smiled at her. "After all the hardship you've been through this year, I'm thrilled you're finally getting your miracle."

On the way out of the office, Brooke and Lizbet stopped by the checkout counter and scheduled her next appointment for September eighteen when they would find out if they were having twins.

"Are you going to call Jamie?" Brooke asked on the way down in the elevator.

Lizbet shook her head. "I want to give him the news in person. He doesn't know we were doing the test today. I wanted to either surprise him or break it to him easy."

"FaceTime me after you tell him. I want to see his reaction. He'll be thrilled."

"I'm so excited, I can hardly stand it." Lizbet skipped alongside Brooke through the lobby and out to the parking lot. "Let's celebrate. I'm treating you to a fancy lunch at The Palmetto Cafe. And I get to drink your Champagne, since you can't have any." Her sister stopped walking. "I'm sorry, Brooke. That was insensitive of me. I know how much you like to party. You're giving up your whole life for me."

"Only for nine months, which will fly by. And it's worth it. You're finally getting your baby." She looped her arm through Lizbet's. "But I want a rain check on the Palmetto Cafe. We only have time for a quick bite and still make it to Dad's condo by one."

Tingles of excitement over the prospect of seeing Grady again danced across Brooke's chest. She was thrilled to have him back in her life. They'd once been so close, and she'd loved him like a brother.

Forty-five minutes later, as the sisters showed Grady around their dad's condo, he opened and closed doors, impressed by the empty closets.

"There wasn't much to clear out," Brooke explained. "Dad had few needs and lived simply."

In the kitchen, Grady peeked inside the dirty oven. "Give it a good cleaning and we'll put it on the market. The week before Labor Day, if possible."

"But that's in less than two weeks," Lizbet protested.

Grady appeared surprised. "We can push it back, if that's too soon. But I suggest you get ahead of the surge of new properties coming on the market after the holiday weekend."

"I still think we should wait until late September or early October," Lizbet said.

Brooke gave her sister a sharp look. "Why? What's the point in waiting?"

Lizbet waved a hand at the living room. "There are so many memories of Dad here."

"What memories? We never spent any time here. Dad never even invited us over for dinner. There's no reason to wait, Liz. We'll put it on the market in two weeks," Brooke said, making the executive decision that being an older sister afforded her.

"I can recommend an inexpensive cleaning crew," Grady said. "You won't have to lift a finger."

"Perfect." Brooke turned to Grady. "Do you have time to walk through the Tradd Street house? I'd like your thoughts on what we must do to get that house ready to sell." When they'd spoken on the phone, Brooke and Grady had devised a plan to get him to the Tradd Street house without making Lizbet suspicious.

"What? Why?" Lizbet's face beamed red. "We agreed to wait."

"We're going to sell it at some point. If we know what's involved, we can plan accordingly." Brooke smiled at Grady. "We'll meet you there in ten minutes."

As Brooke suspected, Grady wasn't as optimistic about

putting the Tradd Street house on the market. "Sorting through all this will be a monumental task," he said about the contents of the sweltering attic.

Brooke felt sweat trickle down her back. "You're looking at three generations of our family's junk. It'll take some time. But we'll get it done."

Lizbet fanned her face. "In October or November when the weather cools."

Brook scoffed, "But that would mean waiting until after the holidays to put it on the market."

"So? What's the hurry? Let's talk about this downstairs. I can't think when it's this hot," Lizbet said and hurried down the stairs.

Brooke gave Grady a helpless look. "I'm sorry."

"She has a sentimental attachment to this house. And understandably so."

Brooke glared at him. "Whose side are you on?"

Grady's hands shot up. "Nobody's. I'm being honest."

"I know," she said with a sigh. "Let me show you the rest of the house."

Lizbet was waiting for them in the foyer. "Since he's here, Grady is going to tell us what needs to be done when the time comes," Brooke said and led them into the living room before her sister could argue.

Grady fingered the silk yellow-and-white striped drapes. "These are dry rotted. I would suggest taking them down."

Lizbet's brow hit her hairline. "And leave the windows bare?"

Grady lifted back the drapery panel. "These aren't just any windows. They are beautiful handblown glass windows." He let the panel fall back into place. "The house has nice bones, but the kitchen and baths are outdated. Whoever buys it will need to renovate. Not all buyers are willing to do that."

They continued the tour of the downstairs with Grady pointing out things that would need to be fixed or replaced before going to market. "Bottom line, you have some work to do to get ready."

"All the more reason to wait until next spring," Lizbet snapped.

Brooke took Lizbet by the hand. "Excuse us a minute, Grady," she said and dragged her sister outside to the front porch. "Why are you being so difficult about this?"

"Because I told you I needed some time to think about it. And I don't appreciate you pressuring me."

"We need to do this now!" Brooke said, her temper flaring. "If we wait until next spring, I'll be in my last trimester of pregnancy, and you'll be getting ready for the baby."

Lizbet wrenched her hand free and moved to the edge of the porch. "But there are so many memories in this house. All Mom's stuff is here."

"But Mom isn't here, Liz." Brooke joined her at the railing. "You heard Grady. The kitchen and baths need updating. We can either renovate or sell. I realize there's a lot of work involved with getting it ready for the market. If you won't help me, I'll do it alone. But I don't want to be packing boxes when I'm seven months pregnant."

"That's why we should wait until after the baby comes."

"Didn't you hear what I just said? We don't have the luxury of waiting. Every day that passes, the house goes into further decay."

"Give me a break," Lizbet said. "The house isn't decaying."

The sisters stare at each other, neither of them blinking, daring to give in. Finally, Lizbet broke the silence. "Just give me a little more time. We can't clean out the attic until the weather cools anyway." She stepped down off the porch. "I should head home. I have to be at work soon."

"I'll walk you to the car." Brooke looped her arm through her sister's as they strolled down the sidewalk. She didn't want Lizbet to leave on a bad note. "Can you believe we're pregnant?"

"No! I can't wait to tell Jamie." When they reached the car,

Lizbet threw her arms around Brooke. "I don't want to leave you. I wish we lived in the same town."

"We'll attempt to see each other as much as possible." Brooke gave Lizbet one last hug before tucking her in the car and turning back toward the house.

Grady was waiting for her on the porch. "Is everything okay?"

"She'll eventually come around. But I will not sit around twiddling my thumbs while I wait. I'm moving forward with getting the house ready for market."

"That's great news! I'll come back tomorrow or Friday to measure your square footage. I need some caffeine before my next appointment. Wanna go with me to Brown Dog Deli for a coffee?"

Coffee was no longer in her diet. But Brown Dog Deli had delicious smoothies. "Sure! I could go for a cool treat in this heat," she said and walked with him out to his car.

On the short drive over to Broad Street, Grady said, "Eliza Erwin is getting married this weekend. Do you remember her? She was several grades below us."

"Vaguely. Is she the pretty redhead?"

"I never thought she was that pretty, but she has auburn hair." Grady waited for traffic to clear before making a right-hand turn on Broad Street. "Because our dads are partners in the same law firm, I've been invited to the wedding. I was wondering if you'd be my plus-one and spare me the humiliation of having to go alone." He grinned over at her. "For old time's sake."

The thought of spending the evening with Grady appealed to Brooke more than it should for a gay woman. "Why not? It'll be like the prom all over again."

"Awesome! Both the ceremony and reception are being held at Magnolia Plantation. It's black tie, and it starts at six o'clock. We should leave no later than five to get there in time."

"I'll be ready." Brooke mentally inventoried the contents of her closet, ultimately deciding she would need to go shopping for something new.

The lunch crowd had cleared out at Brown Dog Deli, and only one person was waiting in line in front of them. They'd no sooner gotten their drinks than Grady's phone pinged with an incoming text.

Glancing down at his phone, he said, "I'm sorry, Brooke. I need to go. My client needs to meet earlier than planned."

"No worries. You go on. I'll walk home."

A worried look crossed his face. "Are you sure? It's super hot out."

She planted a hand on her hip. "I'm a Charlestonian. I'm used to the heat." She held up her pineapple smoothie. "Besides, I have my refreshment."

They exited the cafe together and parted on the sidewalk. As he crossed the street to his car, he hollered, "I'll call you tomorrow to set up a time to measure the house."

She gave him a thumbs-up and headed in the opposite direction toward home. Brooke was grateful for a moment alone. She needed time to process her new reality. She was pregnant. A human being was growing inside of her. Maybe even two. She could not turn back now. She would give up wine and gain thirty pounds. All a small price to pay for the gift she was giving her sister.

She pondered the miracle of childbirth, of a man and woman with different body parts coming together for procreation. The way God had intended for all species. But the world had come a long way since the days of Adam and Eve. Lizbet certainly wouldn't be getting her baby if not for the advancements of modern medicine. Brooke was carrying a baby created by fertilizing her sister's egg with her brother-in-law's sperm. A test-tube baby. How was that for unconventional? Then again, Brooke had never done anything the conventional way. Not so long ago, Brooke and Sawyer had planned to get pregnant by injecting semen from a total stranger into one of their bodies. She'd been all in on the idea but now the process somehow seemed wrong. Against God's will.

Her opinions on several important life issues had shifted since the breakup with Sawyer. Maybe this fresh start she so desperately wanted was more internal than external. Maybe she needed more than a new place to live. What if . . . She dismissed the idea as outrageous, but as she walked the uneven sidewalk toward home, the possibility kept coming back to her. What if she tried being with a man for a change?

Doubt crept into her thoughts as she approached her block. Was she doing the right thing in getting the house ready for the market without her sister's approval? If she waited until spring, Lizbet would be busy with a newborn, even more so if she had twins. The timing seemed right now, but selling their family's home was an enormous deal. What if she was wrong? What if she regretted getting rid of it?

Brooke arrived home to find an old-fashioned red and white For Sale sign taped to the storm door window. She wondered if it was the same sign from the shelf in the back of the gardening shed, the one she vaguely remembered her mother using when she sold her wood-paneled station wagon decades ago. Her mama was sending her a message. Lula was granting Brooke permission to sell the house.

eleven
annie

Everything that could go wrong *did* go wrong in preparing for Eliza Irwin's wedding on Saturday. The bride and her mother, who had spent eighteen months planning every tiny detail for the ceremony and reception, complained about the signature drink being too tart and the lamb lollipops being tough. They insisted they'd asked for ham delights instead of sweet potato ham biscuits and would never have dreamed of ordering deviled eggs.

When Eliza whined about the catering menu being seafood heavy, Annie forced back the urge to wrap her hands around the girl's scrawny neck and choke the life out of her. They'd discussed her future mother-in-law's seafood allergy at least a dozen times during their many planning sessions.

"If she has an allergic reaction and dies during my wedding reception, I'm holding you two personally responsible!" Eliza cried, jabbing a bony finger at Heidi and Annie.

Heidi placated Eliza in the calm tone of voice she reserved for hysterical brides. "You have nothing to worry about, hon. I've catered several events for your mother-in-law in her own home, and she always serves seafood. Guests expect such delicacies at weddings as lavish as yours. After all, Charleston is the seafood capital of the Southeast." She escorted Eliza and her mother out of the kitchen. "Now, you two go pamper yourselves while we do our jobs. Trust me, everything will be splendid."

Annie and Heidi had the least of the problems. The florist and wedding planner had the real headaches.

Eliza had insisted on using blue hydrangeas as the focal point of her bouquets and table arrangements. "The petals match my eyes," she'd claimed. Unfortunately, hydrangeas don't hold up well in the sweltering heat. And Eliza had chosen to marry on one of the hottest days of the summer, the forecast calling for temperatures over a hundred with heat indexes reaching 110.

The heat made everyone thirstier than usual, and the parched bridesmaids began gulping down mimosas when they arrived at noon for hair and makeup. By three o'clock, they were well on their way to being drunk, and the heavy makeup the artist had applied to their faces was dripping onto their pale blue dresses. The wedding planner located an air-conditioned room inside the building where the young women could cool down, sober up, and have their makeup reapplied.

The worst disaster of the day involved the wedding cake. The driver delivering the massive ten-layer cake from Atlanta was unaware his refrigerated compartment had gone on the fritz. When they rolled up the rear door to remove the cake, they discovered all the icing had melted onto the floor of the truck.

Annie's heart sank as she stared at the ruined cake. "What're we gonna do?" she asked her mom. Even though it wasn't technically their responsibility, Annie and Heidi felt obligated to come up with a solution.

"The only thing we can do. Scrape off what's left of the old icing and make a batch of new buttercream frosting."

Annie had been working on the cake for nearly two hours when Heidi returned to the kitchen from outside, where she had been putting the final touches on the food tables. "More bad news."

"Ugh. I'm afraid to ask," Annie said, leaning against the counter, bracing herself.

Heidi stuck her finger in the bowl, licked off the icing, and ran her tongue over her lips. "Yum! That's superb, by the way."

Annie waved the spatula at her. "Come on, Heidi. Out with it. What happened?"

"As you know, the groom's father rented a van to take the groomsman to Kiawah for the day to play golf. Well, the van got a flat tire on the way home. They changed the tire, but they are now stuck in traffic with an ETA of 5:45."

"Not good. That only gives them fifteen minutes to get ready for the ceremony."

"Yep. And there's more. The weather," Heidi said, pointing at the window.

Setting down her spatula, Annie went to the window and looked out at the grand back lawn where a black cloud dominated the sky above the enormous sailcloth tent. "But there's no rain in the forecast."

Heidi came to stand beside her at the window. "According to the radar, it's only a single pop-up thunderstorm. I'm praying it skirts us. Let's look on the bright side. If nothing else, the rain will cool things off."

As they watched, a streak of lightning flashed, and the sky opened. The rain came down in torrents for ten minutes before stopping as quickly as it had started.

Heidi turned away from the window. "Looks like we're in luck. As far as I can tell, the tables under the tent didn't get wet. Let's grab some towels out of the van to dry off the chairs for the ceremony."

As she approached the lawn with her stack of towels, Annie spotted Tyler among the guests sipping cocktails on the lawn. She kept her head lowered while she dried the chairs, hoping he didn't see her. They'd arranged to meet twenty minutes ago, but she'd been so busy, she hadn't even had time to change.

She was carrying the sodden towels back to the catering van when Tyler caught up with her. "Annie! There you are."

She smiled at him. He looked sexy in black tie with his sandy hair slicked back. "Hey, Tyler."

"Where have you been? You were supposed to meet me." He scrutinized her work attire. "And why haven't you changed? The ceremony is starting in a few minutes."

"I'm sorry. You wouldn't believe the day we've had. And that unexpected storm delayed us even more."

His eyes turned cold. "Sounds like a personal problem to me."

Annie tucked the ball of wet towels under one arm. "What's that supposed to mean?"

"I've hardly seen you all week. I'm not sure I can be in a relationship with someone who works all the time."

Annie held his gaze. "As I've said before, this is my career, Tyler. I have little control over my hours."

"You would if you hired someone to supervise some of these parties, like I suggested. You'll never have a social life if you don't." He fingered a smudge of flour off her cheek. "You realize I can have any girl I want, right? I could've asked several other girls to be my date tonight. But I asked you, and now I'm stuck out here drinking my signature cocktail alone while you're mopping up the floor."

"I wasn't mopping up the floor. I was drying off chairs so the guests can sit during the ceremony."

"You *are* a guest. My guest. You need to up your game if you wanna be my girlfriend."

Anger flashed hot within her. "You need to up *your* game by being more supportive of my career. I need to finish up a few things. Then I'll change clothes and come find you."

Continuing to the small parking area behind the kitchen, Annie tossed the wet towels into the back of the van and climbed in behind them. She stripped off her uniform—black pants and a white blouse—and tugged the dress she'd brought with her over her head. She'd been half asleep and distracted that morning, thinking about the long workday ahead, when she'd grabbed the first thing she'd seen in her closet. Her pink dress would've been perfect for the occasion. This gray knit dress with elbow-length sleeves was more appropriate for a business meeting than an August wedding.

The ceremony was beginning by the time Annie sat down in the empty chair beside Tyler.

His lip curled as he inspected her dress. "Seriously, Annie. We're at a wedding. This is a joyous occasion. You're dressed for a funeral in the dead of winter." His eyes fell to her feet. "I think you forgot something."

Annie's eyes followed his to her black running shoes. "Oops. I'll be right back."

"And do something with your hair while you're at it," he called after her in a loud whisper as she slipped away.

Annie hadn't thought to bring any cosmetics, but her mom never left home without her makeup bag. Returning to the van yet again, she applied makeup and tied her hair back as best she could with only the rearview mirror to see herself. When she was satisfied with her appearance, she closed the mirror, stuffed her feet into her black ballet flats, and went to the kitchen. She'd already missed the ceremony. She might as well check on a few things while she was here.

Tyler's frustration with her career was mounting, and she was on the verge of losing him. But she couldn't abandon Heidi during the grandest wedding they'd ever catered. She would do her best to split her time between work and Tyler.

Annie put out several fires in the kitchen before she went in search of Tyler again an hour later. She found him swinging an attractive blonde wearing a lime-green ruffly silk dress around on the dance floor.

Annie waited patiently for the song to end and the band to announce they were taking a break before approaching them. "Sorry that took so long," she said, tucking herself under his arm.

The young woman gave Annie's gray dress a look of disapproval. "Who are you?"

Annie straightened, holding her head high. "I'm Annie. Tyler's girlfriend."

"Seriously?" the blonde said, looking at Tyler for confirmation.

"Seriously," he said with a single nod.

"You're not from Charleston," said the blonde, as though she knew everyone from Charleston. "Where did you go to college?"

"CIA in New York." When the blonde appeared confused, Annie added, "The Culinary Institute of America."

"I mean undergrad. Duh. I was a Tri Delt at UNC."

Before Annie could respond, the groom appeared at the microphone, announcing the bride was throwing her bouquet.

"That's my cue." The blonde kissed her fingers and pressed them to Tyler's lips. "Thanks for the dance."

"Anytime, Jess." Tyler appeared proud of himself, as though he'd accomplished a major feat by asking Jess to dance.

Annie scolded herself as she watched Jess parade off in her lime-green dress. She would have to try harder if she wanted to fit into Tyler's world.

He pulled Annie into his arms. "Where have you been?"

"Working. I'm sorry, Tyler. If I'd known things would be this chaotic, I never would've agreed to be your date."

"You have a choice, Annie. You can be the guest at the top of everyone's A-list. Or you can go through life as the hired help."

Annie gulped back fear. She knew how to serve the privileged class. She had no clue how to be one of them. This was her big chance to have everything she'd ever wanted. She couldn't blow it. "This is my career, Tyler. Heidi and I own this business together. I'm committed to her."

"What about your commitment to me?"

"I'm committed to you too. I promise. I'm sorry I upset you tonight. If you'll give me another chance, I'll make it up to you," Annie said, resting her head on his shoulder.

He kissed her hair. "I'll give you another chance, because I'm really into you. But you are replaceable. Every single girl here would give anything to be my girlfriend."

"I promise I won't let you down." Annie was lucky to have won the coveted role as Tyler Gerry's girlfriend. She had no intention of relinquishing the position.

cooper

Cooper dreaded the wedding. He scolded himself for accepting the invitation. And he almost bailed when Lia insisted they ride on the bus the bride's parents had arranged to transport the younger and out-of-town guests from downtown Charleston to Magnolia Plantation. When he arrived at the venue, he excused himself to use the restroom. He needed to collect himself after spending an hour with the wedding attendees, most of whom were partying like they were back in college. While he had fond memories of his years in college, it was not a place he wanted to be now.

While in search of the men's room, he spotted Tyler and Annie in what appeared to be a heated discussion. Cooper ducked behind a potted plant to eavesdrop. Tyler was apparently irritated with Annie for having to work the reception. He even told her she needed to *up her game* if she wanted to be his girlfriend. Who did this guy think he was? Some people had to earn a living. At least she'd stood up to him. Cooper almost cheered out loud when she told Tyler he needed to up his game by being more supportive of her career.

After using the restroom, Cooper returned to the party, but he kept an eye out for Annie as she hustled back and forth between the kitchen and Tyler. Cooper's heart went out to her. She didn't look her best in that drab dress. Every time Annie turned her back on Tyler, he dragged a different hot chick onto the dance floor.

Despite his concern over Annie, Cooper found himself having a good time. Lia turned out to be an exceptional date. She was an excellent dancer, and she made him laugh with anecdotes of the other guests, many of whom were her parents' friends.

Lia was stunning in her hot pink peekaboo dress that showed off her tanned midriff, and he couldn't help but admire her trim figure and toned legs as he followed her through the crowd. She seemed to know everyone at the reception. Many of the people she introduced Cooper to were already familiar with his work. To those that weren't, Lia delivered her persuasive sales pitch, enticing them to attend the next showing at her gallery.

The crowd had dwindled around eleven o'clock when Lia hooked her arm through Cooper's. "Come on! I want you to meet my brother." She guided Cooper to a cluster of people waiting to bid farewell to the bride and groom. To Cooper's horror, she stopped in front of Tyler. "Cooper, this is my brother, Tyler. Tyler, this is Cooper, the artist I've been telling you about."

Cooper was momentarily speechless, but once he contemplated the connection, he could totally see how Lia and Tyler might be cut from the same cloth.

"Right. Cooper. We met at the gallery opening," Tyler said in a dismissive tone.

"Not officially." Cooper had seen Tyler with Annie that night, but she had not introduced them. He extended his hand to Tyler. "I'm Cooper Hart. Nice to meet you, Tyler."

Tyler shook his hand. "Likewise."

Lia gestured at Annie. "And this is Tyler's girlfriend, Annie."

Cooper smiled at her. "I know Annie."

Annie gave him a shy smile in return. "Hey, Cooper."

Tyler looked suspiciously from Annie to Cooper and back to Annie. "How do you know each other?"

"From Prospect," Annie explained. "Cooper is the first cousin of my half brother Jamie."

Tyler appeared relieved. "So y'all are blood kin?"

A flush creeped up Annie's neck. "Not exactly. Jamie and I have the same father. Jamie's and Cooper's mothers are sisters."

Tyler placed a possessive arm around Annie. "Sounds like incest to me," he said, his comment intended to be funny, but no one laughed.

"What's up with those two?" All eyes followed Tyler's to the only couple remaining on the dance floor. They were entwined in each other's arms and moving slowly around the dance floor, even though the band had stopped playing and was packing up their instruments. "I thought Brooke was gay."

"She is," Annie said. "At least she was. She just broke up with her long-time girlfriend. Who's that guy with her?"

"Grady Ellington, one of my best friends from high school. I haven't seen him since he moved back to town from Atlanta."

As their small group watched, Brooke and Grady drew apart and gazed at each other.

"See!" Tyler swept an arm in their direction. "I'm telling you, something is going on between those two."

Brooke and Grady left the dance floor and walked towards them.

"Grady!" Tyler pumped his old friend's hand. "Good to see you, man. I heard you were back in town. Why haven't you called me?"

"I've been meaning to. But I've been busy with my new job."

A devilish grin tugged at Tyler's lips. "Not too busy to reconnect with Brooke. What's going on between you two?" He wagged a finger at Brooke and Grady. "If I didn't know better, I'd think you two were a couple."

"Be real, Tyler. You know I'm gay," Brooke said.

"Are you sure about that?" Tyler teased.

Brooke rolled her eyes. "What kind of question is that? Of course I'm sure." She smiled up at Grady. "We were close in high school. I'm glad to have my best friend back in town."

"Everyone knows the best relationships begin as friendships. I recognize love when I see it." Tyler pulled Brooke in for a half hug. "You're on the verge of straying to the other side of the street. You just don't know it yet."

Brooke shoved him away. "Shut up, Tyler. God, you're annoying."

Lia stared daggers at her brother. "Give it a rest, Tyler. The subject of Brooke's sexuality is officially off the table."

"Fine," Tyler said, throwing his hands in the air. "Let's talk about my birthday. I'm turning thirty in two weeks. To celebrate, I'm throwing a kick-ass party at the house on Sullivan's Island."

Lia's brow hit her hairline. "Do Mom and Dad know about that?"

"Duh. Whose idea do you think it was? I'm having a house party on Labor Day weekend, and you're all invited. Including you." Tyler fixed his gaze on Cooper. "I've forgotten your name, Ginger."

Anger surged through Cooper, but he kept a straight face. "Surely you can be more original than *Ginger*."

"Original is overrated. You're the only man at this reception with a ridiculous knot of hair on top of your head. I guess that makes you a queer." Tyler burst into a fit of laughter while the rest of their group remained silent.

Cooper glared at Tyler. "Now who's being original? You're the only one here laughing. I guess that makes you . . . not funny. In fact, I'd call you pathetic."

"Who are you calling pathetic, loser?" Tyler slammed a hand into Cooper's chest, shoving him backward.

Righting himself, Cooper stepped close to Tyler and stared down at him. While Tyler was fit, Cooper was a full head taller with broader shoulders. "Are you sure you wanna fight? Little guy like you will lose for sure."

"That's it. Let's go," Tyler said, coming out of his tuxedo jacket and tossing it on the ground.

Annie stepped between them. "Stop! Please! We're at a wedding."

The bridesmaids appeared with baskets of bubbles and handfuls of sparklers. The maid of honor lined everyone up to prepare for the bride and groom's departure.

Turning his back on Tyler, Cooper said to Lia, "I've had enough. Can we go now?"

"No!" she shrieked. "We can't leave before the bride and groom."

Disappointment set in as Cooper endured the newlyweds' departure. The evening had been going so well. For a few brief hours, he'd forgotten about Charles and Maggie. Afterward, he migrated with the crowd to the parking lot for the rowdy bus ride back to town. By the time they arrived at the drop-off destination, Cooper had a splitting headache and longed for his own bed. But he was too tired and tipsy to drive back to Prospect. Lia was a good time, but he didn't want to sleep with her. Especially now that he knew she was Tyler's sister.

On the short walk to her apartment, Lia said, "You'll be my date for Tyler's birthday weekend, won't you?"

Cooper stuffed his hands in his pocket. "After what just happened with your brother, I'm pretty sure I'm not invited."

Lia took hold of Cooper's arm. "Don't let Tyler get to you. He can be a pain in the butt sometimes. He's easier to take in small doses."

"When he's not the center of attention?"

"Exactly. Besides, I can invite whomever I want for Labor Day. It's my beach house too."

"I'll think about it and let you know." He had a lot on his plate at work, and two weeks seemed like a long way off.

When they reached Lia's apartment, she offered him a night-cap, but he asked for a glass of water instead. "I have to be back in Prospect at the crack of dawn. If you don't mind, I'll just grab a couple of hours' sleep on your sofa and sneak out whenever I wake up."

"If you're sure," she said, not bothering to hide her disappointment. She disappeared down the bedroom hallway and returned a minute later with a blanket and pillow.

Cooper dozed, on and off, throughout the night, but he was too worried about Annie to sleep soundly. He slipped out of Lia's apartment just before dawn. The first rays of sunrise greeted him as he crossed the Ashley River and exited onto the highway heading toward Prospect. He tuned into his favorite country music station and tried to focus on the work waiting for him at home. But his thoughts kept drifting back to Annie. Something told him she was way in over her head with Tyler. And there was no longer any question in his mind. He was still very much in love with her.

thirteen
brooke

Brooke and Grady argued over who would drive Grady's car home from the wedding reception. "But I've only had a couple of drinks," Grady claimed.

"And I've only had a couple of sips," Brooke countered. And she'd faked those sips. She'd poured the signature drink out in the grass when he wasn't looking.

"I'm tired of arguing. You win." Grady handed over the keys. "You've changed, Brooke. What happened to the party girl I knew in high school?"

She got pregnant, Brooke thought, but she said, "Everyone has to grow up sometime."

"Everyone but Tyler," Grady grumbled as he got into the passenger seat.

Silence fell over them as Brooke navigated the dark road back to town. She wondered if she would go back to partying after the baby came, or if her life would forever change. Where was the fun in growing up?

Brooke glanced over at Grady, but his head was pressed against the window, his expression a blank slate. Had she offended him in some way?

"You're awfully quiet over there. Is everything okay?" she asked.

Lifting his head off the window, he smiled softly at her. "I was just thinking about Tyler's birthday weekend. Would you like to go with me?" He quickly added. "As friends, I mean."

Brooke tightened her grip on the steering wheel. "I'm not sure I can handle an entire weekend of Tyler."

Grady chuckled. "I agree he can be difficult. But I'm gonna go, since I don't have any plans, and I never pass up a chance to spend the weekend at the beach. Why don't you come with me? We'll have fun."

The idea of spending a beach weekend with Grady both appealed to her and confused her. She let out a sigh. "House parties aren't really my scene with everyone shacking up together."

"You've been to Tyler's beach house before. They have at least ten bedrooms. I'm sure we can figure something out. Do you have other plans for Labor Day?"

"Only cleaning out my attic." Brooke wasn't sure she could endure the drunken party scene for three nights.

Grady, as though reading her mind, said, "We'll do our own thing. We can have dinner at The Obstinate Daughter one night and go for bike rides and long walks on the beach."

"That does sound nice. Let me think about it."

As they neared Charleston, Brooke asked, "Do you want me to drop you at home? You can get your car tomorrow."

"Honestly, I'm fine to drive the short distance. Besides, I don't want you going into an empty house alone."

"I'm a big girl, Grady. I can take care of myself." Secretly, she enjoyed being fussed over. Grady was raised a gentleman, perhaps the last of a dying breed.

She parked on the curb in front of her house, and they strolled up the sidewalk to the porch. Taking her key, he unlocked the door and turned back toward her, hooking an arm around her waist and kissing her on the lips. She tensed at first, surprised, but she quickly relaxed as his lips explored hers. Their bodies fit perfectly, as though they were meant to be together. Given the history of their friendship, perhaps they were.

"What was that for?" she asked in a breathy whisper when the kiss ended.

Grady grinned. "I've wanted to do that all night. I didn't think you'd kiss me willingly, so I had to sneak attack you. And I'm glad I did, because now I know."

She cocked her head to the side. "Know what?"

"What I've always suspected. There may be more than friend-ship between us." He kissed her again, this time with more passion. Her knees grew weak, and her body went limp in his arms.

Brooke had never been kissed so tenderly, and when their lips parted again, she was at a loss for words.

"Sleep on that, pretty lady." He kissed her forehead before leaving the porch. Midway down the sidewalk, he turned around to face her. "By the way, there's a house near Colonial Lake coming on the market soon," he said, walking backward. "You should look at it. It would be perfect for you."

Brooke held out her hands, palms up, as if to say what's the point. "I can't afford to buy a house until we sell Dad's condo."

"We can work out the financing. Besides, you should educate yourself on the current market. And the best way to do that is check out what's available."

"That makes sense, I guess."

Grady got in his car and started the engine. As he drove off, he flashed her a silly face that reminded Brooke of her old Grady from high school. *The best relationships begin as friendships.*

Brooke watched his car disappear around the corner before going inside to the kitchen for a glass of milk. She'd always loved milk. She was thrilled to have the excuse of pregnancy to drink more of it.

She stood at the back window, looking out at the moonlit night. The vision of her mama pruning her rose bushes in her perennial garden popped into her head and brought a tear to her eye. Swiping away the tear, she looked up at the starry sky.

"Hey, Mama. I know you're up there watching over me. Did you see Grady kiss me just now? I sure wish you were down here. I could use some sound advice right about now. I miss not having you and Dad to talk to. You tried, but I don't think you ever truly approved of me being gay. I imagine you would be in full support of a relationship between Grady and me."

Brooke rested her head against the window. She couldn't stop thinking about what Tyler had said at the reception. *I recognize love when I see it. You're on the verge of straying to the other side of the street. You just don't know it yet.*

She'd kissed a few boys in her life, most of them pimply faced teenagers while playing spin the bottle. But she'd only been romantically interested in two people—Annabelle Butler, her high school girl crush, and Sawyer.

The lingering sensation of Grady's lips on hers brought a smile to her face. That kiss was . . . Amazing. Sensual. Delicious. She cautioned herself not to read too much into it. Her loneliness could be confusing her, tricking her into feelings that weren't real. The last thing she wanted was for Grady to be her rebound person. If they hooked up and it didn't work out, it could destroy their friendship. Besides, she was foolish to even be thinking about romance now that she was pregnant with her sister's baby.

She would sleep on it as Grady had suggested. Perhaps her feelings for him would be less complicated in the morning.

Placing her glass in the dishwasher, she went about her nightly routine of turning off lights and locking up the house. She was surprised to find the back door unlocked. A shiver ran down her spine. She was always careful about locking doors. On the other hand, she'd been running late and wasn't ready when Grady arrived. She'd probably just forgotten to check the back knob before leaving for the wedding.

Brooke couldn't shake the uneasy feeling that had settled over her as she climbed the stairs to her bedroom. And when she woke with a start during the night, she was certain she smelled Sawyer's floral perfume. She got up and went downstairs, double-checking that both doors were still locked before returning to bed. Unable to fall back asleep, she tossed and turned for hours. Every little noise set her further on edge. The hum of the air conditioner turning off and on. A siren in the distance and a dog barking on the street in front of the house. Just before dawn, she gave up on sleep and went up to the attic to begin the arduous process of sorting through boxes. She found little of interest—musty old clothing, broken furniture, and toys no child would ever want to play with.

When she could no longer stand the heat around eleven, she came down out of the attic and turned her attention to household chores. Late that afternoon, Brooke was cleaning her bathroom upstairs when she found a wadded-up tissue in the wastebasket. She used tissues to blow her nose, but she usually flushed them down the toilet. Removing the tissue from the wastebasket, she smoothed it out on the marble floor. In the center of the tissue were smudges of Cover Girl's Bronzed Glow lipstick. Sawyer's signature color.

Her heart beat in her throat as she flew down the stairs and double-checked all the windows and doors on the first floor. The house was locked up tight.

Brooke searched every room on both floors from top to bottom, but the only trace of her ex was an old UCLA T-shirt, abandoned on the top shelf in the back of the closet they'd shared.

Brooke yearned for a glass of wine. She took a long walk instead.

On Monday morning, Brooke woke to the tantalizing aroma

of coffee, reminding her of the many mornings Sawyer had brought her coffee in bed. Not yet fully awake, she stumbled down the stairs to find the kitchen empty and Keurig coffee maker turned off.

Since coffee was off the table, Brooke brewed herself a cup of tea. Leaning back against the counter, she said out loud to the empty room, "I don't understand, Mama. What're you trying to tell me? Does this have to do with Sawyer? I realize our relationship ended abruptly. But she was awful to Liz and me after Daddy died." She stared down at her tea. "We were all under a lot of pressure. Was I too hasty in kicking her out?"

Brooke listened closely for an answer that never came.

She put the strange happenings out of her mind for much of the day, but late that afternoon, she arrived home from work to find her laundry folded neatly in the basket on top of the dryer. She'd done a load of whites yesterday, but she'd never gotten around to folding them. Was it possible she didn't remember folding them?

Things got weirder as the week progressed.

On Tuesday afternoon, she discovered an empty Starbucks Cold Brew can beside the swing on the front porch. On Wednesday morning, the smell of frying bacon roused her from sleep, but once again, she found no one in the kitchen when she went downstairs. She came home early from work that afternoon with a splitting headache. When she went to the refrigerator for a glass of milk, an open bottle of wine stared out at her.

With trembling hands, she retrieved her phone from her purse and clicked on her sister's number. "Do you believe in ghosts?" she blurted when Lizbet answered the phone.

"In theory, I guess. Every other household in Charleston has one. But I've never encountered a ghost. Why do you ask?"

Brooke quickly filled her sister in on the strange events of the past few days. "The wine is my favorite brand of pinot grigio. But I have bought none since before we did in vitro."

"Hmm. Maybe it was left over from before. Is it possible it was hiding behind a carton of orange juice?"

"I would've seen it before now. I clean out the refrigerator once a week when I bring home my groceries. What if I'm having withdrawals from wine and caffeine?"

"Wait a minute. Are you suggesting you may have drunk the cold brew and wine but don't remember it?" Lizbet asked in an alarmed tone.

"Yes, but I've been very careful. There's no way I could've done that. Besides, that doesn't explain the tissue and laundry." Brooke dropped down in a chair at the kitchen table. "What if I'm losing my mind, Lizbet? What if I have a brain tumor like Mama? That would explain this splitting headache," she said, massaging her temples.

Lizbet sighed. "You're not losing your mind, Brooke. And you don't have a brain tumor. When's the last time you ate anything?"

Brooke had to think about it. "I had a salad for lunch around noon."

"That explains it!" Lizbet said, relieved. "You have a hunger headache. You're pregnant. You're going to have to eat more often."

"That may explain the headache, but not the other odd incidents."

"You're under a lot of pressure, Brooke. This has been a stressful summer for you, with Dad dying, your breakup with Sawyer, and everything related to the in vitro. Even more reason not to put the house on the market until spring."

Irritation crawled across Brooke's skin. "Maintaining this house *is* my primary source of stress. I've gotta run, Liz. I'm sorry I worried you. I'm sure there's an explanation for everything. I'll talk to you in a day or two," she said, and hung up on her sister.

Brooke stared at her phone. Lizbet was right about one thing. She had been under a lot of stress these past few months. And stress did strange things to people.

She felt a pain in her belly, like a mild menstrual cramp. And as she moved about the kitchen, preparing an omelet for her dinner, the cramping intensified. She took her plate to the table, but she was too worried to eat.

What could be causing the cramping? Please, God, don't let me lose this baby.

Brooke had been moving heavy boxes around in the attic, and she'd been freaking out about all these strange occurrences. What if she'd somehow hurt the baby?

She typed out a text to her doctor. *This is Brooke Horne. I'm having some cramping. Should I be worried?*

Dr. Carroll texted back immediately. *Some cramping is normal. Call me if it persists or if you experience spotting.*

Feeling only slightly relieved, Brooke dumped the omelet down the disposal, dragged herself up the stairs, and stretched out on her bed with a cold washcloth draped over her eyes and forehead. Within minutes, she fell into a deep sleep.

The room was dark when she woke around nine o'clock. She'd neglected to close her blinds and the light from the full moon shone in through the window, casting a golden glow over Sawyer, who was sitting on the edge of the bed beside Brooke.

fourteen
cooper

Cooper was thrilled with his renovations. Painting took longer than he'd expected, but once Carlos delivered his furniture and the accessories his mother had chosen, the cottage felt like home. His home.

In his upstairs study, he mounted an oversized computer monitor to the wall, uploaded his favorite bald eagle photo, and set up his easel. The vibe of his new studio, with soft jazz music playing in the background and a gentle breeze rustling the palm fronds on the trees outside his open balcony doors, settled his nerves and inspired him to paint. As a plein air artist, he'd been limited to painting during daylight hours. But this new arrangement would enable him to work late into the night, leaving the daytime hours free to focus on his growing web design business.

Cooper was working at his desk late afternoon on Wednesday when Lia called. "I have a client who wants to commission a painting. I realize this is last minute, but is there any chance you can come to Charleston to meet him?"

Cooper frowned. "You mean now?"

"Whenever you can get here," Lia said. "My client is in town only for the day. Sorry for the inconvenience, but I think this is worth your time. He's a good client, Cooper, with deep pockets."

Cooper rolled his chair back from his desk. He was at a good stopping point for the day. "Okay. With afternoon traffic, it'll take me an hour to get there."

"I understand. Be careful."

Cooper had never painted on commission before. He painted what inspired him. He wasn't keen about painting what inspired other people. And Lia's client's request baffled him.

"I don't understand," he said to Ira Wade. "Why would you want me to paint the view of the Intracoastal Waterway from your living room, when you have the real deal right in front of your eyes?"

Ira chuckled. "It's not for me. It's a gift for my son. He moved to Kentucky for a career opportunity, but he really misses the Lowcountry."

Cooper smiled. "That makes a lot more sense."

"Your landscapes really move me," Ira said, gesturing at the paintings hanging on the gallery walls. "I believe you're the right artist for the job. But I'd like you to visit my property. I own ten acres on the Intracoastal Waterway up near Pawley's Island."

"I'd like that," Cooper said, and they set a date for the week after Labor Day.

The men talked a few more minutes before Ira had to leave to meet a friend for drinks.

Lia glanced at the wall clock. "It's after six already. Do you have time for an early dinner before heading back to Prospect?"

Cooper hesitated. He was eager to work on his eagle painting. But he hadn't been to the grocery store, and his refrigerator was bare. "If we go somewhere quick."

"We can do that." Lia led him out of the gallery and locked

the door behind them. They stood on the sidewalk out front. "Let's walk up to Amen Street. We won't have to worry about parking, and I doubt there will be a wait at this time of night."

"That works for me," Cooper said, and they headed east on Broad toward East Bay Street.

Lia removed a tube of lipstick from her shoulder bag and smeared the bright pink color across her lips. "So, have you decided about Labor Day?"

"Not yet." The thought of being away from his easel for three days did not appeal to him.

"Can you let me know by Friday? I hate to pressure you, but if you're not going, I'd like to find another date."

He wondered if she had someone else in mind. Someone she was interested in. Or if she just felt the need to have a date. "Of course. I'm just bogged down in work right now. And trying to find time to paint."

"You could always bring your easel with you. There's plenty to paint on Sullivan's Island."

"I'm sure. But to be honest, I've started work on a new painting, and I'm not a lot of fun to be around when I'm obsessed with a project.

Lia pursed her pink lips. "Ooh. Is it one of the bald eagles?"

"Yep," Cooper said, smiling. "Fingers crossed, this might be my best work yet."

"In that case, I want you to work. Our beach house has plenty of room. If you decide to come, I'll make sure you have a private place to paint. Tell me about the composition," she said, and for the rest of the walk, he described his work in progress.

When they arrived at Amen Street, the hostess informed them of a forty-five-minute wait.

"Even for the bar?" Cooper asked. He didn't have time to wait for a table.

The hostess shrugged. "The bar is first come, first served.

Something could open sooner. I'll keep you on the list. Let me know what you decide."

Cooper spotted Annie and Tyler in a booth several rows back. Annie waved at them, motioning them over to their table.

"Can we please not eat with them?" Cooper mumbled to Lia, but she was already making her way through the crowded restaurant toward them.

When Lia explained about the wait, Annie said, "In that case, eat with us. We haven't ordered yet." She moved over to Tyler's side of the table. "Come on. Sit down."

Cooper glanced at Tyler, who appeared as though he'd sucked on a lemon.

To irritate Tyler, Cooper said in a cheerful voice, "Sure! Why not?" He sat down in the booth opposite them, with Lia sliding in close beside him.

The foursome carried on a cordial conversation as they perused menus and placed drink and food orders with the waitress. Cooper cast frequent glances at Annie. She was as lovely as ever, her doe eyes warm and face bright. But Cooper detected a weariness about her he hadn't noticed before. Was she stressed out at work? Or was there trouble in Tyler paradise?

"What plans have you made for your birthday weekend so far?" Lia asked her brother.

Tyler's eyes lit up. "It's gonna be a blowout. I've ordered a bunch of kegs and some food."

Lia's mouth fell open. "Dude! This isn't a fraternity party. You're turning thirty. You need to organize activities that don't involve drinking."

Tyler cut his eyes at her. "Where's the fun in that? This is my last chance to party like a rock star. I'm bidding farewell to my twenties, the best ten years of my life."

"You're hopeless." Lia's yellow-green eyes shifted from Tyler to Annie. "Which is why you and I are taking charge."

"Thank you!" Annie said with a wide grin.

"Hold on a minute," Tyler said in an alarmed voice. "What exactly do you mean by *taking charge?*"

"We'll start by canceling the kegs and ordering some bottled beer." Lia slid off the bench to her feet. "Come on, Annie. We need to talk, and I need to use the restroom."

Cooper waited for Lia and Annie to leave the table before saying to Tyler in a teasing tone, "Looks like your birthday weekend just got shanghaied."

Tyler glared at him. "Shut up, man. Something about you bugs me."

Cooper held his steely gaze. "What a coincidence. Something has bugged me since I first met you, you arrogant prick."

Tyler's jaw tightened. "If you weren't dating my sister, I'd beat the crap outta you."

"I'm not dating your sister. She doesn't do relationships. Shall we step outside?" Cooper asked, gesturing at the door. He'd love nothing more than to kick this guy's teeth in.

Tyler looked at the door and back at Cooper. "What do you mean, she doesn't do relationships?"

"That's what she told me," Cooper said in a nonchalant tone. "You'll have to ask her to explain."

"I love my sister, Ginger Boy. You'd better not hurt her."

Anger pulsed through Cooper. "And Annie is *my* friend. You'd better not hurt *her.*"

Tyler's lip curled. "Do us all a favor and get a haircut. You look like a douche with that furball on top of your head."

Before Cooper could hurl the next insult, Annie and Lia arrived back at the table, followed shortly by the waitress with their food.

While they ate, Lia and Annie tossed around activity ideas for Tyler's birthday weekend. Some of them were silly, but many of them had merit. Tyler was noticeably quiet, and more than once, Cooper caught Tyler glaring at him with his creepy, dark eyes.

Cooper was relieved when the meal ended, and they paid their check. On the way back to the gallery, he said to Lia, "About Labor Day, if you'll still have me as your date, I'd like to go."

"Good! I promise it'll be a fun time." Looping her arm through his, she pressed her body close as they continued down East Bay.

They appeared as lovers to the people they passed on the sidewalk. Cooper felt guilty for leading Lia on, but he suspected she could take care of herself. Annie was a different story. Apprehensive that she was in over her head with Tyler, Cooper wanted to be at the house party in case something went wrong. And he had a sinking suspicion, unfortunately, that something would go wrong.

Truth be told, Cooper wanted to go to be near Annie. She'd gotten under his skin again. Perhaps his feelings for her had always been there, hiding beneath the surface for all these years. He'd had other girlfriends along the way, but he'd never cared about any of them except Maggie. And even his feelings for her paled when compared to his feelings for Annie. But Annie was with another guy, and Cooper had to wait for that relationship to fall apart. And when it did, he would be there to help her pick up the pieces.

fifteen
annie

Annie and Tyler stood outside of Amen Street, neither of them making a move to leave. She'd walked to the restaurant from work, and he'd driven straight from his law office across town.

"Do you wanna come over?" Tyler asked in a tone that suggested he didn't really want her to.

"Why don't you come to my place for a change?" she said, although she knew he'd say no. She'd invited him to spend the night a handful of times since moving into the apartment, but he'd always declined. She wondered if he felt uncomfortable outside of his domain when he wasn't surrounded by all his expensive things.

"I have to be in court early tomorrow." He glanced at his Rolex Submariner. "And I have some work I need to do to prepare. I'll drive you home."

They walked to his car in silence. Tyler was in one of his broody moods, and Annie had learned from experience it was best to let him be.

"Is there something you're not telling me about Cooper?"

Tyler asked as he navigated the evening traffic down East Bay Street.

Annie appeared calm despite her pounding heart. "What do you mean?"

He tightened his grip on the steering wheel. "You know what I mean, Annie. Did you and Cooper ever date?"

"No. What makes you think that?" she said with a laugh that sounded fake, even to her own ears.

"Because Cooper could hardly take his eyes off you during dinner." Tyler stopped for a red light and stared over at her. "Tell me the truth, Annie. I won't get mad. We both have skeletons in our closets. I just need to know what I'm dealing with."

Annie looked him straight in the eye as the lie slid smoothly off her tongue. "I'm telling you the truth, Tyler. Cooper and I have never been in a relationship. I'm close with Jamie's family, and Cooper is Jamie's first cousin."

"Right. So you said." The light turned green, and Tyler stomped on the accelerator. When they arrived at her apartment, he parked on the curb out front. "What're your plans for the weekend? Oh wait! Stupid question. I'm sure you're working."

"Believe it or not, we don't have any events booked for the next two weeks." She didn't mention they would likely be booked solid from Labor Day through New Year's Eve.

"Hallelujah." He took the car out of gear and shifted his body toward her. "I have this work thing tomorrow night. One of the senior partners has invited all the attorneys and their significant others to his house in Mount Pleasant for dinner. Will you come with me?"

She smiled. "I'd like that."

"Outstanding. On Friday night, my friend Penny is having a party, and then we can spend the day Saturday on the water. I'd love for my parents to get to know you better." Tyler brushed a lock of her hair out of her face. "What say we cook dinner for them Saturday night at their house? You can impress them with your culinary skills."

Annie groaned to herself. She'd catered for Tyler's mother for years. Helen Gerry had always been professional, but not overly friendly. When Annie saw them at the wedding last weekend, Tyler's mother had been borderline rude. Maybe Annie could win them over with a well-planned, intimate dinner. "That sounds like fun. I'll come up with a special menu."

She leaned over and kissed him. "Are you sure you don't wanna come inside?"

He straightened, pulling away from her. "I wish I could, but I have a lot of work. I'll call you tomorrow."

Annie got out of the car, and he sped off, leaving her standing on the sidewalk. She hated lying to him about Cooper. But Tyler was the jealous type, and she didn't want to cause trouble for Cooper. Especially since he was dating Tyler's sister.

The thought of Lia and Cooper together summoned a pang of jealousy. And, she had to admit, they made a cute couple. Cooper, despite his man bun, was handsome in a boy-next-door kinda way, and Lia was drop-dead gorgeous. When Cooper broke up with Annie, it had taken her years to get over him. She would not go down that road again.

Annie trudged up the stairs to her apartment. As she was gathering up the mail, her phone slid out of her purse to the floor. Tyler hated when she spent too much time on her phone, and she hadn't checked her messages since before dinner. She had five missed calls from Heidi and a string of text messages about a party she was supposed to work but didn't know about. The tone of the messages morphed from curiosity to irritation to concern about Annie's well-being.

She thumbed off a quick message. *I didn't know about the event. But I'm on my way now. Be there in ten.*

Fortunately, the Hammonds lived a few streets over. She

grabbed her bag and took off on foot. Walking would save the time she would spend looking for parking.

The dinner party was in full swing when she arrived. She jumped right in to help serve the entrees and dessert. She didn't have a chance to speak to Heidi until afterward, when the guests were having cognac in the paneled library and the crew was cleaning up in the kitchen.

"I'm sorry I was late. I didn't have this event on my calendar," Annie said as they worked side by side at the sink.

"It was a last-minute gig," Heidi explained. "I should've confirmed with you. I had a hunch you weren't listening when I told you about it yesterday morning. You've been distracted lately. Is everything okay?"

"Yeah. I'm just going through some stuff with Tyler," Annie said, rinsing soap suds off a silver platter and handing it to Heidi.

"What kinda stuff?" Heidi asked, as she dried the platter.

"We'd like to spend more time together, but it's difficult with me always having to work." Annie turned off the sink faucet and faced Heidi. "What do you think about offering Lydia a promotion? She's certainly earned it. We could use another capable person to help coordinate all these events."

Something resembling annoyance crept across Heidi's face. "I'll remind you, we're currently the most reputable caterer in Charleston. And we've achieved that success by running a hands-on operation. One disaster could ruin everything we've worked so hard to build."

Annie folded the dish towel and draped it over the sink. "I'm not suggesting we hire just anyone. But Lydia is different. She's been our head server for years. She knows this business as well as we do."

"I agree. Lydia is my most valuable staff member. But she doesn't have a stake in the game like you and me. You knew what you were getting into when you entered the food service industry."

"I'm not complaining, Heidi. I'm just suggesting we could make life a little easier for ourselves."

Heidi moved over to the refrigerator. As she stacked leftover containers inside, she said, "You've always known exactly what you want, sweetheart. This sudden lack of self-confidence isn't about you being unsure of your career. It's about a certain young man planting seeds of doubt in your mind."

Heat radiated through Annie. "Hold on a second. Who said I was having a confidence crisis? What's so wrong with me wanting a life outside of my career?"

"You weren't worried about your social life before you met Tyler," Heidi said, closing the refrigerator door.

Annie sagged against the counter. "Why don't you like him?"

"Whether or not I like him isn't the issue. I don't think he's right for you."

Annie folded her arms over her chest. "Why? Because his family is wealthy? You think he's too good for me."

"On the contrary." Heidi palmed Annie's cheek. "I think you're too good for him. He has different values than you. We've had to work for everything we have, and he comes from a privileged background. People like him hire people like us to cook for them."

Annie brushed her mom's hand away. "Where is this resentment toward wealthy people coming from? Have you been cooking for them too long?"

Heidi let out a sigh. "You're angry. And tired. You've been working hard, and you deserve some time off. Since we don't have any events booked until after Labor Day, why don't you take the next two weeks to sort out your life?"

"Fine. I will." Annie grabbed her purse and stormed out of the kitchen.

Heidi followed her outside to the piazza. "Don't leave angry, sweetheart."

Annie spun around to face her. "Why shouldn't I be angry

after the things you just said to me? Not only did you accuse me of lacking self-confidence, you dissed my boyfriend."

"It's my job as your mother and business partner to play devil's advocate, Annie. You've been in the industry now for several years. Catering isn't for everyone, and if you decide to try something new, I'll support you a hundred percent. But with my semi-retirement on the horizon, I need to know I can count on you. If you're not committed, we may want to consider selling the business."

Annie had never been more confused, never felt pulled in so many directions. She very much needed some time to think about what she really wanted out of life.

"You're right. I need some time off to think about my future. We'll talk again after Labor Day." She strode angrily off the porch, letting the wrought-iron gate slam behind her on the way out.

Annie didn't slow down until she reached the end of the street. As she strolled the rest of the way home, she replayed the conversation in her mind in slow motion. As much as she hated to admit it, there was some truth to Heidi's accusation. Annie had lost confidence in herself. Because Tyler was planting seeds of doubt in her mind.

Was it possible Annie had outgrown her life? She'd never considered another career. She loved everything about catering events—the planning, preparation, and execution. What else would she do? She was a trained chef, but working in a restaurant did not appeal to her. She imagined herself being married to Tyler. As his wife, her responsibilities would include raising children, planning trips, and sitting on boards of nonprofit organizations. She would lunch with her friends and learn to play tennis and pickleball. Would that be enough to fulfill Annie? She didn't think so.

What Annie needed now was to clear her head. Maybe it was time for Heidi and Annie to go their separate ways.

sixteen
brooke

Brooke sat bolt upright in bed with knees tucked to chest, putting as much distance as possible between her and Sawyer. "How did you get into my house?"

Sawyer dangled a brass key. "You forgot to ask for your key back."

Brooke's mind raced as the puzzle pieces fell into place. "You're the one who's been making coffee and doing my laundry."

Sawyer grinned. "I wanted to remind you of all the nice little things I used to do for you."

"You've been stalking me." Brooke jumped out of bed to her feet. "You've been living in my house since Sunday. I thought you were a ghost."

Sawyer rose slowly to face her. "I've been here since Saturday, actually. I saw you kiss that guy. Are you straight now?"

"That's none of your business." Brooke extended her arm with palm facing up. "Give me the key. I want you out of my house right now."

Sawyer closed her fingers around the key. "I'm not leaving until we talk. I drove a long way to see you."

A thought suddenly occurred to Brooke. She hadn't noticed Sawyer's car on the street. "Where'd you park?"

"Around the corner. You drove past my car every day to work. You should be more observant."

Brooke shivered. "This is all so creepy. Only psychos do stuff like this."

"You know me, Brooke. I'm not a psycho. I'm taking a leave of absence from the residency program. I was on my way home to California when I had the urge to see you. We left things unsettled between us."

"Things are plenty settled, Sawyer. Maybe our relationship didn't end like we wanted it to, but it was time for it to end."

Sawyer lowered herself to the edge of the bed. "Sit down, Brooke. Just give me a few minutes," she said, running her hand across the mattress beside her.

The sight of Sawyer sitting on the edge of her bed, the bed they'd once shared, brought back memories. They'd spent many happy years as a couple. They were building a life together and planning a family. Despite everything that had happened between them, Brooke still had feelings for her ex-lover. On the other hand, Sawyer could be persuasive, and Brooke couldn't afford to put herself in a vulnerable position.

"Not here. We can talk downstairs," Brooke said and walked out of the room ahead of Sawyer.

In the kitchen, Brooke filled the kettle with water for tea while Sawyer poured herself a glass of wine. "Don't you want wine?" she asked, holding up a second empty glass.

"No thanks. I need a clear head for this conversation." Brooke placed a lavender tea bag in her favorite mug and leaned back against the counter. "What you did was wrong, Sawyer. Sneaking around my house like that. You made me think I was losing my mind. I worried I had a brain tumor like my mother."

"I'm sorry, babe. I didn't mean to hurt you." Sawyer brushed

Brooke's long bangs off her forehead. The tender gesture stirred something inside of her, and she moved away.

"I'm not your babe. And don't touch me again." The kettle whistled, and she poured hot water over the tea bag. "You wanted to talk. So start talking."

"Can we go outside to the porch?" The porch swing had been their favorite spot for deep discussions. They'd often drank wine and talked well into the night, planning their future.

"Sure." Brooke grabbed her mug and followed Sawyer outside, sitting as far away from her on the swing as possible.

"Where did we go wrong, Brooke? I've gone through it all in my head, repeatedly. I can't figure it out."

"*You* went wrong, Sawyer. You were hateful to my sister. I'll never forgive you for the way you treated Lizbet."

Sawyer grimaced, as though the mention of Lizbet pained her. "She lived with us for seven months, for crying out loud. And she was always in a bad mood, moping around here and dragging everyone down with her."

"She was ill, Sawyer. She had an emergency hysterectomy right after you left."

Sawyer pressed her lips thin. "I'm sorry to hear that."

Brooke waited for Sawyer to ask about Lizbet. If she'd recovered from the surgery? If she and Jamie were back together? The silence that ensued was very telling. Sawyer despised Lizbet. Perhaps because she was jealous of the close relationship Brooke and Lizbet shared.

"We both made mistakes, Brooke. At least I'm willing to own up to mine."

"Whatever mistakes I made are nothing compared to what you did. My father had just died, and you were awful to me. You ripped my bedroom apart with a knife and made a drunken fool of yourself in our front yard for all the neighbors to see."

Sawyer hung her head. "And I'm sorry about all that. If you give me another chance, I promise I'll make it up to you. We make a good team, Brooke. We just got offtrack. I'm sure we can talk through our differences."

Brooke's headache came back with a vengeance. She should probably eat something, but she felt too queasy to stomach anything. "Not tonight." She slid off the swing to her feet. "I'm going to bed. I have a splitting headache."

"Can I stay the night? We can talk in the morning."

Brooke lacked the energy to argue with her. "In the guest room," she said, and went inside, leaving Sawyer alone on the porch.

She had a bad feeling about letting her ex-girlfriend sleep in the same house, but she didn't know how to get rid of her. She couldn't risk making her angry by asking her to leave. Sawyer had a short temper, and she might do something to hurt the baby.

Brooke grabbed two Tylenol from the bathroom before going to her room and locking the door. Despite being exhausted, she lay awake for hours listening for sounds of Sawyer moving about the house. But she heard nothing. She eventually drifted into a fitful sleep. When she woke on Thursday morning, there were no smells of bacon frying or coffee brewing, and when she went downstairs, there was no sign of Sawyer in the kitchen.

Brooke was starving. She had to eat something before going to work. She didn't think she could stomach eggs. She was craving something sweet. Rummaging through the refrigerator, the only thing she found that appealed to her was a strawberry ice cream sandwich.

She longed to call in sick, to stay in bed all day under the covers. But she couldn't afford to take more time off. She'd left work early yesterday because of her headache, and she was in the middle of several projects that desperately needed her attention.

She pushed through the fatigue and brain fog that bogged her down all day, but when five o'clock rolled around, she was ready for her bed.

Brooke arrived home to find Sawyer at the stove in the

kitchen, a bottle of rosé wine sitting half empty on the counter beside her.

"You're home. Just in time. I made your favorite dinner." Sawyer spun around to face her, a platter of blackened mahi tacos extended in her hands as though she were presenting Brooke a gift.

Brooke's mouth watered. She hadn't felt like eating much all day, but the smell of the tacos made her ravenous. "Those look delicious."

They sat down together at the table, which Sawyer had set with colorful Mexican-style linens. Brooke added a dollop of avocado cream and a spoonful of mango salsa and gobbled the taco down in three large bites. She was reaching for a second taco when she noticed Sawyer watching her.

"What's with the appetite? You usually eat like a bird."

Heat crept up Brooke's neck. "I didn't eat much today. Or yesterday because of my headache."

Sawyer relaxed her shoulders. "I'll take it as a compliment. You missed my tacos."

Brooke stared at the beautiful young woman sitting across from her. Sawyer's tacos weren't all she missed. She missed the companionship of having a significant other. She hated coming home after work to an empty house. She enjoyed having someone to discuss the day's events with over supper. To lounge with in bed on rainy Sunday mornings. And walk with down to the seawall to watch the sunset. So she'd learned something about herself. She hated being alone. But despite any previous doubts she'd been having about their breakup, Brooke knew with abso-lute certainty that Sawyer wasn't the right special someone for her.

Sawyer moved to pour her some wine, but Brooke held her hand over the empty glass. "None for me, thanks."

Sawyer wrinkled her brow. "Since when do you turn down wine?"

Brooke touched her fingers to her temple. "I finally got rid of that awful headache. I don't want to risk it coming back."

Sawyer reached across the table for Brooke's hand. "Why don't we go away together for Labor Day weekend? We could drive down to Beaufort and stay in one of those charming inns we're always reading about. We can talk through all our problems and start fresh."

Brooke wrenched her hand free and chose a second taco from the platter. "Sorry. But I already have plans for Labor Day."

Sawyer's face fell. "Oh really? Where are you going?"

"To Sullivan's Island. An old high school friend is turning thirty."

"Is this old high school friend the guy I saw you kissing?" Sawyer tried to sound nonchalant, but Brooke could tell she was seething inside.

"No. Tyler is Grady's best friend." Brooke settled back in her chair, eating the second taco more slowly to savor the flavors. "So when are you leaving for California?"

"I'm not sure. I was thinking I might stay in Charleston."

Brooke gulped down the food in her mouth. "But I thought you hated the South."

"Isn't it obvious, Brooke? I wanna stay because you're here." Sawyer drained the last of her wine and poured more. "But thanks to Lizbet, I doubt I'll be able to find a job."

Chill bumps crawled across Brooke's flesh. "What does my sister have to do with your career?"

"She told lies about me to the head of oncology. I almost lost my residency. I had to beg them to transfer me to Mass General."

Brooke pushed her plate away, her appetite suddenly gone. "I don't believe you. Lizbet wouldn't do something so devious."

"I don't blame Lizbet for what she did." Sawyer stared solemnly into her wineglass. "I crossed a line, and she was trying to protect you. Do you think she might retract the things she said about me? If she did, I might find a job."

"Why would Lizbet say she was lying when she was telling the truth? I'm sorry, Sawyer, but you brought that on yourself." Brooke got up from the table, rinsed her plate in the sink, and placed it in the dishwasher. She stood beside the table. "It's over between us, Sawyer. You need to leave. And I want my key back," she said, extending her hand.

Sawyer jumped to her feet. "Don't be like this, Brooke. I have a surprise for you. Come with me," she said, dragging Brooke up the stairs to her bedroom.

Standing in the doorway, Sawyer swept an arm at the candlelit room. "Ta-da!" She had turned the bed covers neatly back and spread red rose petals across the crisp white sheets.

Brooke's stomach soured, and she ran down the hall to the bathroom, locking the door and vomiting her dinner into the toilet. She flushed the toilet and rested her head on the seat.

She had to get Sawyer out of her house and out of her life for good. But she had to proceed with caution to avoid sending her mentally unstable ex over the edge. She had no grounds to file a complaint with the police, and she didn't want Grady to know she'd been in a relationship with a psycho. She had one idea that might get rid of her. But it was a long shot.

After rinsing out her mouth, Brooke opened the door to find Sawyer waiting just outside the bathroom in the hallway.

"I heard you throwing up," she said with concern. "Are you okay? Was it the tacos?"

"No." A wave of dizziness overcame her, and Brooke leaned back against the wall. "I'm pregnant with Lizbet's baby. She had the foresight to freeze some of her eggs before the hysterectomy. We did in vitro fertilization with Jamie's sperm."

Sawyer's face beamed red, and her nostrils flared. "Why would you do something so stupid? You're wasting nine months of your life, and you're getting nothing in return."

Brooke pushed off the wall. She was furious with Sawyer for being so self-centered and with herself for ever falling for such a vile person. "I'm giving my sister the gift of life. The gratification in doing this for her is enormous. But I don't expect you to understand such a selfless act." She grabbed Sawyer's arm and marched her down the hall to the guest room. "Pack your stuff."

Brooke remained in the doorway while Sawyer gathered her meager belongings.

When she finished, Sawyer wheeled her small suitcase across the room and stood in front of her. "I have nowhere to go, Brooke," she said, her chin quivering. "Can't I stay a little longer?"

"You need help, Sawyer. Go home to your family in California." She ushered Sawyer down the hall and out the front door. She gave her a quick hug. "We were never meant to be. I mean this sincerely. I hope you have a nice life."

Brooke didn't bother asking for the key again. She was certain Sawyer had made copies. As she stood on the edge of the porch, watching Sawyer get in her car and drive away, she googled locksmiths. She hit a home run on the third call. Pete with Ryan's Locksmith had just finished up a job in the area and promised to be there in twenty minutes.

Brooke sat down on the swing to wait. She would guard her house in case Sawyer returned. She was sitting there five minutes later, replaying the scene with Sawyer, when Grady's SUV pulled up to the curb. He got out and strolled toward her. The kick in his step told Brooke he was in a good mood.

She got to her feet and greeted him with a kiss on the cheek. "This is a surprise. What're you doing here?"

"I was just leaving work and took a chance you might be home." He gestured at the swing. "Are you waiting for someone?"

"A locksmith." The words slipped out before she could stop herself. "I've been having trouble with my locks sticking, and I wanted one key to fit both doors."

He gave her a skeptical look, clearly not believing her. "Isn't it late for a locksmith to be working?"

"I scheduled him for five o'clock. But he got tied up on

another job." She glanced up and down the street. "He should be here momentarily."

"Then I won't keep you." He shifted his feet but remained on the porch.

"No, stay! It's fine!" She sat back down on the swing. "Did you need to see me about something?"

"That house I was telling you about is coming on the market Tuesday. I made an appointment for you to see it late afternoon. You might need to leave work a few minutes early." He sat down beside her. "Here, look. It's on Rutledge Avenue, right across from Colonial Lake."

He handed her his phone, and she scrolled through the pictures on the MLS listing. The small pink cottage with black shutters and dormer windows enamored her. Colorful summer annuals spilled from containers flanking the steps leading to a porch that had a swing much like the one she was sitting on. The inside boasted pale gray walls, a small but updated kitchen, and lots of windows offering plenty of natural light.

She gave him back the phone. "It's adorable. But I still don't see the point in looking at it when I'm not able to buy it?"

"Your dad's condo goes on the market the same day." He tapped on his phone screen and showed her the condo listing. "We already have ten people scheduled for showings. Waterfront property in downtown Charleston is in hot demand. You will likely get several offers. If the timing works out, you could use the earnest money from the condo to make an offer on the pink house. Or I can hook you up with a loan officer who can help you get a bridge loan."

Brooke let out a sigh. "I guess it won't hurt to look at it." She went back to the previous listing and scrolled through the pictures of the pink house again. She could totally see herself living there. Alone, at first, surrounded by her own things, not her mother's castoffs. And then maybe one day with a new partner.

seventeen
annie

Annie was at a loss, with no work to occupy her time. She obsessed over her menu for Saturday night's dinner with Tyler's parents. She considered everything from pork chops in port wine sauce to skirt steak. She didn't dare consider a new recipe. She couldn't afford to bomb when entertaining such important guests.

Her seafood vendor settled the matter when she consulted him on Friday. "I recommend the sole fish," Mark said. "I have the best of the season so far."

"Dover sole sounds perfect," Annie said and ordered two pounds.

Annie envisioned an elegant dinner with tried-and-true recipes. In addition to the Dover sole with lemon caper sauce, she would serve homemade cornbread, and her southern succotash— a take on the traditional dish with fresh okra, cherry tomatoes, and bacon.

Annie was a nervous wreck about the dinner party, but Tyler assured her everything would be fine. "Mom and Dad are spending the day in Beaufort with my aunt and uncle. We'll have the house to ourselves all afternoon to prepare."

But they ran into a group of Tyler's friends when they were out in the boat on Saturday morning and ended up staying on the water later than expected. Fortunately, Annie had done all her shopping the day before.

She was used to cooking in her clients' magazine-worthy kitchens, but Tyler made her nervous, scrutinizing her every move. After she burned butter for the third time, she assigned him a job to get him out of her hair.

"Since we're running behind on time, you can help by setting the table on the piazza," she said, gesturing at the french doors leading from the kitchen to the first-floor porch.

"The piazza?" Tyler said, taken aback. "But we never eat outside. Mom always insists on having dinner in the dining room."

Annie had served twenty people at his mother's mahogany double pedestal table. The idea of sitting down to dinner with his parents at this mammoth table with the priceless Oriental rug under her feet terrified her.

"Then we should do something different and surprise them. Besides, it's not so hot out for a change."

Tyler gave her a skeptical look. "If you say so."

He opened and closed several drawers, gathering the necessary items, and went outside to the porch. But when she went to check on his progress thirty minutes later, she discovered the table set with the napkins and flatware, and Tyler asleep on the daybed swing.

She nudged him awake and waved a paper napkin in his face. "This is not what I had in mind when I asked you to set the table. Where does your mother keep her linen and china?"

He swung his legs over the side of the swing and rubbed his eyes. "In the butler's pantry. You can use whatever you want."

Annie dug her fist into her hip. "Not without your approval. Can you show me?"

"Okay. Fine," Tyler said, and slowly rose to his feet.

The butler's pantry was a narrow room between the kitchen

and the dining room. Cabinets with glass doors covered the upper walls, with rows of drawers occupying the space below the marble counter.

Annie had never paid much attention to the contents of the cabinets before, but inspecting them now, she counted at least five different china patterns stored within. She opened a cabinet and removed a white plate with blue flowers and gold accents. She knew little about fine dinnerware, but she thought the pattern sweet. "What about these?"

"I told you, use whatever you want," Tyler said, as though he couldn't care less.

Rummaging through drawers, she located a blue-and-white floral linen tablecloth with matching napkins. She spotted four small blue-and-white vases on a top cabinet shelf and instructed Tyler to get them down for her. In the kitchen's walk-in pantry, she found a large hurricane lantern and fat creamy pillar candle. Transporting her treasures to the piazza, she set the table with the linens and china and filled the vases with blue hydrangea from Helen's garden.

Heidi was responsible for the decorating side of their catering business, while Annie mostly handled the food. But as she admired her handiwork, she experienced a different satisfaction, a new inspiration for event planning. She didn't need to change careers. She needed to branch out within her current one.

With thirty minutes to spare before the Gerrys were due to arrive home, Annie showered in the guest bathroom and dressed in a yellow sundress. She was mixing cucumber martinis in the kitchen when she heard voices in the front of the house. She took the tray of martinis out to greet Tyler's parents.

Helen and Eugene Gerry reeked of old Charleston money in their impeccably tailored casual summer attire—Helen in a white pantsuit and Eugene in khakis and a blue houndstooth soft jacket. Helen wasn't a natural beauty like Heidi. Her nose was pointy, eyes beady, and lips permanently pressed thin. But she took care of herself. Her taut skin hinted at a recent face-lift and not a single gray hair was visible along the part of her mahogany bob.

"Welcome home," Annie said, offering Helen a drink.

"What's this?" Helen asked, staring down at the green drink as though it were poison.

"A cucumber martini. My specialty."

Helen sipped the martini and grimaced. "That's the worst thing I've ever tasted. It's way too sweet."

"Really? My brides rave about them."

"That explains it." Helen returned the glass to the tray. "Go fix me a vodka and soda with a splash of cranberry."

Annie's heart sank. Helen hadn't asked her husband or son to fix her the drink. She'd *ordered* Annie to do it. Annie had made a grave mistake. She'd wanted to impress the Gerrys with her cooking. But instead of ingratiating herself to them, she'd secured her place in their lives as their caterer. *The hired help.*

Annie passed the tray to father and son, but they both declined a martini. She whispered to Tyler, "Please make your mom's drink while I check on dinner."

Once she was alone in the kitchen, she paused for a moment to collect herself, taking deep breaths until her racing heart slowed. She had no choice but to see the dinner through, but she refused to be ordered around by Helen Gerry.

When Tyler came in search of her a few minutes later, he seemed miffed to find her at the stove preparing the Dover sole. "Why are you hiding out in here? My parents are our guests for the evening. We need to entertain them."

"I'm cooking the fish. Here. Offer them some of these," she said and handed him a tray of crab-stuffed mushrooms.

Annie had never entertained guests in her own home before. Next time, she would plan a menu where everyone would help cook or where everything was prepared in advance.

When Annie called them to the piazza for dinner, Helen's eyes popped out of her head and her hand shook as she pointed at the table. "That's my Herend china, and my Ming dynasty vases, and the table linens I bought on my last trip to India. Who gave you permission to use my things?"

"I . . . um . . ." Annie waited for Tyler to accept responsibility, considering that he'd insisted she use anything she wanted for the table.

"What's the point of having nice things if you're not going to use them?" Eugene said with a wink at Annie. "The table looks lovely, and the food delicious."

"Thank you," Annie said, offering him a smile of gratitude.

Once they were all seated, Helen reached for the expensive bottle of rosé Annie had painstakingly selected from Tasty Provisions. "I refused to drink this. Rosé is for the wannabes who know nothing about wine." She handed the bottle to Tyler. "Son, please grab the Sonoma-Cutrer out of the wine cooler for me."

Tyler jumped to his feet and scurried away.

Annie stared down at her plate and said little while she ate. She had nothing to contribute to the gossip about people she'd worked for but didn't know socially.

Helen only picked at her food, but much to Annie's relief, both Tyler and his father cleaned their plates. Annie gathered the empty plates and went to the kitchen for dessert. She was placing a dollop of homemade whipped cream on the rum babas when, through the open door, she overheard Helen say, "No one is questioning Annie's culinary skills, son. But you don't have to marry her. Find yourself a proper wife and hire Annie to be your live-in chef."

Annie inhaled a deep breath, swallowing past the lump in her throat, and marched out to the porch with the dessert plates.

"What is this dish?" Helen asked, running her fork tines through the whipping cream.

"A rum baba, a sweetened yeast cake soaked in dark rum simple syrup. They used to be popular in France and have recently been making a comeback." Annie smiled. "A word of warning though. They are potent. The alcohol in the rum syrup has not been cooked off."

"Annie spent all afternoon yesterday making these," Tyler said proudly.

Helen forked off a tiny bite and brought it to her mouth. "It tastes like a rum doughnut. I'm not big on desserts," she said, pushing her plate away.

No wonder she's so thin, Annie thought. *She's hardly eaten anything.*

"I'll have yours." Tyler reached for his mother's plate and devoured the baba in three bites.

Eugene smiled across the table at her. "You'd better drive home, Annie. Tyler has been overserved rum baba."

Annie giggled. "That's probably a good idea."

Eugene pushed away from the table. "Honey, why don't you show Annie your garden while Tyler and I do the dishes."

Helen appeared mortified. "I'm sure Annie's not interested in flowers."

"Actually, I'd love to see your garden," Annie said, already on her feet.

Helen spat the names of flowers at Annie as she followed Helen around the walled-in garden. Annie, who knew a lot about flowers, tried to have a discussion with her about her perennials, but Helen wasn't interested.

Helen stopped in front of the small water fountain. "Surely, you realize you don't belong here."

A feeling of cold dread overcame Annie. "What do you mean?"

"You're not in Tyler's league, Annie. We have high standards, which you do not meet."

"But you don't even know me," Annie said, her voice barely audible.

"I know enough. I'm sure you're a nice girl. But you have nothing to offer our family."

There was no point in arguing with this woman. Helen Gerry

had already made up her mind, and nothing Annie said could change it. "If you'll excuse me. I need to use the restroom."

Annie hurried inside and up the stairs to the guest bathroom. Closing the door, she choked back sobs as tears streamed down her face. Fifteen minutes passed before she pulled herself together. She splashed cold water on her face, grabbed her tote bag, and went downstairs to the kitchen, where Tyler and Eugene were finishing up the dishes.

Despite her efforts to appear normal, Tyler evidently sensed something was wrong. "Are you okay?" he asked.

"Sure. It's just been a long day. I'm ready to go whenever you are."

They said goodbye to his father, and Annie was relieved when Helen was nowhere to be found.

"What did my mother say to upset you?" Tyler asked in the car on the way home.

"Oh nothing. We had a pleasant conversation about flowers."

Tyler gave her a skeptical look. He would be furious with his mom if he found out what had happened in the garden. Even so, Annie had no intention of coming between Tyler and his mother.

Eugene seemed accepting of Annie, but she would have to work harder to win over Helen Gerry. Maybe she would enlist Lia's support. Tyler's sister could be a powerful ally in the battle to earn his mother's approval. Annie and Lia weren't exactly friends, but Lia was approachable. Friendly even. And Annie had the perfect excuse to reach out to her.

Cooper painted the last stroke and set down his brush. He was thrilled with the finished product and could hardly wait to show it to Lia. He began putting away his paints. He'd been at his easel since before noon, and it was already after five. He was facing a long night ahead, catching up on his web design work on his computer. But first, he needed to take a break and clear his head.

Leaving the cottage, he crossed the driveway to the main house, where Sean had created a makeshift weight room in one corner of the game room. Cooper was doing bicep curls when Sean came barreling down the stairs from the main floor.

Cooper set down the dumbbells and wiped sweat from his face with a towel. "What's up, bro? What're you doing here? I thought Sunday was one of your busiest days at the restaurant."

"Usually. But the summer's winding down. Kids are heading back to school. I took the day off to get some stuff done around here." Sean squeezed his bicep. "When did you start lifting again?"

"A few days ago. It's harder to get back into shape than it was to fall out of shape. Why did you let me get so soft?"

"Since when am I your keeper? You've got a mirror."

"Looking at you used to be like looking in the mirror. Before I let myself go." He studied his twin more closely. Sean looked fit and tan and more mature with his unruly waves cut short. Feeling a sudden urge to cut his own hair, he pulled out his phone and checked the hours for his hair salon. "The haircut place is open until seven. Do you have time to go with me? I need you to be my model."

"I'm having dinner with Winnie. But not until later. I will *make* time to go with you to get that rat's nest cut." Sean fished his car key out of his pocket. "I'll even drive in case you try to chicken out."

Cooper snickered. "I won't chicken out. I promise."

On the way over to the shopping center, Cooper added his name to the salon's waiting list, and when they arrived, he was shown to the chair of an attractive blonde stylist named Mel.

"What can I do for you?" Mel asked as she fastened the cape around him.

Cooper pointed at his brother. "Make me look like my twin."

Mel tilted her head one way and the other as she scrutinized Sean. "I never would've guessed twins. You look enough alike to be brothers but not twins."

"We're actually identical," Cooper said. "And I want my hair like his."

"Are you sure?" Mel asked, her scissors positioned to cut. "We are talking about a drastic change."

"I'm positive," Cooper said with a definitive head nod. "Cut it."

Mel went to work, clipping away as long strands of hair floated to the floor around him. When she finished, she stood back and looked from Sean to Cooper. "Whoa. You two really are identical. It's remarkable what a difference hair makes."

Cooper paid the stylist, giving her a handsome tip, before exiting the salon with his brother.

Sean gave Cooper a high-five. "Welcome back, bro. You look like your old self again."

"I *feel* like myself again." When they got in the car, Cooper pulled down the visor and admired his reflection in the mirror. "Who knew getting one's hair cut could be so liberating?" he said, running his hand over his short hair. "I didn't realize how much the long hair was dragging me down."

Sean's phone vibrated with a text. "Dang. Winnie just bailed on me. She's having dinner with her mom. Do you wanna grab a quick bite while we're out?"

"Sure! I think there's a Chipotle nearby."

Fifteen minutes later, they were devouring burrito bowls at the fast casual restaurant when Cooper felt Sean's eyes on him. "What are you looking at?"

"You. I'm trying to figure out why you're suddenly so happy. There's more to it than just your hair."

Cooper shrugged. "What's not to be happy about? Moses is helping me cope with my past demons. My art is growing in popularity, and my web design business is taking off. The cottage feels like home after the renovation. I'm especially enjoying my new studio."

"And?" Sean said.

Cooper looked up from his food. "Isn't that enough?"

"I guess. But I thought maybe a girl was responsible for your improved mood."

Cooper hesitated. "I've seen Annie a few times in recent weeks."

"Dude!" Sean jabbed his plastic fork at Cooper. "I always knew you and Annie belonged together."

"Hold your horses, cowboy. Annie is dating someone. She's really into him, even though he's all wrong for her."

Sean frowned. "In what way?"

"He's a total jerk. But Annie's a smart girl. She'll figure it out soon enough."

"And when she does, you'll be there with a comforting shoulder to cry on."

Cooper grinned. "Exactly."

Cooper rarely saw his brother anymore since Sean had opened his restaurant and started dating Winnie. And he enjoyed hanging out with him, even if it meant procrastinating his work longer. When he finally sat down at his computer around eight thirty, he had an email waiting for him from Nicole asking to meet her for coffee at nine in the morning. "I need to talk to you about something important," she said in her note.

As he responded to her email, he wondered what could be so important. He hoped she wasn't asking for a raise after only two weeks. Or worse. What if she hated her job and was turning in her notice?

When he arrived at Starbucks, he was surprised to see she'd brought along her baby, an adorable little boy with rosy cheeks, bright blue eyes, and a halo of white curls.

"My husband had a meeting and couldn't keep the baby," Nicole explained. "I hope you don't mind if he's here."

"Of course I don't mind." Cooper knelt beside the stroller. "He's a cute kid. What's his name?"

"Danny. Short for Daniel. I named him after my grandfather."

Cooper leaned in close to the baby's face. "Hey there, Danny."

The baby gave Cooper a toothless grin that melted his heart.

The barista called his name, and Cooper went to retrieve his coffee. When he returned, he sat down in the chair opposite Nicole. "What's up? I hope nothing's wrong."

"Not at all. Everything's great. But I have this friend. He's—"

"Looking for a job," Cooper said.

"Not exactly." A smile tugged at Nicole's lips. "He's looking for a partner."

Cooper settled back in the chair, tearing his eyes away from the child. "Go on."

Nicole set down her coffee cup. "I knew Jeff in college. He's a genius when it comes to graphic design. He just quit his job in advertising, and he's interested in creating a large cutting-edge firm. He plans to have designers all over the country but keep the headquarters in the Southeast."

"Where does he live now?"

"In Charleston," Nicole said. "I thought you might be interested. You seem like an entrepreneurial kinda guy. And since your business is growing so fast, it might be a good move for you."

Cooper steepled his fingers. "I need to hire more designers. I'm losing potential clients because I can't service them fast enough. I guess it wouldn't hurt to talk to this guy."

"I think you two will hit it off. I'll text you his contact information."

"That would be great," Cooper said, his eyes back on the child. He was mesmerized watching Danny picking Cheerios off the stroller's tray one at a time and popping them into his mouth. He only half listened as Nicole told him more about Jeff Gomer's credentials.

When Danny fussed, Nicole lifted him out of the stroller.

Cooper surprised himself by asking, "Can I hold him?"

"Sure." Nicole gave him a quizzical look as she handed over the child.

Cooper hugged the child closely. He was soft with rolls of baby fat on his arms and legs, and he had his own distinct sweet scent.

"You're a natural. Do you have children of your own? I can't believe I never asked you. I don't even know if you're married."

"I'm not married. I don't even have a girlfriend." With a chuckle, he handed back the baby. "I should get a wife before I have children."

"That would help, although it's unnecessary in today's world."

"In my world, it is. I'm a traditionalist. I believe in doing things the old-fashioned way."

Nicole smiled softly. "Me too."

Cooper got up to leave. "I have to go. I have another meeting at ten. I'll reach out to Jeff Gomer as soon as I get back to the office. I'm curious to hear what he has to say. Thanks for thinking of me. This could be the beginning of something big."

Nicole, with the baby nestled in her arms, stood to face him. "I certainly hope so, Cooper. Having a partner would give you more time off to look for a girlfriend."

"Maybe so," Cooper said, even though he didn't need to *look* for the girl. He needed to steal her away from her current boyfriend.

Cooper drove to his weekly therapy session in a daze.

"What's wrong, Coop?" Big Moses asked. "You look like a deer in the headlights."

Cooper plopped down on Moses's black leather sofa. "I just had coffee with Nicole, my new web designer. She brought her baby son along, and the kid really got to me."

Moses lowered himself to the club chair beside the sofa. "In what way did he get to you?"

"I asked to hold him," Cooper said, his navy eyes wide. "I've never held a baby before in my life. I've been thinking a lot about . . . you know . . . since . . ." His voice trailed off.

"Since Annie came back into your life?"

"She's not in my life," Cooper snapped.

"But she's in your head."

Cooper didn't argue. Annie was never far from his mind these days. "Maybe my biological clock is ticking. Is that weird for a man to say?"

Moses drummed his fingers on the chair's arm. "I've never really thought about it, honestly. Most men probably wouldn't admit it, but I imagine most of us feel pressured to have our families by a certain age."

Cooper planted his elbows on his knees and buried his face in his hands. "Tell me how to get Annie back."

Moses reached over and mussed his hair. "You made a step in the right direction by getting your hair cut."

Cooper ran his hand through his short hair. "Do you think so, really?"

"Really. You're ten times better looking without that stringy mess hanging in your face. Some people can pull off the man bun. Unfortunately, you're not one of them."

Cooper sat up straight on the sofa. "Dude! Why didn't you tell me that before now?"

"It's not my job to *tell* you anything. It's my job to help you realize these things for yourself."

"Then help me *realize* how to get Annie back. I'm going to her boyfriend Tyler's thirtieth birthday party, and my date is Tyler's sister. It's a house party on Sullivan's Island next weekend. This is my big chance to show Annie what a jerk Tyler is."

Moses's hand flew up. "Hang on a second. First of all, are you using Tyler's sister?"

Cooper's face warmed. "Maybe just a little. I think Lia knows I'm not really into her. And I don't think she's into me. She admitted she doesn't do relationships."

The lines on Moses's forehead deepened. "That may be so, but you'd better not *think*. You'd better make sure she knows where you stand. Don't toy with people's emotions, Cooper."

Cooper wagged his finger at Moses. "Ha! You just told me what to do. You broke your own rule."

Moses chuckled. "I told you what *not* to do. There's a difference."

"Whatever. I get your point, and I have no intention of hurting Lia. I enjoy hanging out with her. And she is seriously hot."

"But she's not Annie. Let the situation progress naturally, Cooper. Be a friend if Annie needs one. But I'd advise against meddling in her relationship with Tyler. If they break up because of you, she could end up resenting you."

While Moses's advice made sense, Cooper worried if he didn't interfere, he might lose Annie forever.

nineteen
brooke

Brooke spotted Sawyer everywhere. Through the window of the coffee shop on her walk to work. On a run down by the seawall. Across the produce department at Harris Teeter. She assumed her mind was playing tricks on her, but short of reaching out to her ex, she had no way of knowing if Sawyer had actually left town.

Brooke was going through the last of the items in the attic before work on Tuesday morning when she stumbled upon an old wooden trunk tucked away in a far corner. She lifted the lid, but it wouldn't budge. There were no latches, only a single keyhole. Curious, Brooke went downstairs for a screwdriver, and when she returned to the attic, the trunk's lid stood open. Lying on top of folded clothes was a worn leather diary. Scrawled across the inside cover in her mother's neat cursive was the inscription: *To my darling girls, Brooke and Lizbet. Always follow your heart.*

She thumbed through the yellowed crinkly pages. The diary appeared to chronicle the events of her parents' courtship and subsequent marriage. She'd often wondered why her parents never spoke of how they'd met.

Brooke had thought a lot about the word *partner* in recent

days. She'd even looked up the definition in her mom's ancient edition of Webster's dictionary. *One of a pair of people engaged in the same activity.* In the case of a marriage, the same activity of sharing a life.

Her parents' traditional marriage—her father the breadwinner and her mother a stay-at-home mom—had always bothered Brooke. She'd never understood how her mother had been content to keep house and raise children. Had she never longed for anything more? Lula took her job seriously. Her garden had been without weeds, her house immaculate, and her husband and children well fed and healthy. Brooke wasn't judging her mother. Lula had been perfectly happy in her role of caregiver. But Brooke wanted something more for herself.

Women were obviously equipped to give birth, but men were just as capable of nurturing the babies afterward. Brooke felt both spouses should have careers. She believed that finding fulfillment outside a marriage was the key to a successful relationship. Maybe this concept had initially attracted her to other women. She wanted someone like herself to share her life. But she no longer thought of herself as gay. Her feelings for Grady changed everything. Was it possible she wasn't gay after all, that she'd convinced herself she was homosexual to satisfy a deep-seated need to . . . To what? Be different? To shock her mother?

Brooke wondered how Grady felt about marriage. Was he an equal-partner type of guy? Or did he want a stay-at-home wife to have dinner on the table every night at seven o'clock sharp? They'd resumed their friendship as though they'd never been apart. But there was still much she didn't know about the grown-up Grady.

From a distant part of the house, Brooke heard someone knocking on the front door, followed by her sister's faint voice calling for her. Stuffing the diary in the waistband of her yoga shorts, she hurried down two flights of stairs and swung the front door open to her exasperated sister.

"What took you so long? And why are you all sweaty? And why doesn't my key work?" Lizbet held up her brass house key.

"I just got back from a walk, and I was in the bathroom. What're you doing here? Why didn't you tell me you were coming?"

"I have a follow-up appointment with Dr. Carroll, and I thought I'd stop by and check on you." Lizbet brushed past her into the house. "What about the key? Did you change the locks?"

"It's a long story." Brooke had been so desperate to get the locks changed, she hadn't thought to get an additional copy of the key made for Lizbet.

"I've got time," Lizbet said, folding her arms and tapping her foot.

"Well, I don't. I have to be at work soon, and I'm starving." Turning her back on her sister, Brooke went into the kitchen, dropping the diary into the junk drawer before she began rummaging through the refrigerator.

Lizbet hip-bumped her out of the way. "Here. I'll fix you breakfast." She removed a carton of eggs. "Poached or scrambled?"

The thought of eggs sent a wave of nausea crashing over her. "Gross! Eggs don't agree with me right now. How about a BLT?"

Lizbet blinked, her eyes wide. "For breakfast?"

"Sure. Why not?" She removed a package of uncured bacon from the meat drawer and handed it to her sister. "Having a sister who's a chef is a bonus. Scratch the lettuce and add a slice of cheddar cheese."

"Yes, ma'am. Although, technically, it's no longer a BLT." Lizbet snipped one end of the bacon package open with scissors and laid out several slices on a paper towel, sliding it into the microwave. "Are you having a lot of cravings?"

"I wouldn't call them cravings. I feel queasy most of the time. So I eat whatever I'm in the mood for." Brooke poured a glass of milk and sat down at the table.

"So, why did you have the locks changed?" Lizbet asked, slicing into a juicy ripe tomato.

Brooke groaned inwardly. Lizbet wasn't giving up until she got her answer. Some version of the truth was probably best. "Sawyer left the residency program in Boston. She stopped by to see me on her way home to California."

"What'd she want?" Lizbet asked, slathering margarine onto a slice of bread.

"She asked if I would give her another chance. And I emphatically told her no. She gave me her house key back, but I realized she may have made copies. I figured better safe than sorry." Before Lizbet could quiz her further about the key, Brooke changed the subject. "Speaking of Sawyer, she claims you got her transferred to Boston."

"In a manner of speaking." Lizbet added bacon, tomato, and cheese to the bread and slid it into the toaster oven. When she turned to face Brooke, guilt pinched her face. "I showed her department head the video I took of her drunken spectacle in our front yard. I was desperate to get Sawyer out of your life. I hope you're not mad."

Brooke smiled at her sister. "How could I be mad when you were only trying to protect me? I'm thrilled to be rid of Sawyer." As the words left her mouth, she had a sneaking suspicion she was far from rid of Sawyer.

Lizbet removed the open-faced sandwich when the toaster oven dinged, placed the sandwich on a plate, and set it on the table in front of Brooke. "Are you having any other pregnancy symptoms aside from the queasiness?" she asked, popping a K-Cup into the Keurig.

"Oh, yeah. You wouldn't believe how bad my boobs hurt," Brooke said, forking off a bite of the sandwich. "I experienced some cramping at the end of last week, but Dr. Carroll told me not to worry about it."

Lizbet's head swiveled toward her. "Cramping? What was that about?"

"Dr. Carroll didn't say. She just told me it was normal." Brooke hunched a shoulder. "Anyway, the cramping is gone now."

"Did you have any spotting? Why didn't you tell me?" Lizbet said, joining Brooke at the table with her coffee.

"No spotting, and I didn't want to worry you," Brooke said as she took another bite of the sandwich.

"That's my baby you're carrying, Brooke. I want to share everything. Including the worry."

"You're right and I'm sorry. I promise to tell you everything from now on."

Lizbet softened, a smile spreading across her lips. "This is a first for both of us. We'll figure it out as we go. I've been wondering when we should tell people you're pregnant. Most women wait until after the first trimester. But you may want to wait longer, since the circumstances are . . . unusual."

Brooke wished she had the luxury of time. She dreaded telling Grady. "I'm afraid I won't be able to hide it for long. My pants are already tight."

Lizbet, who had been poised to take a sip of coffee, lowered her mug. "Seriously?"

"Look!" Brooke smoothed her tank top tight, revealing her growing baby bump.

Lizbet's eyes grew wide. "Whoa. That's early. Maybe it's a sign we're having twins."

"Maybe," Brooke said, showing her sister her crossed fingers.

"Do you have Labor Day off from work?"

"Yep. You?" Brooke picked up the last bite of sandwich and stuffed it into her mouth.

"Sean gave me Sunday and Monday off. Why don't you come down to Prospect? Spend Sunday night and we can go to the beach on Monday."

"I may already have plans with Grady for the weekend."

Brooke wiped her mouth and dropped the napkin on her empty plate. "We've been invited to a house party at Tyler's parents' house on Sullivan's Island. But I haven't decided whether I'm going."

Lizbet pointed at Brooke's face. "There it is again. Your whole face lights up when you talk about Grady. Have you been seeing a lot of him lately?"

"Sort of. He's showing me a house this afternoon," Brooke said and immediately realized her mistake.

Lizbet froze in place, her coffee suspended in midair. "Why? We agreed to wait until spring to put this house on the market."

The cat was out of the bag. Brooke couldn't very well stuff it back in. "I never agreed to anything. If we wait until spring, you'll be busy with the baby. Regardless of when it happens, I will be the one responsible for getting the house ready. Which means I get to decide." Brooke got up from the table and took her plate to the sink. "Besides, I've basically cleaned out the attic."

"What?" Lizbet shot out of her chair. "This is exactly what I warned you about. Moving all that heavy stuff around in the hot attic caused the cramping. That's my baby you're carrying. You need to be more careful. From now on, I want to monitor your every move."

"Ha. Don't count on it. *Your* baby is growing inside of *my* womb. Sorry, Lizbet, but I'm calling the shots. I've gotta go. I'm late for work," she said and stormed out of the kitchen.

Brooke stewed over the exchange with her sister. Lizbet had been out of line, and she owed Brooke an apology. Brooke kept her phone faceup beside her on her desk, but Lizbet neither called nor texted. That afternoon, when she left work early to meet Grady, Brooke forced her sister from her mind.

Grady was waiting on the sidewalk in front of the pink house when she arrived. Brooke's heart danced across her chest. She wasn't sure if she was more excited to see him or the house.

"The house is even cuter in person," she said to him under her breath as they approached the front porch.

Inside was pristine, with reclaimed oak floors and walls painted a soft silvery gray. Upstairs featured three bedrooms. The primary offered a sweeping view of the lake, and the smallest would serve as a home office. The third bedroom would serve as a guest room until it became a nursery. The downstairs formal rooms were charming, featuring intricate woodwork and an old Charleston brick fireplace in the living room. But her favorite part of the house was the chef's kitchen and adjacent family room with paned doors opening onto a small patio and walled garden.

As they were leaving the house, they encountered an attractive young couple with a tiny baby arriving for the next appointment. The house would be perfect for them. What if they liked it? Would they make an offer?

Grady turned to her at the end of the sidewalk. "Well? What do you think? I used to be able to read your mind, but I can't tell if you like it."

Brooke chewed on her lip. "I don't like it. I love it. But . . ."

Grady smiled down at her. "But what? Please continue."

"Isn't it irresponsible to buy the first house that interests me?"

"Not at all. If it's the right fit. Which it seems like it might be."

"I can totally see myself living here. But I would feel better if I had an offer on the condo," she said, immediately thinking to herself, *And if my sister wasn't being so difficult about Tradd Street.*

"Trust me, one is coming soon. We have showings today and tomorrow with the acceptance of contracts scheduled for Thursday."

"*The acceptance of contracts?* Aren't you being a little overconfident?"

"Not at all. That's the way things work in this market. People are beating down the door to see the condo, Brooke. I would be surprised if you didn't get at least one offer."

Panic gripped her chest. Buying a house seemed like an enormous venture. "I've never bought a house before, Grady. I have no idea what to do."

"That's what I'm here for. I'll hold your hand through the entire process." He fished a business card out of his wallet. "Call Jennifer Barton at First Palmetto Bank. She'll help you get bridge financing until you sell the other properties."

Brooke read the card before slipping it into her pocket.

"Let's walk around the lake." Grady held onto her arm as they crossed the street.

When they reached the opposite side of the lake, they stopped and stared back across the water. Brooke felt a sense of belonging, looking at what could be her new home. "Do you know why the current owners are selling? Not that it matters. I'm just curious."

"From what I hear, the house was in terrible shape when the current owner bought it. He's a single guy, a radiologist at MUSC. He apparently flips houses as a hobby. He did all the work himself."

A warm feeling flooded her. "That explains why the house is so pristine. Everything about the property is ideal. The lake is so serene and picturesque. And the size is right. I could grow in this house."

"Yes, you would. Sleep on it. If you decide you want to proceed, Jennifer and I will make it happen for you."

Brooke placed a hand on his cheek. "You're too good to me, Grady Ellington. How did I survive all these years without you?"

Grady took hold of her hand and brought her fingers to his lips. "I've asked myself that same question a thousand times during these past few weeks. Now that we've rediscovered our friendship, I hope we will remain part of each other's lives in the future."

Brooke's gaze shifted slightly right in time to see a silver BMW drive by with a dark-haired woman behind the wheel, wiggling her fingers at Brooke. This was real. This was not Brooke's imagination playing tricks on her. Sawyer was the woman driving the car, making her presence known in broad daylights. Sawyer hadn't returned to California. She was still in Charleston, still stalking Brooke.

Brooke was trying so hard to start fresh, but she stumbled into hurdles at every turn. Sawyer, Lizbet, and, to some extent, even the baby she was carrying—all were preventing her from making the changes she desperately needed.

When she arrived home, she brewed a cup of tea and took her mother's journal out to the porch swing. An hour later, her untouched tea sat beside her on the railing as she read the last word. She closed the journal and stared blankly out at the small yard. Now she understood why her parents kept their stormy love affair a secret.

Lula had been engaged to a man her parents had chosen for her. A wealthy Charlestonian who was twice her age, a divorcé with two grown children. Lula met Brooke's father at the city market. She'd been purchasing a bouquet of fresh wildflowers for her mother's dinner party, and he'd been shopping for sweetgrass baskets. Phillip was a nobody from Nowhere, Nebraska. He invited her to join him for coffee, and they'd fallen in love. Months of arguing with her parents ensued. When they refused to allow her to break off her engagement, Lula and Phillip eloped. Because Lula was their only child, her parents eventually accepted Phillip into their family.

Taking the lukewarm tea to the kitchen, Brooke went upstairs and took a long hot shower to relieve her aching muscles. When she pulled back the shower curtain, someone had drawn a heart shape in the steamed-up mirror. She knew her mama was sending her this message. *Always follow your heart.*

Annie waited anxiously for Lia to call about Tyler's party. On Wednesday morning, when she still hadn't heard from her, she stopped by the art gallery with an extra Starbuck's caramel macchiato. Lia was busy instructing her harried-looking assistant where to hang artwork in an advance of an upcoming opening.

Lia accepted the Starbucks cup. "Aww, caffeine. You're the best."

"I can come back later when you're not so busy. I wanted to see what I can do to help with Tyler's party. I could also use your opinion about something relating to his birthday."

"I could use a break," Lia said. "I'm sure Benny could too."

Benny gave her a grateful nod. "Please, oh wonderful slave mistress."

Lia rolled her eyes at her assistant as she headed for the door. "Let's get some air, Annie."

Annie increased her pace to keep up with Lia as they crossed over East Bay Street to Waterfront Park. They were strolling north on the tree-lined brick promenade when a little boy, running away from his mother, nearly bowled Lia down.

"Watch out, you little brat!" she yelled at him and murmured to Annie, "That's a perfect example of why I'm never having kids."

Annie stared at her, mouth agape. She couldn't imagine not wanting children.

"I've been meaning to call you," Lia said. "But I figured you were busy with work."

"I'm taking this week off. I have plenty of time to do whatever you need for the party."

"Cool! I'm so excited. Kaylie's gonna be in town. Did you know she's an exercise instructor?"

"I don't even know who Kaylie is," Annie said with an awkward laugh.

"Oh, that's right. I forgot you're not one of us."

The comment, whether intended as an insult, was a reminder that Annie was not one of the elite Charlestonians. "Have you known her since childhood?" Annie asked.

"Pretty much. Kaylie's seriously cool. You're gonna love her. She's organizing all these fun activities for the weekend. Stretching and yoga on the beach in the early mornings. Water skiing and sailing and a bike tour of the island on Saturday. Sunday will be more low-key with a volleyball tournament on the beach. Oh, and she's going to fit a wilderness hike in at some point."

When they reached the pineapple fountain, Annie stopped walking and turned to Lia. "Sounds like you've planned an action-packed weekend. What can I do to help?"

"I figured you'd be in charge of the food, since catering is your specialty."

Annie was hoping for nonfood-related tasks, but she would do whatever was necessary to get Tyler's sister's approval. "I can do that. How many people are coming?"

"About twenty. Several couples and the rest singles. I'm putting the guys in the bunk room and the girls in the guest cottage."

"Will Cooper be your date?" Annie didn't know what made

her ask or where the pang of jealousy came from when Lia nodded her head.

"I can hardly wait." A dreamy expression crossed Lia's face. "He's so wonderful. Totally sexy and fun to hang out with. How well do you know Cooper? Other than him being your half brother's cousin."

"Hardly at all." Annie felt herself blush as the lie escaped her lips.

Lia eased down to the fountain's knee wall. "So . . . what do you need my opinion about?"

Annie sat down next to her. "I can't decide what to get Tyler for his birthday. He has everything."

Lia snickered. "That's *so* true. If he wants something, he goes out and buys it."

"I want to get him something special for his thirtieth. I thought maybe you might have an idea."

"Let's see." Lia crossed her legs and tapped on her chin. "Instead of giving him a gift, why not do something special for him? He's already throwing himself a house party, but you could host a party within the party."

"You mean like a surprise?"

"Yes! A surprise! I love it!" Lia clapped her hands like a child. "We haven't yet planned anything for Sunday night. A few people are leaving that morning, so Sunday's dinner will be more low-key. We'll have an intimate dinner for those of us who are left. You could incorporate a theme. He's always talking about how much he loves your cooking."

Annie's doe eyes widened as an idea for the theme popped into her head.

Lia elbowed her in the ribs. "I can see your wheels spinning. What're you thinking?"

"I'm not telling. I want it to be a surprise for everyone. Speaking of surprises, how will I pull this off without Tyler knowing about it?"

"Well, let's see." Lia twirled a lock of dark hair. "We're having the beach volleyball party on Sunday afternoon. You'll have all day to prepare while we're on the beach. We'll make sure Tyler has enough to drink that he'll need a nap afterward. When he comes downstairs for dinner, we'll surprise him."

Annie hated to miss the volleyball party, but it was for a good cause. "That works. I'm excited. This will be fun."

Lia glanced down at her phone. "Oops. I hate to cut this short, but I need to go. Benny is having a coronary about a painting."

Annie waved her on. "No worries. You go ahead. I'm gonna finish my coffee and brainstorm about the surprise party."

The possibilities for a luau were endless. Several Hawaiian dishes immediately came to mind, and the decorations would be relatively easy to find. She remembered Lia's comment. *You're not one of us.* This was Annie's big chance to prove to Tyler that she didn't have to be born and raised in Charleston to be one of them.

Annie was experimenting with a recipe, putting a Hawaiian spin on her popular tuna poke, when Tyler unexpectedly stopped by late on Wednesday afternoon. She greeted him at the door with a peck on the lips. "This is a nice surprise. Come in," she said, stepping out of the way.

He noticed her mess in the kitchen. "What're you making?" he asked, examining the contents of her mixing bowl.

"Nothing special." She placed a sheet of aluminum foil over the bowl. "I'm taste-testing a recipe for this weekend."

"That's why I came by. Lia said you're organizing the food for the house party." He handed her a folded piece of paper. "She came up with this list. She thought you could purchase some items from your suppliers to save on cost. The rest you can pick up at Costco."

She unfolded the paper and scanned the long list. Hamburger patties, hot dogs, and chicken breasts to grill for Friday night's dinner. Two beef tenderloins, and four pounds of shrimp for Saturday night. Five pounds of bacon, and six dozen eggs for breakfasts. Fruits and breads and bags of salad. A variety of snacks took up the bottom half of the list.

Does he expect me to pay for all this? Annie wondered. She was already spending a small fortune on his surprise birthday dinner. She folded the list and slipped it in her pocket.

"Oh! I almost forgot! We need large batches of your pimento cheese and egg salad. And make some of those incredible mini muffins for breakfast. I prefer the blueberry, but I'll let you choose the flavor."

Annie didn't argue. She was too flattered he appreciated her cooking.

He started off across the living room toward her bedroom. "Where are you going?" she asked, hurrying after him.

"To look in your closet," he said over his shoulder.

She watched as he flipped through her clothes, tossing several of her favorite sundresses on the bed.

"Stop!" She stepped in his way. "What're you doing?"

"I want you to make a good impression on my friends this weekend. Especially the ones you've never met."

She shoved him out of the way and closed her closet door. "You don't need to pick out my clothes, Tyler. I know how to dress."

Tyler cocked an eyebrow. "Really? I'm not so sure after that awful dress you wore to Eliza Erwin's wedding."

"Why do you keep bringing that up? I told you I was stressed out about the wedding, and I just grabbed the first thing I saw. I promise to pack more carefully for the weekend."

He retrieved the dresses from the bed and handed them to her. "Make sure you pack these and leave those ratty old shorts at home."

She glanced down at her favorite pair of cutoff jean shorts and bare feet. "I'm cooking, Tyler. I like to be comfortable when I'm working." She returned the dresses to the closet and followed him to the door.

He kissed her goodbye. "Can you do something about your hair?"

Annie grew still. "What's wrong with my hair?"

"It's the color of dirty dishwater." He started off, but turned back around when he reached the porch stairs. "By the way, I'm going to the beach early on Friday. I'll send you the address, and you can drive down later that afternoon."

Irritation flickered through her as she watched his sandy head disappear down the stairs. He'd just dumped the responsibility of purchasing all the food for *his* friends in *her* lap, and he couldn't be bothered to help her transport it? Was she his date for the weekend? Or his caterer? His mother's words came back to her. *You don't have to marry her. Find yourself a proper wife and hire Annie to be your live-in chef.*

Annie pulled out her phone, called her hair salon, and sweet-talked the receptionist into squeezing her in for highlights the following morning.

Brooke wavered between stressing about Sawyer and obsessing about the pink house. She considered reporting her ex to the police, but she had no evidence to prove Sawyer was stalking her. So she called Jennifer Barton, the loan officer at First Palmetto Bank, instead. After a lengthy discussion regarding her finances, Jennifer basically guaranteed her the loan and sent her the documents to fill out.

Grady was waiting for her on the porch when she arrived home from work. "So, what are you thinking about the house? Shall we make an offer?"

Brooke flashed him a mischievous grin. "I think so. I just finished filling out the paperwork Jennifer sent me. I have my heart set on this house, Grady. I don't want to lose it."

"Then let's write an offer they can't refuse," he said, moving over to make room for her on the swing.

Brooke dropped her work bag on the porch floor and sat down beside him. He tapped notes in his phone as they talked about dollar amounts and contingencies.

"I'll draw up the contract for you to sign tonight. Then we'll be all ready to go tomorrow." Grady got to his feet. "The owner is accepting offers at six o'clock, which coincidentally is the same time we're accepting offers on your dad's condo. We'll have much to discuss. Is it okay if we meet here?"

Brooke stood to face him. "That would be great."

He kissed her cheek. "Perfect. I'll pick up some takeout on the way over and meet you here at six."

As she watched him hurry out to his car, Brooke brought her fingers to her cheek where he'd kissed her. She longed to feel those lips on hers again.

The next twenty-four hours passed at a snail's pace. Brooke spent Wednesday night roaming around the house, deciding which furniture she would take with her and where it would fit in the pink house. She was as anxious about the sale of her father's condo as she was about her offer on the pink house, and by the time six o'clock on Thursday evening rolled around, her stomach was twisted in knots.

Grady arrived a few minutes late with a file folder tucked under one arm, a shopping bag from Tasty Provisions in one hand, and a bottle of chilled white wine in the other. "I'm sorry I'm late. I got held up talking to Heidi at Tasty Provisions." He handed her the shopping bag. "I hope you like chicken Parmesan."

"Who doesn't like chicken Parmesan?" Brooke said with a smile, even though the thought of marinara sauce made her stomach burn. She was more concerned about the wine anyway. If she was going to spend the weekend with him, she needed to come up with a logical explanation why she wasn't drinking.

"About the wine . . . there's something I should tell you. I haven't been entirely honest with you." *And I'm being more dishonest now,* she thought. "I quit drinking a few months ago. I was worried my alcohol consumption was getting out of hand."

"No big deal. We won't have the wine," he said, and put the bottle in the refrigerator.

"It may not be a big deal tonight, but it will be at Tyler's drunkfest this weekend. I don't want to prevent you from having a good time. I'm thinking maybe you should go without me."

"No!" Grady spun around to face her. "I won't go, if you don't go. Besides, I talked to Lia. She's working hard to keep this weekend from being a drunkfest. Kaylie, who apparently is now a fitness instructor, is organizing activities to keep everyone busy, so we aren't sitting around drinking all weekend."

Brooke twirled her finger in the air. "Woo-hoo. Kaylie. I can hardly wait to see her."

Grady gave her a scolding glare. "Be nice, Brooke. I never have understood what you have against her."

Brooke leaned back against the counter. "I'm sorry. She just rubs me the wrong way." She picked at a loose thread on her blouse. "What about the sleeping arrangements for the weekend?"

"Lia and I discussed that as well. There are more singles than couples coming. All the guys will sleep in the bunk room, and she's putting the girls out in the guest cottage. There are two bedrooms. You might not get your own bed, but you'll be comfortable."

At least the pressure was off to sleep with Grady. Not that she wasn't constantly fantasizing about doing just that.

Grady moved closer to her. "Come with me, Brooke. It's a free place to stay for Labor Day weekend. If the partying gets out of hand, we'll just do our own thing. I had to pull some major strings to get a reservation at The OD on Friday night. I can't cancel them now."

Brooke weighed her options. She very much wanted to spend the weekend with Grady. The alternative was to stay home alone and wait for Sawyer to come after her. She would be safer in a house full of people. Even if they were all drunk. "In that case, how can I say no to The Obstinate Daughter?"

Grady's eyes were like gold coins. "So you'll come?"

"As long as you promise we'll leave if things get out of hand."

"Deal!" He waved the file folder at her. "I have contracts! You're gonna be pleased."

"Cool. I'll get us something to drink." Opening the refrigerator, she grabbed herself a San Pellegrino. She looked back at Grady over her shoulder. "Beer or wine?"

"Beer's fine. I'll take the wine home with me if it's too tempting. Did you go to rehab? I feel like I would've heard about something like that."

Guilt tugged at Brooke's heartstrings. She hated lying to Grady, but she wasn't ready to tell him about the pregnancy. "No, it was nothing like that. I just needed to take a break. I have just as much fun when I'm not drinking, and I definitely don't miss the hangovers."

Grady laughed. "I don't imagine you do." He popped the beer cap and took a long sip. "Let's talk about the pink house first. The owner has received such overwhelming interest in that property, he's extended the showings through the weekend. Contracts are now due by noon on Monday."

Brooke's mouth fell open. "Can he do that?"

"Of course. It's his house. Although he's made a few agents angry."

"I can see why." Brooke collapsed in a chair at the table. "I'm not sure I can wait that long."

Grady sat down beside her. "The weekend will fly by. We'll be having so much fun at the beach."

"Ugh." Brooke slumped down in her chair. "I want this house, Grady. I can hardly think of anything else."

"Our contract is very competitive. If it goes to a bidding war, I would be very surprised if we're not included. With your permission, I'll extend your offer until six on Monday."

"That's fine. This is so nerve-wracking. I won't be able to sleep until this is over."

"Yes, you will." Grady opened his file folder. "You're gonna sleep like a baby when you hear these offers for the condo."

Brooke placed her phone on the table in front of her. "Let me get Lizbet on speaker. She needs to be part of the decision-making process."

Brooke hadn't heard from her sister since their argument two days ago. She hated to be the one to cave by calling her first. She was giving up nine months of her life to have Lizbet's baby. Her sister should be the one bending over backward to make Brooke happy.

Lizbet answered on the third ring. When Brooke explained why she was calling, her sister said, "The restaurant is slammed right now. I trust you to make the right decision."

Brooke looked over at Grady, who nodded. "Hey, Lizbet, it's Grady. Watch for a DocuSign email from me later. I'm going to need your signature."

"Will do," Lizbet said and hung up.

Brooke gestured at his file. "Let's hear them."

"We've received three contracts. Two are better than the third." He picked up the top two contracts and compared them. "I was wrong. I only glanced at them earlier. I didn't notice this one is way better than the other two. Considerably more than asking price. All cash. No contingencies. Closing in three weeks," he said, sliding the contract in front of her.

Brooke's eyes popped when she saw the offer amount. "Wow! This is the best news ever." She came out of her seat, throwing her arms around his neck and accidentally landing on his lap. "I'm sorry. I got carried away."

When she tried to get up, he pulled her back down. "I'm not. This is where you belong. Right here, on my lap."

Brooke let out a sigh. "If only it were that easy."

"It's totally that easy." He kissed the tip of her nose. "Our friendship is morphing into something deeper. And I believe you feel it too."

Through the back window, Brooke spotted Sawyer staring in at them. Brooke jumped to her feet. "Everything is happening too fast," she cried, raking her fingers through her pixie hair. "I just got out of a long-term relationship. I'm selling my family's home and buying my first house." *And I'm pregnant with my sister's baby,* she thought to herself.

Grady stood and took her in his arms. "We'll take it slow, Brooke. I'm in no hurry. I agree. You have a lot going on, and I'm here for you. As your friend. You decide when you're ready for something more."

"Thank you for being so understanding." Brooke rested her head on Grady's shoulder as her heart rate slowed and breath steadied. When she summoned the nerve to look back at the window, Sawyer was gone.

L ia instructed Cooper to pick her up at one o'clock on Friday afternoon. "And don't be late or we'll get stuck in traffic," she demanded.

"I won't," he assured her. "I have an early meeting in Charleston. I should be finished in plenty of time."

His meeting with Nicole's friend, Jeff Gomer, took longer than expected. To Cooper's surprise, they had the same ideas about growing their web design firms, and by the time their lunch at Mercantile and Mash ended, they'd agreed to partner up. Cooper was beyond thrilled. He didn't even argue when Jeff suggested Charleston as their headquarters. He hoped to be spending more time in the city once he won Annie back.

Slow traffic on East Bay made him five minutes late in picking up Lia, but they made it from downtown Charleston to Sullivan's Island in record time. His guilt over using Lia to get to Annie mounted as she chatted excitedly about the weekend plans. He promised himself he would be honest with Lia about his feelings. Hurting her was the last thing he wanted.

He was relieved to find several others had arrived ahead of them. A stunning young woman with a super fit body wearing a blue ruffled bikini hurried out to greet them. She pulled Lia out of the car and into her arms. "I haven't seen you in *so* long. We have *so* much to catch up on. Go put on your bathing suit."

Lia laughed. "Slow down. I just got here. I want you to meet my date for the weekend. Kaylie, this is Cooper." Lia smiled at her friend. "Kaylie is my high school bestie."

Kaylie slid her sunglasses down her nose and pursed her fake lips as she gave him the once-over. "You must be something special to have scored a date with Lia. She doesn't let many men get close."

Lia flicked her wrist, dismissing her comment. "Cooper and I are just friends."

"Yeah, right. Time will tell." Kaylie gave Lia's arm a squeeze. "Hurry and change. I'll be out by the pool with Tyler and the others. Believe it or not, they're already drinking." She blew a kiss over her shoulder as she sauntered off with sexy hips swaying.

"Ugh! I warned Tyler not to turn this into a fraternity party." Lia retrieved her purse and beach bag from the front seat and strode off toward the house.

Grabbing their suitcases out of the rear, Cooper followed Lia through the back door into the kitchen. He immediately thought of Annie when he saw the stainless-steel appliances, handsome navy custom cabinets, and brass hardware. It would be hard to get her out of this kitchen this weekend.

Lia deposited her stuff on the marble countertop and turned to him. "Just leave my suitcase beside the door. Because we have a packed house this weekend, I had to give up my bedroom to one of the couples. I'll be staying in the guest cottage with the single girls, and you'll be in the bunk room with the guys. I hope you don't mind."

Relief washed over Cooper. He'd worried about the sleeping arrangements. "Not at all. That's perfectly fine with me."

She showed him upstairs to the bunk room, which featured three sets of built-in bunk beds, twins over queens. Since someone else had already claimed the queen beside the window, Cooper tossed his duffle bag onto the one nearest the door.

"I'm going out by the pool with Kaylie. We need to go over the activities we've planned for the weekend. You're welcome to come hang out, but I figured you'd want to work. Did you bring your art supplies? You can set up your easel from the balcony off my parents' bedroom."

"I didn't bring art supplies, but I have my camera. Don't worry about me. I can entertain myself. I will probably walk over to the beach and explore for new inspiration."

Lia flashed him a brilliant smile. "There's definitely plenty to explore on Sullivan's Island."

Cooper took himself on a self-guided tour of the L-shaped house. He dated the original part of the house back to the 1920s or '30s, with the extension off the rear added more recently. Despite being updated with modern conveniences, the house still had the charming old beach cottage vibe. He counted nine total bedrooms, including the luxurious primary suite in the back corner of the addition with sweeping views of the inlet.

He continued downstairs to the first floor, where sliding glass walls in the living and dining rooms opened onto the pool where Tyler and his friends were sitting on the edge with their feet dangling in the water. The house was on the Intercostal Waterway side of the island. A fleet of boats in different shapes and sizes was tied up at a dock extending from the property.

Slipping out the back door, Cooper headed east on foot and cut across the grounds at Fort Moultrie, an old Civil War fort, to the ocean. He tugged off his shirt and strolled up the beach to the lighthouse. While the afternoon sun was too harsh for photographs, he enjoyed the fresh air and feel of the sun on his shoulders. He would return tomorrow at dawn, when the sun was soft and the wildlife was beginning to stir.

When he returned to the beach house a few minutes before five, Annie was struggling to remove a cooler from her car.

"Here! Let me help you with that." Hip-bumping her out of the way, he took the cooler from her and set it on the ground.

Annie glanced at him and then did a double take. "You cut your hair. It looks *so* much better."

"Thanks. I think. I see you've changed your hair as well," he said, noticing the new streaks of white blonde.

Annie smoothed back her hair. "Heidi hates it. She says I look like an albino zebra."

Cooper laughed. "That's not very nice. But I don't know why you would dye it. Your hair is the color of the first rays of sun breaking the horizon at dawn."

She scrunched up her nose. "That's so corny. Who says stuff like that?"

"Artists, who spent an inordinate amount of time thinking about color."

"Okay. That's fair." Annie laughed, and then let out a sob.

Cooper lowered his voice. "Hey. What's wrong?"

Annie swiped at her eyes. "Heidi and I had a fight earlier. It's not a big deal," she said and reached inside the car for a second cooler.

He took the cooler from her. "It is if you're upset."

"I don't want to talk about it."

Cooper decided not to press her. He would find out more about the fight after she composed herself.

The cooler was heavy, and they both had to lug it to the kitchen. They made three more trips to her car before everything was unloaded.

"Why isn't Tyler helping you?" Cooper asked, tearing off a sheet of paper towel and mopping the sweat from his face.

Annie's brown eyes traveled to the french doors. She smiled at the sight of Tyler and his friends playing Marco Polo in the pool. "It's his birthday, and he's having fun with his friends."

"Still, he could take time out to help you unload the car. What's in here anyway?" Cooper opened a cooler and stared down at the assortment of meat neatly packed inside. "Did you rob a butcher? There must be a thousand dollars' worth of meat in here."

"Way north of that. You obviously haven't been shopping for meat lately. I got good deals from my supplier, but still these prices are ridiculous."

"I hope Tyler's paying you back."

"He'd better be," she grumbled.

Cooper handed the items to Annie as she stored them in the refrigerator. Two beef tenderloins wrapped in butcher paper. Two boxes of hamburger patties. On and on it went. "I hope Tyler doesn't expect you to cook all this."

Annie spread her arms wide. "How could I possibly mind cooking in this amazing kitchen?" The tightness in her jaw suggested she'd rather not spend all weekend cooking.

"So what did you and Heidi fight about besides your hair?"

Annie sucked in a breath. "Heidi's upset because I'm thinking of quitting Tasty Provisions."

Cooper removed the last package of shrimp and slammed the cooler lid shut. "Why? I thought you loved your job. You've worked so hard to get where you are."

"I love my job, but all I ever do *is* work. I have no quality of life. Look at me, I'm at the beach on Labor Day weekend, and I'm still working."

"I hate to say it, Annie, but you set yourself up for that. You should've told Tyler to buy the food. These are his friends, not yours."

"That's what Heidi said too." Annie removed two beers from the refrigerator, handing one to Cooper. "Compensation for helping me unpack."

"I would've done it for free, but I won't turn down a beer."

They walked together to the french doors and stared out at the pool party in progress.

Cooper took a swig from his beer bottle. "How long have you

been feeling like you have no quality of life? Is this something new?"

Annie chewed on her lower lip. "Sorta."

"Tyler is pressuring you to take more time off, isn't he?"

"Maybe. But it's not Tyler's fault. Any guy who works normal hours would feel the same way. Regardless of who I end up marrying, my irregular hours will be a problem when we start a family."

"Not necessarily. If your husband loves you, he'll pick up the slack with the kids while you're at work." Cooper would never consider asking Annie to quit a job she loved.

Tyler spotted them in the window and waved. "Hold this," Annie said, thrusting her beer at Cooper. Rummaging through her tote bag, she removed a baseball cap and tugged it on over her head. "Maybe Tyler will be too drunk to notice the highlights."

Tyler will have to be blackout drunk not to notice, Cooper thought.

Tyler and his friends entered the kitchen in single file, with Lia and Kaylie bringing up the rear. He introduced Annie to everyone, but he ignored Cooper as though he were invisible.

"Why are you wearing a baseball cap?" Tyler asked, snatching the hat off Annie's head before she could stop him. "Wow! What did you do to your hair?"

Annie grabbed the cap back and returned it to her head. "I got highlights. Like you suggested."

"Ha. I assumed you had a reputable stylist, not some city worker who paints lines on streets," Tyler said and everyone in the room laughed except Annie and Cooper.

"Tyler! Stop being so mean!" Lia squealed in a fake voice.

"Annie knows I'm kidding. Don't you, babe?" He glanced down at Annie's cropped white jeans. "Why don't you go put that hot body into one of your teeny weenie bikinis?" he said, grabbing a handful of her butt.

Cooper was surprised when Annie merely smiled at Tyler. The Annie he'd known, the girl who never took crap off anyone, would've smacked Tyler's hand away.

Annie glanced at her Apple Watch. "It's getting late. Aren't you going to shower before dinner?"

"We're on island time, Annie. When we come to the beach, we go whichever way the wind blows us. And right now, the wind is taking me back outside to the pool." Tyler held his arms out straight, like wings on a plane, and glided through the french doors.

Cooper seethed inside. It took everything ounce of restraint he could muster not to go after Tyler, to give him the ass whooping he deserved.

Annie cast Cooper a shy glance. "Someone needs to feed this drunken crew. If I don't cook, I have a hunch they won't eat."

Cooper looked down at his shorts and flip-flops. "I'm all sandy from the beach. I need to shower first. Then, I'll help you."

Annie appeared relieved. "That's an offer I can't refuse."

When he came back down thirty minutes later, the party had moved out to the dock. Some guys were doing cannonballs from the tuna tower of Tyler's dad's sport fishing boat. Someone was going to kill themselves. It would solve all Cooper's problems if that someone was Tyler.

The DJ was setting up his equipment at the far end of the pool, and Annie, who had changed into a yellow sundress, was picking up empty beer bottles from the deck. Why was she picking up after them? Did she not have any pride? She really had it bad for this guy. Worse even than Cooper thought.

Cooper yearned to leave this house and never come back. But his gut told him this weekend would not end well for Annie, and she would need all the support she could get when things went south.

twenty-three
brooke

Brooke and Grady left Charleston after work on Friday and got stuck in traffic on the way to Sullivan's Island. By the time they arrived at the Gerrys' beach house, it was almost seven o'clock. They followed the sound of loud music to the pool where Annie and Cooper were cooking hamburgers on the grill.

"Sorry we're so late," Brooke said. "Traffic was a nightmare."

"Where is everyone?" Grady asked, looking around the empty pool deck.

"I assume they're getting dressed for dinner," Annie said. "Although some of them might be passed out drunk."

Brooke cut her eyes at Grady. "I told you. Drunkfest," she said under her breath.

Grady winked at her. "I hate to be rude, but we're in a bit of a hurry. Our dinner reservation is in thirty minutes. Do you have any clue where we're staying?"

"I do, actually. Lia left instructions for you." Annie waved her spatula at the guest cottage. "Brooke, you're staying in the guest cottage, and Grady, you're in the bunk room in the main house."

"Thanks," Brooke said. "We'll catch up with you all tomorrow."

Grady walked Brooke around the pool and down a garden path to the guest cottage, which was tucked away behind a stand of palmetto trees. They heard laughter as they approached, but when they entered the cottage, the sitting room fell silent.

Lia jumped up to greet her. "Brooke! You're finally here. Come on in."

"I'll meet you at the car in twenty minutes," Grady said to Brooke, seconds before Lia closed the door on him.

Kaylie held up her martini glass. Her hair was wrapped in a towel, and she sat with her long legs dangling over the arm of a club chair. "Go, Brooke! Grady is looking seriously sexy these days. I assume y'all are together. Are you straight now?"

"We're still just friends." Brooke had no intention of discussing her sex life with Kaylie.

Kaylie swung her legs around in the chair as she sat up straight. "Cool! Then you don't mind if I hit on him."

"Have at it." Brooke chuckled. "But I wouldn't get my hopes up if I were you. You're not exactly his type."

Kaylie's face fell. "What's that supposed to mean?"

"Grady is a super nice guy, Kaylie. He's way too good for you."

"You little bitch." When Kaylie jumped to her feet, her silky robe gaped open and exposed her nipple.

Brooke's eyes traveled to the bare breast, out of instinct, not interest.

"Ooh. Gross. Stop looking at me, you little lesbian creep," Kaylie said, tying the robe sash tight.

Brooke laughed. "Don't worry. You're not my type either. You and Tyler should never have broken up. You two deserve each other. Too bad he's with Annie now."

"Get out!" Kaylie's arm shot out with a finger pointed at the door and the liquid sloshing out of her martini glass. "I refuse to sleep under the same roof with a lesbian."

Brooke turned toward Lia, who appeared to be enjoying the exchange. "Do you want me to stay somewhere else?"

"Of course not. We have two bedrooms." Lia gestured toward the short hallway leading to the bedrooms. "You can have one, and the rest of us will take the other."

Which meant five young women would share one room. Which would get real uncomfortable real fast. But it wasn't Brooke's problem. Served the homophobes right.

"Great! Thanks. I need to get changed. Grady and I have dinner reservations at the OD." Brooke felt Kaylie's eyes burning a hole into her back as she left the sitting room.

Choosing the smaller of the two bedrooms, Brooke quickly freshened her face and changed into a pale blue, flowy sundress. She'd packed only loose-fitting clothes to accommodate her rapidly expanding midsection.

When she returned to the driveway, Grady was waiting for her in the Gerry's golf cart.

"Yay! I love riding in style," she said, jumping in beside him.

He put the cart in gear. "I hope you don't mind if your hair gets windblown."

"Are you kidding? You can't mess up a pixie cut," she said, grabbing hold of the handrails as he peeled off.

"It's gonna be a long weekend," Brooke yelled over the hum of the tires on the pavement. "I'm pretty sure every girl here hates me now."

Grady glanced over at her. "Uh-oh. What happened?"

"Kaylie happened. I should warn you, she has a major crush on you."

He returned his attention to the road. "She's not my type."

Brooke laughed. "That's what I told her."

The hostess, a cute young girl with a perky blonde ponytail, fell all over herself to accommodate Grady. She even gave up one of the coveted tables outside on the patio.

"Your server will be right out. Let me know if I can get anything for you in the meantime," she said, and flashed Grady a brilliant white smile before scurrying off.

Within minutes, the waitress, an attractive brunette about their age, appeared at the table. "Can I get you started with something from the bar?"

Grady hesitated, and Brooke said, "Go ahead. Get whatever you want. Don't worry about me."

He smiled at the waitress. "In that case, I'll have a glass of the house pinot noir."

"And I'm fine with water. Can we hear your specials, please?" Brooke asked.

The waitress ran down the short list of specials. Soft-shell crabs caught her attention, but the thought of seafood did not appeal to Brooke's squeamish appetite. She ordered the Miss Carolina pizza, their simplest pie with green and red tomatoes, mozzarella, and basil.

Grady looked at her as though she'd lost her mind. "Seriously? You're passing up soft-shell crabs?"

Brooke shrugged. "What can I say? I'm in the mood for pizza."

Grady looked up at the waitress. "Well, I'm having the soft shells."

"Coming right up," she said, winking at him.

Brooke, her mouth wide open, watched the waitress walk away. "Is it my imagination, or does every woman you encounter flirt with you?"

"It's your imagination," he said with lips pressed thin, as though he didn't enjoy the attention.

During dinner, they discussed their plans for the next day. They would take a long bike ride in the morning and spend the afternoon on the beach. "If we get an early start, we can go for a boat ride while the others are still sleeping," Grady suggested.

"That would be fun. Will Tyler mind if you borrow a boat?"

Grady shook his head. "I used to do it all the time, but I'll check with him just to be sure."

On the way home from the restaurant, Brooke asked if they could make a detour by her family's old oceanfront cottage.

"I have a better idea. Why don't we walk by your cottage instead? The moon is bright. You should be able to see it well from the beach." He took a sharp left, drove to the end of the street, and parked the golf cart in one of the spaces provided for beach access.

Slipping off their shoes, they ran, laughing like children, down the sandy path to the beach. The moon, a yellow ball high in the sky above the ocean, cast a radiant glow over the white sand and crashing waves. *Tonight is a night made for romance,* Brooke thought as Grady took hold of her hand, and they walked past the light-house to her family's old cottage.

Her father had sold the cottage in the months following her mother's death. The beach had been her mother's favorite place on earth, and none of them could bear the thought of being in the cottage without her.

Brooke was grateful to see the new owners had remodeled it beyond recognition. "It doesn't even look like the same place," she said. "I guess that's a good thing. Now I don't have to be sad."

"Good. Because I hate seeing you sad." Placing his hands on her hips, Grady drew Brooke in and kissed her. Their lips parted and warmth flooded her body all the way down to her toes.

When the kiss ended, Grady said, "Wow. We need to talk about that."

"Let's do it again first," she said in a throaty whisper. When they kissed again, her body ached with desire. She'd never known such sexual yearning before.

"Now it's my turn to say *wow*," said Brooke.

"Right? That kind of chemistry doesn't happen very often. I have certainly never experienced it before."

"Me either. And I find it confusing." Brooke scrunched up her brow. "Technically, I'm still a virgin."

"Have you ever kissed a guy before, Brooke?"

"Only playing spin the bottle in high school." Brooke remembered what Kaylie said earlier. *Stop looking at me, you little lesbian creep.* "Doesn't it gross you out to kiss someone who's gay?"

"No. Because you're obviously not gay. You're a passionate young woman who falls in love with the person, not their gender." Realizing what he'd said, Grady added, "I'm not suggesting you're in love with me . . ."

"I've always loved you, Grady. But that love is deepening into something I'm not sure I'm ready for." Brooke turned away from him and headed back toward the golf cart.

He caught up with her. "Hey! Why are you holding back? Is it because you just got out of a long-term relationship?"

Brooke stopped walking. "There's a lot you don't know about me, Grady. Things I'm not sure you'd approve of."

"There's a lot you don't know about me too. We'll take our time getting to know each other again." Grady brushed her bangs off her forehead. "I'm really into you, Brooke. I just want to spend time with you."

"I want that too." She ran her thumb over his bottom lip. "I'm sorry, Grady. So much is happening at once."

"If you let me kiss you again, you'll see that we belong together."

"Then kiss me. But kissing is all I can handle right now."

"I understand. And I promise not to pressure you."

But kissing made her want to do so much more, and she had to push him away before things went too far. She would have to tell him about the pregnancy, sooner rather than later.

They arrived back at the house to find a party in full swing. Country music was blasting from the speakers, and the pool deck had become the dance floor for the drunken mob. Through the crowd, Brooke spotted Tyler swinging Kaylie around while Annie stood off to the side, watching.

Grady followed her gaze. "What a jerk!"

"I never understood how you two were such good friends when you're nothing alike," Brooke said.

"We used to be more alike. I've grown up, and he hasn't. Do you wanna hang out?" he asked, his voice lacking enthusiasm.

"Not really. I'm tired. I think I'll turn in. But don't let me stop you."

"I'm tired too. My Kindle is calling me."

Brooke smiled. "Mine too."

They'd always shared a love of mystery novels. As he walked her to the guest cottage, they discussed which books they'd downloaded on their Kindles.

"Can I kiss you goodnight?" he asked.

"Yes, you may. But you don't have to ask me every time you kiss me."

Brooke was relishing the feel of his soft lips and his firm body against hers when Lia blew past them on her way inside the cottage.

"Get a room. Oh wait. You already have one," Lia snarked before disappearing into the bathroom.

"Oops," Grady said, and Brooke pressed her lips together to keep from smiling.

Grady squeezed Brooke before dropping his arms from around her. "Shall we meet in the kitchen for coffee at seven?"

"Seven? Are you crazy? We're on vacation. Can we say eight?"

"Eight o'clock it is. Sweet dreams," he said, kissing her lips one last time.

Brooke was still standing in the doorway, watching Grady's tall frame stroll down the garden path, when Lia emerged from the bathroom. "Sorry. Tampon emergency."

No wonder she's sleeping in the guesthouse and not with her date, Lia thought.

Lia looked from Grady to Brooke. "You two make a cute couple. I'm sorry about earlier. You know how rude Kaylie can be. I can't believe she's still hung up on Tyler after all this time."

"Kaylie needs to accept he's with Annie now," Brooke said.

Through the rustling palm fronds, they glimpsed Tyler, who was now slow dancing with Annie.

"Kaylie is a much better fit for him. Do you know any scoop on Annie? Isn't Lizbet married to Annie's brother or half brother or whatever?"

"Half brother. And I know nothing," Brooke said, even though she knew all about what happened between Annie and Cooper in high school.

"Come on, Brooke. Everyone has skeletons in the closet. You might as well tell me. I know tons of people from Prospect I can ask."

"Then ask them. But you won't find out anything. Annie is the salt of the earth. You should be thrilled a nice girl like her is dating your brother."

Lia let out a humph. "He can do better. No matter how hard she tries, Annie will never be one of us," she said and stormed out of the cottage.

"Thank goodness for that," Brooke called after her, kicking the door shut behind her.

Brooke conducted her nightly routine in the bathroom and went into her bedroom, locking the door and sliding a chest of drawers in front of it. She didn't trust any of these girls. She was liable to wake up with an ink mustache or toothpaste in her hair.

Despite being exhausted, the music kept Brooke awake until the wee hours. She replayed the scene on the beach with Grady over and over in her head. She could no longer deny she was falling for him. Being with him felt so right. She wondered what sex with a man would be like. She imagined Grady would be a tender lover.

Her pregnancy complicated the situation. Her body was changing. She would soon be visibly pregnant. If they were together, people would assume the baby was his. Would he be turned off by having sex with a woman who was carrying another

woman's child? What if he suggested they postpone their relationship until after the baby came? Brooke didn't want to wait.
She wanted to be with him now. But it wasn't just up to her. She
needed to tell Grady the truth. If he really cared about her, he
would be supportive. If not, it was better to find out now before
she fell even more deeply in love with him.

twenty-four
annie

Annie was scooping honeydew balls, preoccupied with the events of last night, when a voice startled her out of her reverie. She flinched, and the melon baller slipped out of her hand, clattering to the counter. She looked up to see Cooper standing on the other side of the island. "Geez, Cooper! You scared me."

"Sorry." He handed her the melon baller. "You were a million miles away. What's on your mind?"

"Nothing really. Just thinking," she said and went back to digging melon balls.

"I thought I was the only one awake. Why are you working so early? The sun isn't even up yet."

"I'm planning a surprise for Tyler's birthday." She scooped the last of the melon, dropped the rind in the trash, and reached for a cantaloupe.

"You're giving him fruit for his birthday? He'll be thrilled."

"Ha ha. I'm having a surprise dinner for him tomorrow night." She waved the melon baller at the oven. "I'm just killing time while I wait for his birthday cake to finish baking." She gave

Cooper the once-over. He wore a baseball cap and had a camera and backpack slung over one shoulder. "Why are *you* up so early?"

He held up his camera. "I'm going exploring for inspiration. Wanna come?"

"That sounds like fun. But I can't leave until the cakes are done. Which should be soon." As the words left her lips, the oven timer went off. "Right on cue." She removed the round cake layers and tested them for doneness. "If you can give me five minutes, I'll go with you."

"Sure. Is there any coffee?"

"I just brewed some." She gestured at the coffeepot. "I want some too. See if you can find us to-go cups."

While she transferred the cakes to wire racks, Cooper searched the cabinets for to-go cups, finally locating two Tervis tumblers with lids. By the time he'd finished adding cream and sugar, she was ready to go.

They drove to the beach in the golf cart and walked down the long boardwalk in bare feet. The beach was serene with the waves gently lapping the shore, and the horizon glowing a golden pink hue from the first rays of dawn.

They'd only walked a short distance when Cooper whispered, "Follow me," and led her into the sand dunes.

"Why are we whispering?"

Cooper chuckled. "I'm not sure. I don't want to disturb the peace, I guess."

Annie laughed. "Makes sense."

They crouched down behind the dunes, and Cooper aimed his superzoom lens through the beach grass. Annie watched as he snapped dozens of pictures of the scenery. He sat back on his haunches and scrolled through the images on the camera's display. He let out a frustrated sigh. "These are no good."

"Let me see." She took the camera from him and scrolled through the images. "What do you mean? These are great!"

"They don't do justice to the beauty of the sunrise."

"You'll do it justice on canvas. Isn't the idea to use the pictures as inspiration for your paintings?"

"True. I'm painting more and more from photographs, although I still prefer to work in real time."

They left the sand dunes and strolled south while they finished their coffee.

"Have you given any thought to what you'll do if you quit Tasty Provisions? You have a good eye. You could try something totally different, like graphic design."

Annie shook her head. "I can't see myself sitting behind a computer all day." She kicked at the sand. "To be honest, I love everything about my job. I thrive on our hectic schedule, and food excites me. I understand the service industry."

"I admit, you have a special knack for catering to the needs of others."

Annie cut her eyes at him. She couldn't tell whether he meant that as a compliment. "The tenant is vacating the building next to the gourmet shop. It would be an ideal place for a sandwich shop. Unfortunately, in order to afford the lease, I'd have to serve dinner as well. And then I'm right back to working all the time."

"You could hire a night manager."

"Heidi doesn't believe in paying someone to do what we can do."

"But you wouldn't be opening the restaurant with Heidi. Isn't the point to go out on your own?"

"Yes, but the idea scares me to death."

"Of course it does. You've reached a fork in the road. You must choose between taking the easy road or traveling down the unknown path. I can totally relate to how you're feeling. When my friends died, I ran straight home to my family. But they couldn't help me. Only I could help myself."

Annie tried not to let her surprise show. She did not know his *troubles* were so serious. Who were these friends? Was one of them his girlfriend? "I'm so sorry about your friends. How did they die?"

Cooper's blue eyes were wet as he shook his head. "It's difficult to talk about. Maybe I'll tell you another time."

It broke Annie's heart to see how much he was hurting. They'd once told each other everything, no matter how troubling. "You mentioned that you're seeing Moses. Is he helping?"

Cooper gave a solemn nod. "We're working through my grief. But he's also coaching me on life skills, teaching me to trust my gut in making major decisions."

"Maybe I need to sign up for some sessions with Big Mo," Annie said in a lighthearted tone, although she wasn't teasing. She didn't trust her gut. When it came to love, she listened to her heart. If Tyler was the wrong guy for her, why were her feelings for him so strong? Professionally, she believed in Heidi's method of success. Her track record proved it. But Annie thought her way of doing things had merit as well.

Annie squinted at something off in the distance. "Whoa. Are those sea turtles?"

Cooper followed her gaze. "That's surprising. They usually crawl out of their nests at night."

"It hasn't been daylight for long."

Cooper knelt and focused his zoom lens. "Okay, this is spectacular," he said, holding the shutter button down as the tiny creatures inched their way to the surf.

"Now these are some outstanding pics," Cooper said as he and Annie looked at the images together on the camera. "I've never painted anything like this."

"There's your composition!" Annie pointed at an image of a baby sea turtle at the water's edge. "I'd buy this painting in a heartbeat."

Cooper shivered in excitement. "I can hardly wait to get to work."

"I know how you feel! I experience that same thrill when I

discover a new recipe. Do you know how lucky we are to have discovered our passions? So many people never do."

Cooper flashed her a smile. "All the more reason for you to reconsider giving up catering."

"I know. You're right. I can't imagine doing anything else."

He stored his camera in the backpack, and they headed back in the direction they'd come. As they neared the beach access lot, they came upon an exercise class in progress. They slowed their pace as they watched Kaylie, dressed in black skin-tight exercise shorts and tank top, instruct her students in the art of stretching.

"Do you think Kaylie is pretty?" Annie whispered.

"Nope," Cooper whispered back without hesitation. "She's obnoxious."

"I didn't ask what you thought about her personality."

"Personality is way more important to me than looks. Although it helps if the girl is at least cute."

Annie nudged his arm. "Do you think Lia's cute?"

"Lia is a mystery. I'm still trying to figure her out."

Lia, as though sensing they were talking about her, scrambled up from her towel and hurried over to them. "Where have you two been so early in the morning?" she asked in a suspicious tone.

"Cooper let me tag along on his discovery mission," Annie explained. "We saw some baby sea turtles crawling out to the water. Wait until you see the images."

Cooper nodded agreement. "Totally amazing."

Lia hung onto Cooper's arm, pressing her body against his. "Cool! Show me the pics!"

Annie started walking backward, putting distance between them. "I'm gonna run. I'll see y'all back at the house."

"Take the golf cart," Cooper said. "I'll walk home with Lia."

Annie gave him a thumbs-up and turned toward the sand dunes. She experienced a heady sense of loss in leaving Cooper with Lia. Where were these feelings coming from? She would always care about Cooper. He had been her first love. But this felt like something new. She'd enjoyed the sunrise walk. The serenity of the beach at daybreak. And the turtles were special, not something one sees every day. Cooper was easy to be with and nonjudgmental. Perhaps she'd missed their friendship more than she realized.

Annie dismissed her feelings as she got in the golf cart and drove off. She arrived at the house to find the kitchen packed with hungover guys, eating everything in sight.

Tyler threw his arms around her. "There you are! Will you make us some food?" He smelled like booze, and Annie suspected he was still drunk.

"I already made breakfast." She opened the warming drawer and removed a sausage, egg, and hash brown casserole. She served healthy portions on plates with spoonfuls of melon balls.

As the guys gathered around the pine table, Annie imagined many years of Labor Day weekends ahead. His parents would eventually accept her, and Lia would become her best friend. She and Tyler would have a brood of children running around, begging to swim in the pool or go for a boat ride.

Annie was brought back to the present when Rich, a fraternity brother of Tyler's from South Carolina, pushed abruptly away from the table and shot down the hall to the bathroom.

"I hope it wasn't something he ate," Annie said, her tone concerned.

Tyler winked at her. "I think it was something he drank last night."

Tyler's childhood friend, Jeremy, planted an elbow on the table, supporting his head while he shoveled in the food. "Dude, I feel bad. I need some hair of the dog. Do you have any Bloody Mary mix?"

Annie stood near the table, watching the motley crew eat. "You guys need to sober up before you start drinking again."

"Where's the fun in that?" Tyler said, and when Annie gave

him a scolding look, he added, "You're right. After I let my food digest, I'll go for a run to sweat it out."

"What *are* we doing today?" Annie asked, wanting to know when she might ice his cake.

"We're going water skiing," Tyler said with a silly little boy grin.

"I'd rather lounge by the pool," Annie said.

"No way. You're going with me."

She felt flattered that he wanted to spend time with her. After the way he was dancing with Kaylie last night, she'd wondered if something was going on between them. Tyler was the most desirable bachelor in Charleston. She would need to get used to women always throwing themselves at him.

twenty-five
cooper

C ooper agreed to go along on the skiing outing, even though he had a sick feeling something terrible would go wrong. He'd detected a glimmer of jealousy in Annie's eyes on the beach earlier, when Lia was hanging all over him. Perhaps he was slowly worming his way back into her heart.

"What's in the cooler?" Cooper asked as Tyler and Jeremy loaded the Yeti into the boat.

Tyler rolled his eyes. "Beer, dude. What do you think?"

"I think you've been drinking all morning and have probably had enough." This guy was really grating on Cooper's nerves.

"Chill, Ginger. Are you always such a bore?"

"I'm being responsible, Tyler. I'd hate to see anyone get hurt. I grew up on the water. I've seen more boating accidents caused by drunk drivers than I care to remember."

Tyler cut his eyes at his sister. "Can't you make your date lighten up?"

Lia shook her head. "Sorry, Tyler. I agree with Cooper this time. Let someone else drive the boat."

"I'm fine. Nothing's gonna happen," Tyler said, and started the outboard engine.

From Cooper's perspective, there were too many people—six in all—to go skiing in a twenty-two-foot boat, but he kept his opinion to himself.

Kaylie hopped onto the leaning post beside Tyler. "Can I go first? Puh-lease."

"Sure thing!" When they were far enough away from the dock, Tyler took the boat out of gear and tossed the rope in the water. "Get in."

Kaylie slipped a life jacket on over her black bikini and cannonballed into the water. When Tyler sped up, she popped right out of the water and skied for twenty minutes without falling. There appeared to be nothing she couldn't do when it came to sports, either on dry land or in the water.

"You're up next, Ginger," Tyler said as Kaylie was climbing into the boat.

"I'll pass," Cooper said.

Tyler peered at Cooper over the top of his Ray-Ban sunglass frames. "Because you don't know how to ski? Or because you're chicken to ski after Kaylie's phenomenal performance."

"Neither. I'll ski," Cooper said, snatching the life jacket from Kaylie.

Tyler looked around at the water skis littering the bottom of the boat. "Oops. I forgot to bring the trainers."

"Ha ha. I learned to slalom when I was seven." Cooper threw the ski into the water and dove in after it. When he was ready, he gave Tyler the thumbs-up. Tyler slammed down the throttle and jerked Cooper out of the water. The boat was moving so fast, he could barely grip the handle. When Cooper finally let go, Tyler circled around at full speed to retrieve him.

Cooper hoisted himself into the boat and shoved Tyler from behind the steering wheel. "I'm driving. You're too drunk. You're gonna get us all killed."

Tyler threw up his hands. "Fine. I'm tired of driving anyway."

Grabbing a beer out of the cooler, he went to the front of the boat and squeezed in between Annie and Lia.

"Who's up next?" Cooper asked.

"It's Annie's turn," Tyler said, shoulder-bumping her.

Annie gave her head a vigorous shake. "No way. I don't know how to ski. Besides, you forgot to bring the trainers."

"You can use two slaloms," Cooper said. "Try it. I'll coach you."

Their eyes met, and she smiled softly at him, as though she was also remembering the times he'd tried to teach her to ski when they'd dated.

"Okay." Annie stripped off her cover-up and fastened the life jacket around her torso. Cooper helped her into the water and handed her one ski at a time as she slipped her feet into the boots.

When he turned back around, Lia was watching him, her face pinched in an expression he couldn't read. "What's the deal with you and Annie? I saw you two alone on the beach this morning, and now you're making goo-goo eyes at each other. Did y'all used to date or something?"

Cooper hesitated, unsure how to respond. He didn't know what Annie had told Tyler about their past. "A long time ago, when we were in high school."

Tyler's face reddened with anger when he heard that.

Cooper turned his attention to Annie. "Are you ready?"

She bobbed her head.

"Hold your legs together," Cooper hollered. "And stay in a crouched position until you're up."

When he eased the throttle forward, the boat pulled Annie out of the water. Cooper let out a whoop, cheering her on, but the other passengers remained quiet. She skied for a couple hundred yards before she lost her balance and fell.

Cooper quickly circled back to her. "Wanna go again?"

"No thanks. My arms are tired."

"You did great," Cooper said, helping her out of the water.

Annie was all smiles, but Tyler sat with his arms folded, glaring at her with an angry scowl on his face.

"I'm next." Jeremy fastened a life jacket around him and dove into the water.

Tyler grabbed a ski and launched it into the water after him. The ski struck his head, and Jeremy screamed a stream of expletives. Touching his fingers to his head, he cried, "I'm bleeding, man. You cracked my head open."

Cooper killed the engine and moved to the stern of the boat. "Forget about the ski. I'll get it in a minute. Can you swim over to the boat?"

As Jeremy dog-paddled close to the boat, Cooper could see a large gash about two inches long on the right side of Jeremy's head. "Put your foot on the motor," Cooper instructed, and hauled Jeremy into the boat.

Up close, the laceration appeared much worse, and there was blood everywhere, streaming down his face and dripping onto the boat.

"You're bleeding all over my boat." Tyler tossed Jeremy a towel. "Here! Use this."

Jeremy held the towel to his head. "I feel lightheaded."

"You may have a concussion. You're going to need some stitches." Cooper helped Jeremy find a seat in the bow of the boat before turning on Tyler. "What is wrong with you? You cracked his head open with a water ski, and you're worried about blood on the boat? Did you ever hear of a water hose?"

"Shut up, Ginger. You're really pissing me off," Tyler said, giving Cooper a shove.

"You pissed me off the first time I met you." Cooper pushed Tyler backward three times until he was on his butt on the bench seat. "Now shut up and let me get *your* friend to the emergency room."

Cooper retrieved the water ski and sped back to the house. By the time they'd tied up at the dock, Jeremy had gone very pale and was shivering beneath the towel. Cooper and Annie supported him on either side as they walked him down the dock toward the house.

Rich, who was sitting by the pool, jumped up when he saw them coming. "What happened?"

"He got hit in the head with a ski," Cooper said. "He needs stitches. See if you can find his wallet. Hopefully, he has his insurance card with him."

"I'm on it," Rich said, and disappeared inside.

Annie and Cooper settled Jeremy into the front seat and closed the door.

"I'm going with you," Annie said, and climbed into the back seat.

"I wouldn't do that if you care about your relationship with Tyler," Cooper said in a grave tone.

Annie got out of the SUV. "What do you mean?"

Cooper let out a sigh as he leaned against the SUV. "When you were in the water, Lia asked if you and I had ever dated. I told her for a while in high school. Based on his reaction, this was news to Tyler."

"So that's why he's mad. He suspected we had. I shouldn't have lied to him when he asked about it."

"I'm sorry, Annie. I didn't know."

Annie shook her head. "It's not your fault."

Rich came running out of the house with two beach towels, a dry shirt, and Jeremy's wallet. "I couldn't find his phone. I assume he has it with him."

Cooper opened Jeremy's door. "Do you have your phone?"

Jeremy looked up at him with dazed eyes. "I don't think so." He patted the pockets of his wet bathing suit. "I must have left it on the boat. I think I put it in the cup holder. Can someone get it for me?"

"I'll get it," Rich said, taking off at a sprint across the yard to the dock.

Cooper noticed Annie's worried expression. "You can come with me. But I don't think Tyler would be too thrilled about us being together."

Annie glanced over at the pool where Tyler and Lia were sitting with long faces. "You're right. I should stay here and do damage control. But text me and let me know what the doctor says."

"For sure." Cooper spotted Rich returning with the phone and went around to the driver's side.

"Ugh, my head is killing me," Jeremy complained on the drive over to Mount Pleasant. He rested his head against the seat with his eyes closed and the towel pressed to his bleeding wound.

Cooper shook his arm. "I'm pretty sure you have a concussion, and you need to stay awake."

"Don't worry. I'm awake. I'm too pissed off at Tyler to sleep."

Cooper sensed there was more to his anger than Tyler throwing the ski at him. "I'm sure Tyler didn't mean for you to get hurt."

"Right. It was an accident. A careless one. As usual, Tyler was being immature and showing off. I used to think his behavior was funny. But now I find him pathetic. This is the final straw. Annie needs to get away from him. He's bad news. Tyler only cares about himself."

"I agree," Cooper said. "Unfortunately, she is blinded by her feelings for him."

Jeremy unlocked his phone, clicked on a number, and brought the phone to his ear. "Hey, man. Sorry to bother you on a Saturday. I got hit in the head with a water ski. Can you meet me at the hospital in Mount Pleasant?" He listened for a minute. "Thanks. I owe you one." He dropped the phone in his lap. "You can let me off at the emergency room. My brother's meeting me there."

"I'm not leaving you alone. I'll wait until he gets there."

"You're a good dude, Cooper. I don't know how you got messed up with Lia. But she's not much better than her brother."

Something told Cooper he could trust Jeremy. "I'm not here for Lia. I'm here because of Annie. She's in over her head with Tyler, and I'm worried about her."

Jeremy winced as he repositioned his head. "You're playing with fire. Tyler is possessive when it comes to his women, and he has a nasty temper."

"Thanks for the warning, but I can take care of myself."

When they arrived at the hospital, they checked in with the receptionist and located seats in the crowded waiting room.

"I'm not going back to the beach," Jeremy grumbled.

"I don't blame you. We can figure out a way for you to get your car."

"I didn't drive. I rode out to Sullivan's with Rich. I'll get him to bring me my clothes when he comes home on Monday."

They sat in silence until a nurse called Jeremy back to the examining rooms.

Cooper stood with him. "I'll wait out here for your brother."

"That'd be great. His name is Bruce, and he should be here soon." Jeremy showed Cooper a picture on his phone of a guy who appeared to be an older version of himself.

Cooper smiled at Jeremy. "I'm sorry this happened to you. Let us know what the doctor says."

He'd no sooner sat back down than Bruce hurried into the waiting room. They introduced themselves, and Bruce said, "Let me guess. Tyler is responsible for this."

Cooper didn't think it was his place to tell him about the accident. "I'll let Jeremy explain."

"I take that as a yes. Maybe this will get that punk out of my brother's life once and for all."

"Maybe. He's upset about it. They just took him back," Cooper said, gesturing at the door leading to the examining room. "I'm gonna take off."

Bruce slapped him on the shoulder. "Thanks for taking care of him."

"I only wish I could've done more."

Cooper arrived back at the house to find Annie alone in the kitchen, spreading lemon-yellow frosting on a cake. Tyler and Lia and some others were out by the pool, playing Ping-Pong and listening to loud music. "The others forgot about Jeremy's accident in a hurry, didn't they?"

"Yep." Annie scraped the last of the icing from the bowl with a spatula and spread it on the cake. "How is Jeremy?"

"He was being examined when I left. His brother is with him now. Bruce is going to drive him home."

"Oh, good." Annie placed the bowl in the sink and looked up at him with red-rimmed eyes, as though she'd been crying.

"Uh-oh. What happened?"

"Tyler and I had an argument. He's being a jerk."

Cooper watched Tyler chug a beer through a beer bong. "He clearly feels no remorse about splitting Jeremey's head open. If you want to leave, I'll go with you."

"Thanks, but I'm going to stick it out. I planned this big surprise party. I'm hoping that'll make him forgive me. But I need to keep my distance from you. He's convinced that I lied about our past because there's something still going on between you and me."

Cooper went around to her side of the counter. "I'm telling you this as a friend, Annie. He's playing you for a fool and he's dangerous, as evidenced by what happened today on the boat."

"I refuse to listen to you bash him like that," Annie said, pressing her hands to her ears. "Maybe Tyler was right. Maybe you are still in love with me."

Cooper didn't deny the allegation. "I don't care what Tyler thinks." He jabbed a finger at the pool. "Those people are not your friends. They would turn on you to protect Tyler in a heartbeat. Tread carefully, Annie. Anything you say or do could set him off," he said and headed out of the room.

"Where are you going? Are you leaving?" she called after him in a panicked voice.

"No." He turned back to face her. "I'm staying in this nuthouse on account of you. Because I *do* still . . ." He stopped himself from confessing his love for her. "I care about you, Annie. And I'm terrified for your safety."

"You're being melodramatic."

"Maybe I am exaggerating the situation. But I don't trust Tyler or Lia or Kaylie, who has it bad for Tyler, in case you haven't noticed."

"You don't know what you're talking about." Annie held her chin high in defiance. Tyler had cast his spell over her, and she wouldn't recognize danger if she looked it in the eye.

twenty-six
brooke

Brooke couldn't take her eyes off Grady's hot body in the beach chair beside her. Burning with desire, she closed her eyes and fantasized about being in bed with him. She didn't know how much longer she could resist her feelings for him. But to move forward without telling him about the pregnancy was so wrong.

"Brooke? Is that you? What a small world."

The voice sent chills down Brooke's spine despite the ninety-degree day. Shielding her eyes from the sun, she looked up at Sawyer. "Not that small. I told you my friend was hosting a house party for his thirtieth birthday."

"Did you? I must've forgotten. I'm cat sitting for some locals who went out of town for the weekend." Sawyer unfolded a beach chair and plopped down on the other side of Grady. "Hi! I'm Sawyer, Brooke's ex." She offered him a handshake. "We were together for eight years. A word of warning. She's fickle. She ditched me out of the blue. She will probably do the same to you. She's never been with a man before. How's that working out for you?"

Grady appeared bewildered. "I . . .um . . . We're just friends."

"No, you're not. I've seen you kissing." Sawyer stretched her legs out in front of her. "Wow. The sun feels amazing. I think I'll go for a swim." She hopped up, stripped off her cover-up, and glided down to the water, her slim figure elegant in a red one-piece swimsuit cut high on her hips.

Grady tore his eyes away from Sawyer's shapely body. "What's going on, Brooke?"

"Let's walk," Brooke said, already on her feet.

Grady caught up with her. "I'm confused. I thought you told me your ex moved away."

"She did. To Boston. But then she came back. She's been . . . . Ugh, there's no point in sugarcoating it. She's been stalking me." Brooke gave him the abbreviated version of what had been going on with Sawyer.

"Is that why you had your locks changed?" he asked, and she nodded. "Why didn't you call the police?"

"Because I was worried that would set her off, and I wanted her to go away peacefully."

"I don't understand. How could you be with someone like that?" Grady asked, his accusatory tone cutting her like a knife.

"She's a very accomplished individual, actually. She comes from a prominent family in California, and she's incredibly smart. She's an oncology resident. Or she was. I don't know what happened to her. She changed in recent months. She used to be warm and considerate."

"Stop being so naïve, Brooke. People don't become psycho overnight," he said, his voice now angry.

"I don't think she's psycho, Grady. I think maybe she's suffering from a chemical imbalance. Even Mom fell for her."

His tone softened. "That's saying something, I guess. Lula was a tough judge of character. Still, this woman is dangerous, Brooke. She was living in your house without you knowing it. Why didn't you at least tell *me*?"

"Because I thought I'd handled it. I told her our relationship was over, and I convinced her to go home to California. I honestly thought she'd left town," Brooke lied. She knew full well Sawyer was still in Charleston. But following her to Sullivan's Island was a bold move, even for Sawyer.

"This is seriously uncool, Brooke," Grady said, raking his fingers through his hair.

"I'm aware. Why are you being such a jerk? You've never spoken to me like this. Not even when we were just friends."

"Because she's going to ruin our weekend," Grady said, and headed back in the direction they'd come. His stride was longer and faster, and by the time Brooke got back to their chairs, he'd packed up his stuff and left the beach.

"He seemed pretty angry," Sawyer said, rubbing sunscreen on her wet skin. "I don't blame him. He'll have a difficult time explaining to his friends about his girlfriend, who was gay but is now straight and is pregnant with her sister's baby."

The color drained from Brooke's face. "You didn't tell him about the pregnancy, did you?"

"Nope. He didn't stick around long enough." She dropped her sunscreen in her beach bag. "But he'll eventually find out, and when he does, he'll be the laughingstock of Charleston. He won't want anything to do with you. You might as well kiss that relationship goodbye."

Anger raged through Brooke. "Leave me alone!" she yelled, not caring if the other beachgoers heard her. "Even if you run Grady off, I'm not getting back together with you. Go home to California. You don't belong in Charleston."

"Oh, but I do. Didn't I tell you? I convinced the director to let me back in the residency program."

Brooke was at a loss for words as she packed up her belongings. She would never be free of this woman.

Sawyer jumped up and grabbed Brooke's arm. "Don't go away angry. Can't we at least talk about us?"

Brooke jerked her arm away. "For the last time, there is no us.

If you don't stay away from me, I'll get a restraining order against you."

Dread overwhelmed Brooke as she traipsed through the scorching sand to the beach access road. She'd made a terrible mistake in telling Sawyer about the pregnancy. Sawyer was a ticking time bomb. She would wait until the opportune time to use this information to destroy Brooke's relationship with Grady.

Grady had taken the golf cart, and Brooke had to lug her chair and beach bag a half mile in the afternoon heat back to the house. She was dripping with sweat, and her stomach was cramping by the time she arrived. She spotted Grady drinking a beer with Tyler by the pool. He didn't call out to her, and she didn't look his way as she walked past them on the way to the guest cottage.

Brooke locked the bedroom door and collapsed onto the bed. She wanted to leave this god-awful place. She checked her phone, but the closest Uber was an hour away and would charge over a hundred dollars to drive her back to Charleston. She tossed the phone onto the bed. She wished she was anywhere but here. But there was no hiding from Sawyer, who was obviously keeping close tabs on her. If Brooke left Sullivan's Island, Sawyer would know about it, and she'd come after her.

Brooke rolled onto her side, buried her face in a pillow, and screamed out her frustration. Why hadn't she reported Sawyer to the police when she had the chance? Who knew what Sawyer was capable of? She would stop at nothing to get Brooke back. Would she go so far as to hurt Lizbet's baby?

Removing the pillow from her face, she closed her eyes and fell into a fitful sleep. She dreamed she was on the beach, running from Sawyer, who was chasing her with three black cats on leashes. But Brooke couldn't get away because her feet were stuck in the sand. She woke herself when she cried out for help.

The sun was low in the sky as she eased herself up in bed. Checking her phone, she had a text message from Grady. *Hanging out by the pool. Come join me.* There was no mention of what had happened on the beach earlier. No apology for taking the golf cart and making her walk home in the heat.

She thumbed off a response. *Be down in a few.*

Brooke showered off the sunscreen and dressed in Bermuda shorts and a white sleeveless top. As she passed through the sitting room, she noticed Lia sleeping with her mouth wide open on the sofa.

At the pool, she found Tyler and Grady deep in conversation. Neither glanced up when she walked by. Tears stung her eyes as she continued to the kitchen.

"Wonder what those two are talking about," she said to Annie, who was shredding lettuce for a salad.

"Ha. I'm not sure I wanna know. They've been talking with their heads pressed together like that for over an hour. Everyone else went to another party down the beach."

"Not Lia. She's passed out on the sofa in the guest cottage. Who's having the party?"

Annie shrugged. "Somebody with the last name Bromley."

"Never heard of them." Brooke poured herself a club soda from the bar cart and went to stand beside Annie. "Do you want some help with dinner?"

"Sure! You can finish the salad while I peel the shrimp. "Annie slid the salad bowl in front of Brooke and removed a package of shrimp from the refrigerator.

"How much salad should I make?"

"There are only six of us here. Lia and Cooper. You and Grady. And Tyler and me. The others will have to fend for themselves." Annie eyed Brooke's club soda. "I noticed you haven't been drinking. Are you feeling okay?"

"The party girl is on hiatus," Brooke said with an irritated tone she hadn't intended.

"I'm sorry. I didn't mean to hit a nerve."

"You didn't. I'm just overly sensitive these days. The truth is, I'm pregnant with Lizbet and Jamie's baby." Brooke didn't need to explain the situation. Annie had been with Lizbet the night she had an emergency hysterectomy.

Annie let out a woo-hoo as she jabbed the air with her shrimp deveiner. "That's the best news ever. How far along are you?"

"Only six weeks. We're waiting until after the first trimester to break the news, but I'm sure Jamie will tell you sooner than later."

"Well, I'm glad you did. I will act surprised when they tell me," Annie said, and returned to deveining shrimp.

Brooke felt a pang of guilt. Lizbet and Jamie should be the ones to share their news about their baby. But Brooke felt uneasy about everything that was happening, and she needed an ally. And she trusted Annie, who'd been her sister's best friend for years.

"Have you told Grady yet?" Annie asked, rinsing the shrimp and placing them in a plastic bag with the marinade.

"Not yet. I'm waiting for the right time. It's not an easy situation to explain." Brooke covered the salad with plastic wrap and placed the bowl in the refrigerator.

"He seems like a nice guy. I admit I'm surprised you two are together though. I thought you were . . . you know."

"Gay? Trust me, our relationship came as a surprise to me too." Brooke's eyes traveled to the window. Tyler and Grady had moved out of their chairs and were nowhere in sight. "Things are different with men. I'm not as good at reading them as I am women. Sawyer was on the beach today, stirring up trouble, and now he's being a jerk."

Annie's brown eyes widened. "You mean your ex—Sawyer?"

"Yeah. She's been harassing me. She wants to get back together, but I'm not interested."

"By harassing, do you mean she's threatening you?"

Brooke hesitated. If she told Annie the truth, she would go straight to Lizbet and Jamie. Which is what Brooke *should do* and *will do* once the weekend is over. "It's nothing like that. She's just being a crazy ex. I'll go set the table," she said and disappeared into the dining room.

Brooke threw open the sliding walls and set six places at the weathered oak table with rattan woven placemats, whitewash china, and turquoise linen napkins. She was lighting creamy pillar candles in the hurricane lanterns when Grady entered the room wearing a coral striped polo with his hair still damp from the shower.

"Brooke! There you are. I've been looking all over for you."

She finished lighting the candles, blew out the match, and turned to face him. "You left me stranded at the beach. Why'd you take the golf cart?"

Confusion crossed his face. "It's not that far. I didn't think you'd mind walking."

She wouldn't have minded if she weren't pregnant. "If it's not that far, why didn't you walk? It was blazing hot, and I had to carry my chair and beach bag," she said in an uncharacteristic whiny tone.

"I think I liked you better when we were just friends. When you weren't so uptight."

Her throat tightened. *When she wasn't pregnant,* she thought. *When her emotions weren't all over the place.* "I'm sorry, Grady. I'm not myself right now." She was as angry at herself as she was at him.

"I'm sorry too. Taking the golf cart was inconsiderate. But that scene on the beach with Sawyer really got to me. I've never seen you with another woman, and meeting your ex-lover kinda freaked me out."

"Is that what you were talking to Tyler about?"

"And other stuff. Guys talk, too, you know?" He hesitated as though he wanted to say something else. "Whatever. I'm gonna get a drink."

She could no longer hold back the tears as she watched him go. She sensed him slipping away. She knew she'd have to make sacrifices to have the baby. Giving up her social life was one thing.

But giving up the man she loved seemed unfair. Especially when her sister was so unappreciative.

The thought of Lizbet brought on more tears, and she stepped outside to collect herself. She was alone in this pregnancy. She would live in seclusion in her little pink house until the baby was born. Nine months would pass quickly, and she would have her life back. She would not count on another person to make her happy. Finding fulfillment and joy in her life was entirely her responsibility.

Annie finished carving the tenderloin, placed the tray on the server, and called the others to dinner. She'd worked in the kitchen all afternoon, but Tyler paid little attention to the food as he loaded his plate with heaping helpings of tender, juicy beef, spicy grilled shrimp, creamy hash brown casserole, and home-made flaky yeast rolls. He sat down at one end of the table, and when she took the seat beside him, he motioned her to the other end.

"As the hostess for the weekend, you should sit opposite me," he said in a tone one might use when speaking to a young child.

Annie followed his instructions, even though she didn't see what difference it made where she sat.

Brooke and Grady took the seats facing the open wall of windows, and Cooper sat down opposite them, next to Annie.

Annie spread her linen napkin on her lap. "Where's Lia? Did you tell her we're eating?"

"I haven't seen her since I got back from the hospital," Cooper said. "I've been out on the beach with my camera all afternoon."

"Has anyone heard from Jeremy?" When no one answered,

Annie set her gaze on her boyfriend. "Tyler? Have you tried to call him?"

"I've been busy," Tyler mumbled.

Cooper glared at Tyler. "Don't you think you should make time to check on him? Since you're the one who split his head open?"

An awkward silence fell over the room. Tyler's face reddened, and Annie could tell he was going to rip Cooper a new one, when Lia and Sawyer appeared in the open doorway.

Lia gave Sawyer a half hug. "Everyone, I want you to meet my new friend, Sawyer. She's cat sitting at the house next door."

Annie glanced over at Brooke, whose face had gone pale.

Sawyer approached the table. "I've known Brooke and Annie for years. And I met Grady on the beach earlier today."

Cooper flashed her a wave. "I'm Cooper."

Sawyer shot a finger pistol at him. "Right. You're Jamie's cousin."

"Oh my gosh!" Lia exclaimed. "It's such a small world. Everyone in the South knows everyone else."

"That's so true." Sawyer turned to Tyler with a bright smile. "And you are?"

Tyler shot out of his chair. "I'm Tyler, Lia's brother. Nice to meet you, Sawyer. I hope you'll stay for dinner. Here, let me pull up a chair." He dragged a spare chair across the floor, positioning it at the table next to him.

"Come on. Let's get some food." Lia led Sawyer to the buffet, where they filled their plates with small portions from each dish.

"What're you drinking?" Tyler asked Sawyer when they returned to the table.

Sawyer eyed his glass of beer. "Do you have anything other than beer?"

Tyler winked at her. "We have whatever you'd like."

Lia was already back on her feet. "Making new friends calls for a celebration. Since we're having red meat, we'll open a bottle of

Daddy's bordeaux. He'll never miss it." She disappeared into the kitchen, returning a minute later with a wine bottle bearing a black-and-white label featuring a French chateau. She handed the bottle and wine opener to Tyler, who removed the cork and poured a glass for each of them.

"Anyone else want some?" Tyler asked, holding up the bottle. His gaze traveled the table, landing on Brooke. "Would you like some, Brooke? You've been awfully dry this weekend."

"You've drunk enough for both of us," Brooke said with a humph.

"In that case, I'll have your share," he said, and gave himself a healthy pour.

Sawyer clinked glasses with Tyler and Lia. "Cheers." She sniffed the wine first before taking a sip. "This is excellent," she said and spoke about notes of black currants and cedar like an expert.

Tyler sipped his wine and set down his glass. "So, Sawyer, how do you know Brooke and Annie?"

"Brooke and I went to college together in California. I met Annie through Brooke's little sister, Lizbet."

Tyler popped a shrimp into his mouth. "Are you from California?"

"I am. From Napa. My family owns a small boutique vineyard," Sawyer said, picking at the hash brown casserole with her fork.

"Cool! Which one? I've been to California a few times."

When Sawyer named the vineyard, Annie googled it on her phone under the table. It appeared to be legitimate, although the owner's last name was not Glover.

Sawyer blabbed on to Tyler about the vineyard as though he were the only one in the room. She tossed her hair, made eyes at him, and laughed a fake laugh that made Annie want to smack her.

Annie felt Cooper watching her, but she didn't dare look at

him. She risked a glance at Brooke, who was staring daggers at Sawyer. Brooke's face was beet red, as though she might explode with anger.

Finally, Brooke cried out, "Stop lying, Sawyer! Your father doesn't own a vineyard. He's a criminal attorney."

Annie chimed in, "She's not straight either, despite the way she's coming on to you."

Tyler met Annie's gaze. "What did you say?"

"I said she's not straight. Sawyer is gay."

Anger crossed Tyler's face at having been played a fool. "Of course she is. All the hot girls are gay." His dark eyes widened. "Wait, a minute. I get it now. You and Brooke didn't just go to college together. You were lovers."

Grady, who hadn't said a word throughout the exchange, tapped his knife against this beer bottle. "Bingo."

Brooke stood abruptly. "Excuse me. I've lost my appetite," she said and took her plate to the kitchen. Seconds later, Annie saw her pass by outside on the way to the guest cottage.

Annie waited for Grady to go after her. When he remained seated, she pushed back from the table and hurried outside. "Brooke! Wait up!"

Brooke increased her pace, and Annie ran to catch up with her. "I'm sorry, Brooke. I shouldn't have said that about Sawyer being gay."

"Why? It's the truth. I'm not mad at you, Annie. I just can't be here right now." Brooke pulled out her phone and clicked on the screen. "Dang it. There are never any Ubers on this Island."

Annie followed Brooke into the cottage and down the hall to the bedroom. "I don't blame you for being upset. But do you really want to leave?"

Brooke plopped down on the bed. "What I want is for Sawyer to leave me alone. I wasn't entirely honest about her when we talked earlier. She's been more than harassing me. She's been stalking me. I can't get away from her. She's everywhere. "Fat tears spilled over Brooke's lids and streamed down her pretty face. "And my raging hormones are making everything so much worse. I cry all the time now. I can't seem to stop myself."

Annie hated seeing Brooke so upset. She'd always been envious of Lizbet for having such a badass for a big sister. But the pregnancy and trouble with Sawyer were taking their toll on her.

Annie sat down on the edge of the bed beside her. "You have to tell Lizbet and Jamie. They have a right to know their child's safety is at risk."

Brooke inhaled an unsteady breath. "Lizbet will be furious. We're already in a fight about selling the house."

"You poor thing." Annie pulled Brooke close. "You have a lot on your plate right now. But you don't have to go through any of this alone. You're doing an amazing, selfless thing for Lizbet and Jamie. And I'm sure they realize that. Let them help you. Jamie will get rid of Sawyer for you."

"You're right. And I realize I need to tell them, but I'm going to wait until Monday. I don't want to spoil their weekend." Brooke wiped her eyes with the hem of her blouse, leaving mascara and makeup smudges on the white fabric.

"My car is here. If you really want to go home, I'll drive you."

Brooke shook her head. "Sawyer will only follow me. I'll get Grady to take me in the morning." She smiled at Annie. "Thank you for being so kind."

"Sure thing." Annie dropped her arm from around Brooke's shoulders. "You would do the same for me."

Brooke patted her knee. "Are you okay? Sawyer made a spectacle of herself, coming on hard to Tyler like that. And he was eating up the attention. Don't let him jerk you around, Annie."

"Ugh!" Annie fell back on the bed. "He's not usually such a jerk."

"Wrong," Brooke said. "I've known Tyler most of my life, and he's always been a jerk. Tyler has never loved anyone but himself. Except for maybe Kaylie when they dated."

Annie sat bolt upright. "They dated? When was that?"

"The summer before we went to college. It didn't last long. All they ever did was fight. Watch out for Kaylie. She's been in love with him as long as I can remember."

"That explains why she's been hitting on him all weekend." Loud music blasted outside the cottage. "I guess the others are back from the Bromleys' party." Annie slid off the bed to her feet. "Wanna come hang out with me?"

"No, thanks. I'm exhausted. I think I'll read for a while and turn in early." Brooke stood to face her. "I'm here for you if you need to talk."

She gave Brooke a hug. "The same goes for you."

Annie wandered slowly down the garden path, thinking how wrong Brooke was about Tyler. It was his birthday weekend, and he was just having fun. So what if he was flirtatious by nature? She couldn't let it get to her when other women made passes at him.

As she neared the pool, Annie heard her name mentioned, and she ducked behind a palmetto tree. Listening closer, she recognized Lia's voice.

"Our plan is working. Tyler is finally starting to see what a gold digger Annie is."

A second voice said, "I know! Isn't it fabulous? If only Annie would take the hint that she doesn't belong."

Annie peeked out from behind the tree. Through the thick vegetation, she saw the top of Kaylie's dark head standing beside Lia.

"She's clueless," Lia said. "My mom point-blank told her she was not in Tyler's league, and that Annie didn't meet our high standards."

"Ouch! That's harsh," said Kaylie. "I almost feel sorry for her."

"Don't! Annie is a conniver. She came running to me after Mom said those things. As if I'd be her ally. She made up an excuse about needing advice on Tyler's birthday present, but I knew what she was up to."

Kaylie gasped. "You didn't tell me that. What did you do?"

"I called you." Lia giggled. "Having you here this weekend is making things juicy. If I could get some dirt on Annie, I could drive the nail into her coffin."

Annie fingered the round scar on her lower back near her spine. She knew exactly what dirt would be the nail. Suddenly finding it difficult to breathe, she slipped from behind the tree and headed off in the opposite direction, not stopping until she reached the end of the dock. She kicked off her flip-flops and sat down on the edge of the dock with her feet dangling over the side.

The water was still, and the stars bright in the dark sky. Voices rang out in her head. Brooke saying that Tyler had never loved anyone but Kaylie. And Kaylie: *If only Annie would take the hint that she doesn't belong.* But Lia's jab about Annie being a gold digger cut her to the core. Maybe because she was acting like one—poor fisher's daughter chasing after the most eligible bachelor in town. Annie would prove them all wrong if it was the last thing she did.

She leaned against a piling and closed her eyes, imagining how pleased Tyler would be when she surprised him with her special dinner. He would realize what a jerk he'd been this weekend and make it up to her.

Her thoughts shifted to Brooke and the baby she was carrying for Lizbet and Jamie. She imagined what it would be like to be married to Tyler and pregnant with his child. They would buy a small house downtown, and when the baby was born, she would quit her job at Tasty Provisions and become a stay-at-home mom. They would have more children, and she would survive without her catering career. When the children were older, she would find other ways to occupy her free time. Maybe she'd open a clothing boutique or a coffee shop or start a wedding cake business.

Her eyes were still closed, her mind a million miles away, when she sensed a presence hovering over her. She opened her eyes to find Cooper staring down at her.

"Are you okay, Annie? You seemed so peaceful. I thought maybe you'd fallen asleep."

Annie sat up straighter against the piling. "I'm fine. I was just chilling."

"That was some scene at dinner. What's up with Sawyer?"

"I'm not sure. I think she's jealous because Brooke is with Grady." Annie didn't think it her place to tell him Sawyer was stalking Brooke. "Why aren't you partying with the others?"

"Because I'm beat. Jeremy's accident wore me out." He sat down next to her. "Speaking of which, I finally got an update from Rich. Jeremy has a concussion, and it took six staples to close the gash in his head. His brother drove him home to their parents' house. Apparently, Jeremy's parents are pretty ticked off at Tyler. They are talking about suing him."

"Why? It was just an accident," Annie said, even though she knew Tyler had been reckless in throwing the water ski.

Cooper's brow hit his hairline. "You realize it could've been one of us who got hit in the head with the ski, don't you? Tyler was driving like a maniac when he pulled me. If I'd fallen, I could've gotten hurt. I don't see what your attraction is to Tyler. He's a spoiled rotten punk."

Annie hugged her knees to her chest as she stared out into the inky water. "You don't understand, because you were raised with money. This is my one chance to have everything I've ever wanted."

"Money makes life easier, Annie. But too much money corrupts people, makes them greedy for more money and strips away their code of honor. You, as the daughter of a fisherman, have had to work for everything all your life. Which makes you stronger in character than anyone at this party. You believe in yourself, Annie. You have an inner strength most people will never possess."

Annie's throat tightened. "Wow. That's the nicest thing anyone has ever said to me."

Cooper looked over at her. "That's a shame. You deserve to have someone tell you nice things about yourself every single day. You also need someone who will tell you the truth. Everyone makes mistakes, Annie. When it comes to Tyler, you're making a terrible one." He tossed a thumb over his shoulder at the party. "Those corrupt people will eat you alive and bury you in their family's cemetery plot."

Annie responded with silence. She wasn't yet ready to admit he was speaking the truth.

"I didn't mean to upset you. I just need to get that off my chest," Cooper said.

"And I needed to hear it," she said. "Do you ever wonder what would've happened if I hadn't gotten shot?"

"I know what would've happened. We would've gotten married, and you would've had the baby, followed by three or four more. We would be living a comfortable life at Moss Creek with our brood of children and a pack of dogs."

Annie admitted this life sounded way less complicated than Tyler's and Lia's. "Do you ever think about the child we lost?"

"All the time. Even more so since you came back into my life. You and I needed to go our separate ways, to experience life on our own for a while. But fate has brought us back together. Your judgment is too clouded by your feelings for Tyler to realize it now, but you and I belong together. And one day we will be. I'm willing to wait as long as it takes."

Cooper got up, pulled Annie to his feet, and took her into his arms. Annie resisted at first, but she eventually relaxed against his body. The years fell away, and they were teenagers again, experiencing love for the first time. How could she be feeling this way about Cooper if she was so in love with Tyler?

He held her at arm's length. "I would kiss you, but I don't think you're ready."

Her body ached for him. She wanted nothing more than to feel his lips on hers. But an inner voice shouted at her to run away from him as fast as she could, or she would risk losing Tyler. "I don't think Tyler would like that very much."

"I don't care what Tyler likes. Maybe one day you won't either." He glanced up at the house. "Are you going back to the party soon?"

"I think I'll stay down here awhile," she said, even though she was planning to head up soon. Tyler would be furious if he saw them coming up from the dock together. "What about you?"

He let go of her arms. "I'm going to call it a night. Lia wins the prize for the worst date ever."

This tidbit of information sang to Annie's heart. Was it because she thought Lia all wrong for him? Or because she wanted him for herself? "Are you staying until Monday?" She didn't want him to leave. Either the dock or the island.

"I'm not sure. I'll play it by ear. Even though the party scene isn't my thing, I'm enjoying my time on the beach. I've gotten some excellent photographs." Cooper kissed her cheek. "I'm here for you, Annie. If you need anything, you come find me. Watch your back. You're in enemy territory here."

He turned and walked away. She watched him go and disappear up the dock. *Enemy territory?* Was it that obvious Lia and Kaylie were ganging up on her? Heat pulsed through her body. They were making a fool out of her. And she was letting them.

Annie marched up the dock and across the lawn to the pool deck. She would stake her claim on her man. She would not hand Tyler over to Kaylie without a fight. But neither Tyler nor Kaylie were anywhere in sight.

brooke

Brooke woke on Sunday morning with a heavy feeling in her gut that had nothing to do with last night's drama. She got out of bed, threw on some shorts, and began stuffing her belongings in a suitcase. She was calling for an Uber when a text from Grady appeared on her phone. *I'm so sorry about yesterday. I was a real jerk. Can we talk?*

She texted back. *I'm going home. My Uber is on the way.*

Brooke was brushing her teeth a few minutes later when there was a knock on the bathroom door. She spit out the toothpaste and opened the door. Grady was leaning against the doorjamb with a handful of blue hydrangeas.

"I come bearing gifts. Your favorite."

"How did you know?"

"I remembered. I remember a lot of things about you, Brooke. You like your pizza without red sauce. You drink a glass of milk every night before you go to bed. And you cheat at Monopoly."

"I do not," she said, smacking his tight abs with the back of her hand.

His face turned serious. "I don't blame you for being angry. I was an ass yesterday, and I'm so, so sorry. Can we at least talk? I'd like a chance to explain. If you still want to go home, I'll drive you myself."

How could she say no to this sincere man with his disheveled hair and cheeks rosy from the sun? "I've already ordered an Uber. They'll charge me if I cancel."

"I'll buy you brunch at the Sea Biscuit Cafe to pay you back."

"And if I still wanna go home, you promise to drive me?"

"I promise. Cross my heart," he said, with his hand pressed against his chest.

"Fine." She pulled out her phone and canceled the Uber. "You owe me ten bucks, which should at least buy me an omelet."

"I'm willing to splurge on hash browns and sausage as well," he said with a devilish grin.

Brooke retrieved her flip-flops from the bedroom, and they headed off on foot toward the beach. The sky was still golden from the sunrise, and only a few dog walkers occupied the beach.

"How was the party last night?" she asked, curious what he'd done after she'd stormed out during dinner.

"I wouldn't know. Everyone went back to the Bromleys'. I'm not sure they ever came home. If they did, they were quiet. Cooper and I played a couple of games of pool and went to bed before eleven. He's a nice guy. I really like him."

"I agree. He's too good for Lia. Fortunately, I don't think she likes him. He and Annie belong together."

"I can see that." Grady reached for Brooke's hand. "I hardly slept last night. I tossed and turned, thinking about us. I wasn't turned off at the thought of you being with another woman. The thought of you being with *anyone* else struck a nerve. My feelings for you scare me. I fell hard for you fast." He stopped walking and turned to face her. "But I had a revelation as the sun came up. I've been in love with you all along, since the first day of our freshman year in high school when you entered my English class wearing that yellow sundress. I thought your diamond nose piercing was the sexiest thing I'd ever seen."

"Ha. My mama didn't think so."

Grady chuckled. "I admit, I'm glad you got rid of it," he said, touching her nose where the piercing used to be. "I was relieved when you went to college in California. Because of your sexuality, I could never have you. But here we are, and things have changed. Is there any chance you feel the same way about me?"

Brooke wanted to lose herself in his golden eyes. "I admitted that the other night. My feelings for you have deepened beyond friendship. But there's something you need to know about me. This is kinda hard to explain." Her voice trailed off when she noticed Sawyer hurrying toward them. Her stomach did a somersault, and she thought she might vomit in the sand.

"Yoo-hoo! Brooke!" Sawyer called out, flagging them down. She was out of breath by the time she reached them. "I've been looking all over for you."

Brooke shot Sawyer a sharp look. "What do you want, Sawyer? Grady and I are having a private discussion."

"I was worried after you left the dinner party so abruptly," Sawyer said, in a sickly sweet fake voice. "It isn't good for the baby for you to get so upset."

Grady's forehead puckered. "What baby?"

Sawyer draped an arm around Brooke's neck, as though they were still a couple. "Didn't Brooke tell you? She's pregnant."

With an expression of disbelief, Grady's eyes traveled from Sawyer's face to Brooke's. "Is this true?"

Brooke shoved Sawyer away. "I was just getting ready to explain. I—"

"Keep your explanation." Grady threw up his hands. "I'm out. This has gotten too weird for me."

Brooke jabbed a finger at Sawyer's face. "I'm warning you, for the last time, get out of my life." She took off after Grady, calling, "Wait! Grady! Please!"

He kept marching toward the sand dunes, with head bowed and shoulders slumped.

Her stomach cramped as she broke into a run. When she reached him, she grabbed his elbow and spun him around. "Listen to me."

"I don't understand this. Did you use a sperm donor? Do you have a stranger's baby growing inside of you?" he asked, his handsome face set in stone.

"No! It's not like that. The baby belongs to Lizbet and Jamie."

"Okay, that's even weirder." Grady kicked at the sand. "Why would you do something like that?"

"Because I can. If Lizbet needed a kidney, I'd give it to her in a heartbeat. This is not that different."

"This is totally different. You're as psycho as your girlfriend." He jerked his head in Sawyer's direction. "How high are the statistics for surrogate women who become too attached to the babies they're carrying?"

"Not as high as you think. Most surrogates understand they aren't giving up a child. They are giving the child back to their parents."

Recognition crossed Grady's face. "So this is why you haven't been drinking? You lied to me. You told me you were worried you had a drinking problem. What else have you lied to me about, Brooke?"

"Nothing! I promise. Lizbet and I agreed not to tell anyone I'm pregnant until after the first trimester."

"You should've told me before you agreed to go away with me for the weekend."

"I was getting ready to tell you when Sawyer walked up. It's all so new. I'm still adjusting to my new reality myself."

"*Your new reality*? You have a psycho girlfriend stalking you, and you're pregnant with your sister's kid. This new reality is way more than I'm prepared to deal with. I'm sorry, Brooke. I can't do this."

This time, when he walked away, Brooke let him. She would worry about Grady later. For now, she needed to get to the doctor.

She sensed something was wrong with the baby. The heaviness and cramping weren't normal.

She walked as quickly as she dared back to the cottage. When she used the bathroom, the sight of blood in her panties confirmed her suspicions.

She called the doctor and quickly explained the situation.

"Meet me at the hospital in Mount Pleasant," Dr. Carroll said without hesitation, even though it was a holiday weekend.

Brooke thanked the doctor, ended the call, and clicked on the Uber app. The closest car was forty minutes away. She would get someone from here to take her. Tossing her duffel bag over her shoulder, she left the cottage and walked over to the house. She was relieved to find Annie alone in the kitchen, preparing food for Tyler's birthday party tonight.

"Can you give me a ride to the hospital in Mount Pleasant? I think I might be having a miscarriage." The reality of the situation hit home, and Brooke burst into tears.

"Oh, no! I'm so sorry." Annie washed and dried her hands and gave Brooke a quick hug. "Everything will be fine. But we need to hurry. Go get in the car. I'll grab my bag and be out in a second."

Brooke's crying escalated on the way to the car, and by the time Annie emerged from the house, she was nearly hysterical. "This is all my fault! I killed my sister's baby."

Annie fastened her seat belt and started the engine. In a stern voice, she said, "Listen to me, Brooke. You are not responsible. These things happen sometimes. For the baby's sake, you need to calm down. Take some deep breaths."

Brooke inhaled a big gulp of air and expelled it slowly.

"Good girl! Keep doing that," Annie said, throwing the car in reverse and backing out of the driveway.

By the time they crossed the Ben Sawyer Bridge, she felt marginally calmer. "I shouldn't have come here. The entire weekend has been a disaster, with Sawyer showing up and Grady acting like an ass," she said, blowing her nose.

Annie glanced over at her. "Did something happen with Sawyer this morning?"

Brooke nodded and told her about the scene on the beach. "He called me psycho. He asked about the percentage of surrogates who grow too attached to their babies."

"I'm playing devil's advocate here, but that's a legitimate concern. Are you worried about becoming too attached?"

Brooke placed a hand on her belly. "I love this baby already. As its aunt. I remind myself several times a day that this baby belongs to Lizbet. Jamie and Lizbet are the ones I envision driving it home from the hospital. They will christen it and teach it to tie its shoes and pay for its college. I love my sister. I feel so blessed to do this for her. I would never cause her the heartache of trying to take her baby away from her."

Annie smiled at her. "Of course you wouldn't. Men don't understand these things. Grady will calm down once he's thought about it."

"I'm not so sure. I thought I knew him. He's not the same guy he was in high school." Brooke removed her phone. "I need to call Lizbet."

Her sister answered in a cheerful voice, as though they weren't at war over selling the Tradd Street house. "Guess what I'm doing! I'm painting the nursery. I went with yellow to play it safe."

Brooke's heart sank. "You'd better put down your paint roller. I'm having some cramping and spotting. I'm sure it's nothing, but Dr. Carroll wants to see me just in case. I'm on the way to Roper hospital. The one in Mount Pleasant."

"What're you doing in Mount Pleasant?" Lizbet asked, the cheerfulness now gone from her voice.

"I was with Grady at a house party on Sullivan's Island."

"You didn't tell me that," Lizbet said, a hint of accusation in her voice. "Jamie's at work. Let me locate him, and we will be there as soon as we can."

Brooke ended the call and stared out the window. "I dread

telling Jamie and Lizbet about Sawyer. If I lose the baby, they will either blame her for stalking me or me for not calling the police."

"They will not blame you, Brooke. Why don't I talk to Jamie for you?"

"Maybe it would be better coming from you. I'm not sure I can bear their disappointment." Brooke said, her throat thickening.

Annie reached over and squeezed Brooke's hand. "There's nothing for anyone to be disappointed about yet. Think positively."

Brooke inhaled, drawing herself tall. "You're right. Everything will be fine," she said with more confidence than she felt.

At the hospital, they entered the emergency room, and Brooke gave her name to the pretty blonde receptionist. "Dr. Carroll called from the road," the receptionist said. "She's stuck in traffic, but she asked me to be on the lookout for you. We'll take you back and get you settled while you wait." She offered Brooke a soft smile. "Don't worry, hon. I experienced a similar situation with my first pregnancy, and everything turned out fine."

Some of the tension left Brooke's body. "That makes me feel better. Thanks for telling me."

The receptionist motioned them to the waiting room. "Have a seat and a nurse will call you in a minute."

They located two empty seats near the window and sat down. Brooke bowed her head and closed her eyes, asking God not to take the baby to heaven. Lizbet had her heart set on having this baby in April. She would be heartbroken if they had to start over. And she only had but so many eggs to fertilize. Brooke would never forgive herself if she lost this baby. But if a miracle occurred and she didn't miscarry, she would be extra careful for the next eight months, even if it meant moving to another city to get away from Sawyer.

twenty-nine
annie

Lizbet and Jamie arrived before the doctor, who had sent another message that she was still stuck in traffic. Annie waited until after Brooke had explained her symptoms to Lizbet and Jamie before announcing her departure.

"I really need to get back to the beach. I have to prepare for Tyler's surprise birthday dinner tonight." She puckered her lips, blowing a kiss to Brooke. "I'm sure everything will be fine. But let me know what the doctor says."

"I don't want Grady to know what happened. If he asks, just tell him you took me home."

"I understand." Annie locked eyes with her brother. "Will you walk me out? I have something important I need to talk to you about."

"Okay." With a reluctant backward glance, he followed her out of the room.

In the hallway, she said, "Walk fast. I have to meet the guy who is bringing the pig smoker in thirty minutes."

Jamie stepped in line beside her. "Is this necessary, Annie? I don't want to miss the doctor when she arrives."

"Not only is it necessary, it's vital to your child's safety. It'll only take a minute."

They passed through the waiting room and exited the building onto the sidewalk. "Tell me what's going on, Annie. You're scaring me."

"Brooke asked me to talk to you," she said, and told him everything she knew about Sawyer stalking Brooke.

"Do you think this has something to do with . . . with why we're here?" Jamie asked, as though unable to bring himself to say *possible miscarriage*.

"I can't answer that. I'm not a doctor. I do know she's under a lot of emotional stress. She and Grady are now fighting about Sawyer." Fishing her sunglasses out of her bag, Annie cleaned them with the hem of her shirt and slipped them on her face.

"Why didn't she come to us about this problem with Sawyer?" Jamie asked, his dark eyes like black coals.

"She was waiting to tell you on Monday. She didn't want to spoil your weekend. Whether or not you know it, Brooke and Lizbet are in a fight about selling the Tradd Street house."

Jamie nodded. "Lizbet mentioned that. Poor Brooke. We should be supporting her, not making things more difficult for her."

"I don't think Brooke realized how serious things are with Sawyer. She's dangerous. You must help Brooke, regardless of what happens with the baby."

Jamie squared his shoulders. "Don't worry, I will. I'll get Eli involved, if necessary," he said about his stepfather who was the chief of police in Prospect.

Annie checked her watch. She had just enough time to get to the beach house before the smoker arrived. "I need to get on the road."

"And I should get back inside. But first, tell me how things are going with Tyler."

Annie stared down at the car key in her hand. "Not great. These house parties aren't really my scene."

"I heard Cooper's on Sullivan Island with some girl."

"Yep. That girl is Tyler's sister. I don't think things are going great for them either."

Jamie chuckled. "Because you and Cooper belong together. Everyone knows that except you."

"Whatever, Jamie. I gotta run. Take care of your wives and baby," she said, play-punching him in the arm.

"You're funny." He chucked her chin. "Thanks for taking such good care of Brooke. I'll let you know what we learn from the doctor."

Annie felt a twinge of regret as she watched him disappear inside the emergency room. She hated leaving the hospital. Jamie and Lizbet and Brooke were her fam, and she belonged here with them during this critical time. But she'd rented the smoker and spent hundreds of dollars on food and decorations. She had to see this party through.

She was hurrying to the car when a text came in from Tyler. She'd sent him a string of texts during the night. He'd never responded. And he'd spent the night out, presumably at the Bromleys', possibly in Kaylie's arms.

Her blood boiled when she read his text. *Where are you? We're hungry. Can you fix us some breakfast?*

She typed back. *There's plenty of food in the fridge.*

Annie started the car and sped out of the parking lot. She was tired of Tyler treating her like the hired help. Cooper and Jamie had been raised by loving parents. And they turned out to be compassionate sons and husbands. Tyler and Lia had been raised by narcissistic snobs. And they turned out to be just like their parents.

Traffic was stop and go leaving Sullivan's Island, but her side of Ben Sawyer Boulevard was clear, and she cruised back to the house, arriving just as the smoker was being delivered. She hoped

Lia had kept her word to have Tyler out of the house by ten thirty.

She instructed the driver to back the trailer into her vacated spot in the driveway. He attempted to give her recommendations on roasting a pig, but she dismissed him. She'd done this many times.

Annie let out an audible groan when she discovered the mess in the kitchen—dirty dishes piled high in the sink and empty food containers littering the counter. She dropped her purse on the table and went to work cleaning up. She was placing the last plate in the dishwasher when Lia breezed in wearing a white crochet cover-up over a yellow string bikini and sunglasses to hide what Annie assumed were bloodshot eyes.

"Ugh! I'm so hungover." She removed the Zing Zang Bloody Mary mix from the refrigerator and the bottle of Tito's vodka from the freezer, pouring equal amounts of each into a tall tumbler. She guzzled down a quarter of the drink and licked her lips. "Ah. Better already."

"Where did y'all sleep last night? There was no one here when I woke up." Annie tried to sound nonchalant, as though she didn't care where her boyfriend spent the night.

"We all crashed at the Bromleys'. The party was insane."

"Where's Tyler?" Annie asked as she wiped down the countertops.

"Gone to the beach with the others, as planned." Lia peeled a banana and stuffed half of it into her mouth. "You'll have the house to yourself to get ready for his party. If we bring Tyler back around four, you can put up the decorations while we nap and shower. I've told everyone to arrive promptly at six twenty. We're up to thirty now."

Annie stopped wiping and looked up at her. "Thirty what?"

"Thirty people, duh. We invited everyone staying at the Bromleys'. They're all so excited about the surprise."

Annie's brow hit her hairline. "But we agreed to a small, low-key dinner for those of us staying in *this* house. The dining room table only seats twelve."

"So we'll have a buffet. It'll be more fun anyway. We had the intimate dinner last night." Lia freshened her drink and glided toward the back door. "I'll be at the beach if you need me." She stepped outside and stuck her head back in the kitchen. "Oh, I almost forgot. We're having Co-Op cater our lunch, so you don't need to worry about packing us a picnic."

Annie stared slack-jawed at the door while Lia's words replayed in her mind. *You'll have the house to yourself to get ready. You can put up the decorations while we nap and shower. . . . You don't need to worry about packing us a picnic.*

With a guttural roar, Annie balled up the dish towel and threw it at the door.

Cooper chose that moment to enter the kitchen. "Whoa! I'm glad that wasn't a baseball. I'm almost afraid to ask who you're angry at."

"Lia! Your girlfriend! I'm sick of her walking all over me."

Cooper cocked his head to the side, a bemused expression on his face. "Then why are you letting her? You'll never win with people like the Gerrys."

Annie balled her fists, longing to hit something, as fierce determination shook her to her core. "I refuse to give up."

"Give an inch, and they'll take a mile. If you're not careful, you'll lose sight of who you really are."

"Give me a break, Cooper. I'm sick of your theatrics." Annie opened the refrigerator, surveyed the contents, and slammed the door shut.

Cooper dug his thumb into his chest. "*My* theatrics. You're the one throwing wadded-up dish towels at doors. And you're the one considering giving up the career you're passionate about for a guy you admit is walking all over you."

"I didn't say Tyler was walking all over me. I said Lia is."

"Looks to me like they both are," he mumbled.

Deep down, she knew he was right. Both Tyler and Lia were walking all over her, and she was letting them. Although not because she felt obligated to cook for them, or because she wanted to please anyone, but because this kitchen was where she belonged. Where she chose to be, where she felt the most comfortable. Catering was her purpose in life. Giving it up would be like . . . *losing sight of who she really was.*

She marched across the kitchen and flung open the back door.

"Where are you going?" Cooper asked on her heels as she headed to the garage.

"To smoke a pig," she said over her shoulder.

"I'll help you," he said, stepping in line beside her.

"I'm sure you have better things to do today?"

He opened the garage door for her. "Not really. I plan to photograph the lighthouse at some point, but that can wait."

"Suit yourself," Annie said in an indifferent tone, even though she was grateful for the help.

Together, they wrestled the beast out of the Gerrys' spare refrigerator and onto the smoker. Annie adjusted the temperature and closed the lid. "Now we wait."

"I've never cooked a pig before. What did you do to prepare it?"

She was describing the process of butterflying and marinating the pig when Grady zoomed into the driveway in the golf cart.

"Have y'all seen Brooke?" he asked, pressing the brake pedal into park.

"I drove her home a little while ago," Annie said.

With a pinched face, Grady got out of the golf cart and walked over to them. "Did she say anything about me?"

"She told me everything." Annie glared at him with cold eyes. "She's doing a very special thing for two people she cares about, and you made her feel like she was doing something dirty. You don't deserve Brooke."

Grady hung his head. "I know. You're right," he said and lumbered off toward the house.

Cooper watched Grady disappear inside before turning to Annie. "What was that about? You were awfully hard on him."

"I didn't tell you the whole truth last night," Annie said, letting out a deep breath. "Sawyer is more than jealous. She's been stalking Brooke. And Grady is upset because he found out Brooke is pregnant. She's a surrogate for Lizbet and Jamie's baby."

"Whoa," Cooper said, his ocean-blue eyes wide. "I don't want any details on how that process works, but I'm excited for them. I know how much they want children. What relationship does that make me to the kid?"

Annie worked out the blood connection in her head. "First cousin once removed, I think. But don't quote me on it." She tilted her face to the sun. "What a nice day. Since everyone else is at the beach, I'm going to spend the afternoon by the pool. *After* I finish my kitchen chores."

"Those chores will get done faster with two people. Then you can lounge by the pool while I go to the lighthouse."

Annie suddenly felt weary. So much had happened, and it wasn't even noon yet. A few hours to herself in the sun would help clear her head.

"That's an offer I can't refuse."

On the way inside, Annie said, "Since those vultures devoured all my party food, I'm going to have to modify my elaborate luau menu."

"Did they seriously eat all your food?"

"Pretty much. Everything except the watermelon. And only because it hadn't yet been cut." She began removing items from the refrigerator. "I don't even care anymore. I'll serve barbecue, coleslaw, and baked beans. My efforts are wasted on this crowd anyway. They're more concerned about what they drink than food."

Annie and Cooper set to work, preparing a large bowl of

coleslaw and a casserole dish of baked beans. Annie blended and strained the watermelon for a spiked punch while Cooper made tomato sandwiches for their lunch. They ate their sandwiches at the umbrellaed table by the pool before going their separate ways.

Lathered up with sunscreen, Annie stretched out on a lounge chair with Elin Hilderbrand's hot new summer release. She was still there around three o'clock when she received an update from Lizbet.

L izbet and Jamie left the examining room while the nurse drew blood for the tests the doctor had ordered. When they returned, Brooke could tell from their grim faces they'd been talking about Sawyer. She wanted to know what Annie had told them, but before she could ask, the doctor bustled into the room wearing white jeans and a sleeveless blue blouse, her stethoscope dangling around her neck.

"I'm sorry it took me so long to get here. There was an accident on the Isle of Palms connector, blocking traffic in both directions. I had to drive down through Sullivan's Island, and the traffic was bumper to bumper."

"We're so grateful you came, Dr. Carroll," Lizbet said, and Brooke added, "I'm sorry we dragged you out on a holiday weekend."

The doctor smiled. "No worries. I don't have any big plans. And we need to figure out what's causing the spotting and cramping."

Brooke bit down on her quivering lower lip. She knew what was causing it.

The nurse entered the examining room. "Dr. Carroll! You made it!"

"Finally. If you're headed to Wild Dunes today, I suggest you change your plans."

The nurse frowned. "I heard about the accident. Two of the victims were taken to MUSC in critical condition."

"That's awful. I'm sorry to hear it." The doctor flipped open her tablet. "Your tests results are back. Your hCG levels look good."

Lizbet, Jamie, and Brooke breathed a collective sigh of relief.

"That doesn't mean the baby is out of danger." The doctor glanced over at the nurse. "Bring me the cart. I'm going to do a transvaginal ultrasound."

Lizbet nudged her husband. "You should step outside."

"Why? What's a transvaginal ultrasound?"

Lizbet's cheeks pinkened. "It goes between her legs."

Jamie's lips formed an O. "In that case, I'll be out in the hall if you need me," he said, and bolted from the examining room.

The doctor laughed. "You'll need to toughen him up before she delivers. I don't want him to miss the birth of his child."

The doctor's optimism set Brooke at ease.

The nurse returned with the cart, and the doctor prepared the wand for use.

Lizbet stood beside the bed, biting on a hangnail. "What if you don't see a heartbeat?"

"We'll check again in a couple of days," Dr. Carroll said. "We're still very early in the pregnancy."

Lizbet placed a hand over Brooke's. "We still have each other, regardless of the outcome."

Brooke nodded and looked away, unable to stand the fear in her sister's gray eyes.

Brooke placed her feet in the stirrups, and the doctor inserted the ultrasound. The muffled sound of a heartbeat filled the room.

"There's your heartbeat. Hmm." The doctor looked more

intently at the computer screen. "What do we have here? Looks like a second heartbeat."

Lizbet squealed and clamped a hand over her mouth.

Jamie cracked opened the door. "Is everything okay in here?"

"I think we're having twins. Is that right, Doctor?" Lizbet asked.

Jamie entered the room, seemingly unconcerned about Brooke's junk spread out in the open.

Dr. Carroll nodded, her eyes still on the screen as she moved the wand around inside Brooke. "You're having twins. Everything looks good. As far as I can tell, both babies are healthy."

Tears of relief welled in Brooke's eyes. "Oh, thank God."

Wrapping his arms around his wife, Jamie lifted Lizbet off the ground and swung her around. "I can't believe it. This is the best news ever."

The doctor removed the wand. "Any idea what's causing the cramping and spotting? Did you lift anything heavy or do any abnormal physical exertion?"

Brooke pressed her legs together, covering herself with the white sheet. "I think it's emotional stress. I'm having some personal problems," she said, reaching for a tissue to wipe her eyes.

Jamie set Lizbet down, and she returned to the side of the bed. "We're going to deal with all of those problems together," she said, smiling down at Brooke.

Dr. Carroll squeezed Brooke's arm. "I want you to go home and rest. Call me Tuesday morning. If you're still having these symptoms, we'll run some more tests. Try not to worry. Everything looks fine. I'm sure this is your body's way of warning you to eliminate the stress from your life."

Brooke dressed while they waited for the release paperwork, and then the threesome walked out of the hospital together. Once they were in the car, she blurted, "I'm so sorry. This is all my fault."

Lizbet shifted in the passenger seat so she could see Brooke. "Stop! It most certainly is not. This is Sawyer's fault. And we've come up with a plan to get rid of her."

Jamie nodded at the phone in his wife's hand. "The first step in that plan involves Annie. See if you can get her on the phone."

Lizbet clicked on a number, and the sound of a ringing phone filled the car. Annie picked up right away. "Finally! I've been worried out of my mind!"

"You're on Bluetooth," Lizbet said. "I'm in the car with Jamie and Brooke, and we're heading back to Charleston."

"What'd you find out from the doctor?"

"Good news! The babies are okay," Lizbet said with a mischievous grin.

A beat of silence filled the car. "Wait, a sec! Did you say *babies*? As in more than one?"

Jamie smiled. "That's right. The doctor did an ultrasound. We're having twins."

Annie's squeal reverberated through the car, and Brooke covered her ears. "That's fantastic. I'm so excited for you," Annie said.

"We're pretty excited ourselves," Jamie said, and his tone turned serious. "But now we must deal with Sawyer. Have you seen her since this morning?"

"Not yet. She's probably down at the beach with the others."

"When you see her, tell her you drove Brooke home this morning. Then call or text us right away, so we can be on the lookout for her."

Annie hesitated. "Okay. But I hope you know what you're doing."

"Don't worry. Eli is in charge. He's meeting us in Charleston."

From the back seat, Brooke said, "Hey, Annie, it's Brooke. Have you seen Grady today?"

"Yes. He was looking for you earlier. I told him you had gone home like you asked. I also told him he didn't deserve you, that you are doing a very special thing for two people you care about."

Brooke pressed her fingers to her lips to hide her smile. "What did he say?"

"He agreed with me and went inside."

"Good!" Lizbet winked at Brooke. "Brooke's too good for Grady."

Jamie ran his finger across his throat, signaling to Lizbet to end the conversation. "I need to hang up now, Annie. Please stay in touch."

"For sure," Annie said and ended the call.

"Tell me about Eli's plan," Brooke said in a skeptical tone.

Jamie locked eyes with her through the rearview mirror. "Eli thinks you need more than a restraining order. He wants to scare Sawyer off. If he can catch her trying to break into your house, he'll have her arrested and bring charges for breaking and entering."

"Great. So he's using me as bait to set his trap."

"Not exactly," Lizbet said, and Jamie added, "You won't be in the line of fire."

Brooke chewed on a hangnail. "I'll go along with Eli's plan as long as I don't have to see Sawyer."

"You won't have to see her," Jamie said. "I promise."

Lizbet pulled a funny face. "You'll be upstairs in your room, and I'll be feeding you chicken noodle soup."

"I'd prefer salted caramel ice cream and fried chicken tenders."

Lizbet made a funny face. 'That's an interesting combination."

"I've been having some strange cravings. And I'm so emotional. Everything makes me cry. And now I understand why." Brooke's heart raced at the idea of having twins. "There's a reason people get married before having children. I can't do this alone."

"You won't have to." Lizbet climbed over the console into the back seat with Brooke. "I promise not to let you down again. I was so wrapped up in the idea of having a baby, I never really considered the sacrifices you are making."

"Sacrifices I will gladly make for you." Brooke brought a hand to her sister's cheek. "I'm used to doing everything for myself, and this scare has made me realize I need help. For the sake of the babies."

Lizbet rested her head on Brooke's shoulder. "I'm so sorry I've been difficult about selling the house. I have no excuse, other than I'm having a hard time letting go of the past. But you deserve to have your own place if that's what you want. Jamie and I will do everything. You won't have to lift a finger. We'll put Tradd Street on the market as soon as possible, find a house for you, and move you in."

"Actually, I made an offer on a house last week. It's a long shot. A lot of people are interested in it."

"The one you mentioned?" Lizbet asked, and Brooke nodded. "Tell me more about it. Where's it located?"

"On Rutledge Avenue across from Colonial Lake. I'll show you the listing." Brooke pulled up the listing on her phone and handed it to her sister.

"Ooh. Pretty," Lizbet said as she scrolled through the pictures. She handed the phone back to Brooke. "When will you find out if you got it?"

"The deadline for offers is noon tomorrow. I should hear sometime tomorrow afternoon."

Brooke grew silent as they crossed the Ravenel Bridge, and her thoughts drifted as she stared out the window at the Cooper River. Grady was a professional. She knew he would see her contract through. She remembered what Annie had said. Is it possible Grady regretted the way he'd treated her? Even if he apologized, she wasn't sure she would forgive him. If she couldn't count on him, she couldn't afford to have him in her life. Especially now.

thirty-one
cooper

Cooper encountered a massive party underway on the beach. He estimated at least sixty people playing volleyball, throwing Frisbees, and wandering around in varying stages of drunkenness. When Lia spotted him, she brought him an ice-cold beer from a nearby cooler.

"I'm glad to see you're finally joining the party. I'd written you off as a dud date."

He refused the beer. "I am a dud date. And you're too much for me to handle."

She let out a booming laugh. "I'm a lot. I admit it. That's why I'm never getting married or having children."

Cooper chuckled. "The right guy, God help him, will eventually come along and sweep you off your feet." His smile faded. "In all seriousness, I hope we can still be friends. You're a badass art dealer, and there's no one else I trust to represent me."

"Absolutely," she said, offering him a high five. "Ooh, there's Ian Bromley. I've had a crush on him since forever. Bye, Cooper. Thanks for your honesty." Lia wiggled her fingers at Cooper and took off across the sand.

Cooper, feeling relieved as he watched her flirt with Ian, was glad his personal relationship with Lia had never taken off. They'd been a match made in hell.

He noticed Sawyer heading this way, but he didn't have time to hide from her. If she asked him about Brooke, he wasn't sure what to tell her.

"Have you seen Brooke? Grady's been here all afternoon." Sawyer gestured at Grady, who was sitting in a beach chair and staring blindly out at the ocean. "He looks like he lost his best friend. I assume they had a fight, but he won't talk to me about it. I'm worried about Brooke, and I want to make sure she's all right."

"I haven't seen her today. I think Annie may have driven her home earlier." Cooper figured this was a safe answer. Sawyer couldn't bother Brooke if she wasn't on Sullivan's Island.

"Thanks," Sawyer said, pushing him out of her way as she headed off toward the sand dunes.

Cooper, with his camera backpack slung over his shoulder, left the party and headed up the beach. He was surprised to find the lighthouse deserted, especially on a holiday weekend. He was covered in sweat by the time he climbed to the top. The salty breeze cooled his skin as he looked out over the ocean. He took a minute to enjoy the peaceful setting before fastening his zoom lens to his camera. Surveying his surroundings, he picked up the trail of a ghost crab skimming across the sand. He was following the crab with his camera when a naked man and woman having sex in the sand dunes appeared in his viewfinder. *What the heck?* He zoomed in on their faces. Tyler and Kaylie. He wasn't surprised, but he was furious, and he would make Tyler pay for betraying Annie. He pressed the shutter button, holding it down while the camera recorded several dozen images.

Cooper placed the camera in his bag and began the journey down the stairs. By the time he reached the bottom, Kaylie and Tyler were gone. Retracing his steps back to the party, he dropped his camera bag onto an empty beach chair and went in search of

Tyler. He found him talking with a group of friends near the keg. Grabbing him by the arm, Cooper swung Tyler around and punched him in the eye. Tyler stumbled backward, laughing, too drunk and numb to realize what had just happened to him.

Cooper waited for Tyler's friends to pounce on him, but they just stood there, some of them laughing while others bit their lips to hide their smiles.

"Dude! What was that for?" Tyler said, his hand pressed to his eye but still laughing.

Cooper longed to beat the living daylights out of Tyler again, but he wouldn't stoop so low as to take advantage of a man in Tyler's condition. He pointed his finger at Tyler's face. "That's for Annie, you cheating bastard. I saw you and Kaylie in the sand dunes."

"Oh. That." Tyler shooed him away. "Run on along. I know you're dying to tell Annie I banged Kaylie. Everyone here knows you're in love with Annie. With me out of the picture, maybe you have a chance."

"You should be the one to tell her," Cooper said. "Then again, why should anyone expect you to do the right thing when there's not a decent bone in your body?"

"That's it. I'm gonna tear you apart." Tyler tried to stand straight, but he stumbled again.

"Okay! That's enough! Time for you to take a nap," Lia said, hooking an arm around her brother's waist and guiding him away from the crowd.

Cooper retrieved his camera bag and followed them off the beach. Lia drove Tyler home in the golf cart, and by the time Cooper arrived on foot, Lia was helping her brother up the stairs.

Annie stood nearby, watching them. "This excessive partying is disturbing."

"Agreed. I'll be happy when this weekend is over." Cooper wanted nothing more than to go home to his peaceful cottage in Prospect. But he couldn't leave Annie here alone, an innocent prey surrounded by vicious animals. "What do you have left to do for the party?"

"Decorate. I bought so much stuff." Annie went to the dining room closet where she'd stored her decorations. "If you're looking for something to do, I could use some help. The band is supposed to arrive at five. I'd like for everything to be ready when they get here."

Cooper blinked hard and opened his eyes wide. "You actually hired a band for this gig?"

Annie gave him a shove. "Not a party band, silly. A small four-piece band. They play all kinds of music. They'll start with Hawaiian tunes for ambiance and take it from there."

Cooper didn't know how to respond. A band cost a lot of money, no matter the size. Annie had gone completely overboard in planning this party for a guy who was sleeping with another girl.

For the next hour, they set tiki torches around the pool, hung paper lanterns in the dining room, and strategically placed tiki towers, fake palm trees, and pink balloons spelling out the word *aloha*. They arranged six tall vases down the center of the dining room table, each bearing a single bird of paradise stem, and filled baskets with brightly colored leis for the guests to wear.

Everything was ready by five when the band arrived. Annie, who couldn't contain her excitement, bounced around on her toes as she watched them set up.

"Calm down Annie. Everything's gonna be fine," Cooper said.

"I can't help myself. I just can't wait to see Tyler's face."

Cooper's heart broke for her. He hated to be the one to burst her bubble, but she had a right to know Tyler was cheating on her.

Annie glanced down at the phone in her hand. "Jamie is calling me. In all the excitement, I forgot to text him." She accepted the call. "I'm sorry, Jamie. It's been crazy here. I meant to text you. I haven't seen Sawyer today."

"I have," Cooper said.

"What?" Her neck snapped as she looked up at him. "Cooper's here. He says he's seen Sawyer. I'm going to put you on speaker."

She clicked the speaker button, and the cousins greeted each other.

"Where and when did you see Sawyer?" Jamie asked.

"On the beach, around three. I wasn't sure what to say, so I told her Annie had driven Brooke home this morning."

"Which means she's probably already on her way here," Jamie said. "I've gotta run. I'll let you know what happens."

"Please do." Annie ended the call and stuffed her phone in her pocket.

"Do you know if everything is okay with the baby?" Cooper asked.

"Everything is fine." Her lips parted in a broad smile. "If anyone asks, you didn't hear this from me. But Brooke is carrying two babies. Lizbet and Jamie are having twins."

"Yes," Cooper said, punching the air. "That's outstanding news."

She dropped her smile. "Unfortunately, I just screwed up their plan. They've set a trap for Sawyer, hoping to catch her in the act of stalking Brooke. I should've thought to ask you if you'd seen her on the beach. I hope I haven't put their lives in danger."

"I wouldn't worry. Sawyer doesn't seem very dangerous to me."

"You have no idea. From what Brooke has told me, she appears to be having a mental breakdown. Which makes her extremely dangerous."

B rooke woke from a long nap, feeling even more exhausted than she had before she went to sleep. She would need days to recover from the emotional trauma of the near miscarry.

Hearing voices in a distant part of the house, she plodded in bare feet down the stairs to the kitchen where Jamie, Lizbet, and Eli were all huddled around the table, deep in conversation. They all stood at once when she entered the kitchen.

Eli enveloped her in a warm hug. "Congratulations, little surrogate mama."

"Thank you," Brooke mumbled, still hazy from sleep.

"Here. Sit down." Lizbet gestured at the chair she'd vacated. "Let me fix you something to eat. While you were napping, I went to the Harris Teeter to pick up some things for dinner. I bought your ice cream and chicken tenders."

Brooke lowered herself to the chair. "I'm not sure I can eat. My stomach feels queasy."

Lizbet's brow pinched in concern. "What have you eaten today?"

She and Grady had been planning to go to brunch when hurricane Sawyer hit. "Only a few crackers the nurse gave me."

Lizbet relaxed. "That explains it. You need to get something on your stomach. I'll make you anything you feel like eating."

"I guess I'll have some ice cream." She smiled up at her sister and added, "Please." She wasn't sure how long she could tolerate her sister fussing over her. She'd asked for the help, and she needed their support, but they would have to find a happy medium.

When Lizbet placed a bowl of salted caramel ice cream on the table in front of her, Brooke took a bite and moaned. "This might seriously be the best thing I've ever tasted."

"Good! There's plenty more where it came from." Lizbet showed her the ice cream carton before returning it to the freezer.

Jamie folded his hands on the table. "At the risk of spoiling your appetite, we just received an update from Annie. Cooper ran into Sawyer on the beach around three o'clock. And it's almost six now. She's had more than enough time to get here."

"Maybe she's not coming," Eli suggested.

"She's coming." The bottom dropped out of Brooke's stomach, and she pushed away the ice cream bowl. "Sawyer hasn't let me out of her sight in the past week. At least not for long. Every time I've turned around, she's been there, watching me. We're sitting ducks."

"We're well protected," Eli said. "I have an unmarked car with two plainclothes detectives stationed at the end of the block. I've shown them Sawyer's picture and given them the description of her car. They will call me *if* they see her."

Brooke's heart jumped into her throat at the sound of loud banging on the front door. "Right on cue."

"Let me in, Brooke! We need to talk."

Eli picked his phone up from the table. "The detectives just texted," he whispered. "She slipped past them. She must have parked several blocks away."

"I hear voices in there! I know you're here! Let me in so we can talk," Sawyer shouted, ringing the doorbell over and over.

Brooke's eyes met Eli's, and he nodded at her to answer. "Go away, Sawyer! There's nothing to talk about."

Eli motioned for Jamie to take Lizbet upstairs.

"What about Brooke?" Jamie said in a low voice.

"I won't let anything happen to her," Eli said. "But you two are in the way."

Jamie dragged Lizbet out of the kitchen and up the stairs.

The creak of the front storm door was followed by the brass knocker—clang, clang, clang. "I'm not joking, Brooke! Let me in. I hear footsteps. Who else is in there with you?"

Anger drove Brooke to her feet. She'd had enough of this crazy person stalking her. She marched into the foyer. "I'm not joking either, Sawyer. Leave me alone. For the last time, I want you out of my life."

Brooke heard footfalls on the porch, followed by a deafening silence. With Eli peering over her shoulder, she peeked through the side window at the empty porch.

"She's gone," Brooke said.

"Not for long. She won't leave until she gets what she came for."

An explosion of breaking glass came from the kitchen. Brooke spun around and Eli jumped back, out of the line of sight from the kitchen.

Sawyer stood in the kitchen with feet planted wide and one hand behind her back. She was dressed from head to toe in black, her mahogany ponytail pulled through the back of a black baseball cap. Her brown eyes shone brightly, wide and wild as they bounced around the room. "I can tell you're up to something, Brooke. Who are you hiding?"

"No one. I'm here alone." She didn't dare glance over at Eli, who was pressed against the foyer wall.

"Liar!" Sawyer shrieked. "Someone is in here with you. I saw them. Is it another man? Another woman? I know it's not Grady.

He's still pouting at the beach. Whoever it is isn't good enough for you. Only I'm good enough for you. The sooner you realize that, the sooner we can get on with our lives." She withdrew her hand from behind her back, revealing a small black pistol.

Brooke's pulse raced. "Since when do you own a gun?" she said to let Eli know about the gun in case he couldn't see it from his vantage point.

"Since that creep followed me home from work. Remember? Happened about a year ago. I told you I was buying a gun for protection, but you must not have been listening. Which is part of your problem. You never listen."

"Do you even know how to use the gun?" Brooke asked, buying time, hoping the detectives would appear soon.

"I know it's loaded." Sawyer looked down the barrel of the gun. "All I have to do is pull this little thingy," she said, placing her finger on the trigger.

Brooke felt sweat trickle down her back. "You're a doctor. Why would you want to hurt me, Sawyer? Especially when I'm carrying my sister's twins."

"You only have yourself to blame, Brooke. You should never have broken up with me. I can't let you be with anyone else. Which means you have to die." Sawyer held the gun in front of her, pointed in Brooke's direction.

Eli stepped out of the shadows, shielding Brooke with his body as he aimed his own gun at Sawyer. "Drop the gun, or I'll shoot."

Sawyer let out a maniacal laugh. "I'm not afraid of you."

"Freeze! Charleston PD here!" yelled an unfamiliar voice from the kitchen.

Brooke peeked out from behind Eli at the two men wearing khaki pants and polo shirts. They stood behind Sawyer with guns trained on her.

"Drop your gun, then turn around with your hands over your head," ordered the taller of the two.

Sawyer did as she was instructed and slowly turned around to face them. "Thank goodness you're here, officers. That man is an intruder. He tried to shoot us."

"Yeah, right, lady. That man is Eli Marshall, chief of police in Prospect." The shorter of the two men twisted Sawyer's arm behind her back, handcuffing her. "You're under arrest."

Brooke glanced into the living room at her mama's portrait. When Lula winked at her, she was certain her mind was not playing tricks on her. Relief washed over Brooke. Everything would be okay. Lula, her guardian angel, was looking out for her.

Eli turned to face her. "That was close. Are you okay?"

"I think so. You saved my life. If you hadn't been here."

"Don't even go there," Eli said, pulling her in for a hug.

Jamie came barreling down the stairs with Lizbet on his heels. "Are y'all okay?"

"We're fine. Although a little shaken up." Eli walked Brooke to the table and eased her into the chair.

As reality set in, Brooke's body trembled and her teeth chattered. The woman she'd once planned to spend the rest of her life with had just threatened to kill her. *Which means you have to die.*

"I'll make you some passionflower tea," Lizbet said, setting the kettle on the stove.

Brooke watched the detectives wrestle a feisty Sawyer out of the house. Jamie closed the door with the broken window behind them. "I hope that's the last we've seen of her."

"I'm certain of it," Eli said, with a hand still resting on Brooke's shoulder. "At a are minimum, she'll be charged with stalking and criminal trespassing."

Brooke grunted. "Her father's a criminal attorney. He'll get her off."

"Not this time. I'm afraid Daddy can't help his little girl out of this mess." Eli sat down in the chair next to Brooke. "The gun surprised me. I ran a background check. There are no firearms registered in her name."

"She probably bought it off the street," Brooke mused.

Lizbet placed a cup of hot water with the steeping tea bag in front of her. "Or she may have stolen it from someone."

Brooke tuned out the others as they discussed potential charges against Sawyer. She suddenly knew what she had to do, what she should've done a long time ago. She stood abruptly, knocking the teacup over. "I can't stay in this house."

Lizbet grabbed the roll of paper towel and mopped up the spilt tea. "You don't have to be here alone, Brooke. Jamie and I will stay with you."

Brooke shook her head. "You don't understand. I can't be here. There are too many memories of Sawyer in this house. I'll book a hotel room if I have to." She cried for what seemed like the hundredth time today.

"Oh, honey." Lizbet dropped the sodden paper towel into the trash can and took Brooke in her arms. "I didn't realize you felt this way. You'll come home with us. And you can stay as long as you like. Even until the baby comes, if that's what you want."

Brooke nodded into her sister's shoulder. "You won't get stuck with me for that long. But maybe a couple of weeks. If I don't get the pink house, I'll find something to rent."

Jamie patted Lizbet's back. "Honey, go upstairs and pack Brooke's things. The sooner we can get her out of this house, the better."

"Is that okay with you, Brooke?" Lizbet asked, her voice soft in her ear.

"That's fine. Just grab a bunch of clothes. My toiletries are already packed from the weekend in the duffel bag in my room."

"I'm on it," Lizbet said and dashed out of the room and up the stairs.

Jamie placed a hand on Brooke's back. "Let's you and I go get the car."

Eli said, "While you do that, I'll clean up the glass and find something to tape up this window."

"Thanks, Eli. That would be great," Jamie said, and walked Brooke to the front door.

Outside on the porch, Brooke turned to Jamie. "Do you mind if I stay here while you get the car? I just need a minute alone."

Jamie hesitated, as though concerned about leaving her. "Are you sure?"

"I'm fine. Sawyer is in custody. Thanks to Eli, we have eliminated the threat."

"True. Eli is inside if you need anything." Jamie jogged off to where Lizbet had hidden her car from Sawyer.

Brooke sat down on the swing, her favorite spot in the house. The memories of her time spent on this swing were all good, and she would take the swing with her when she moved. Other than a few other pieces of furniture, she would buy everything new, a clean slate for a fresh start in her new life.

Ten minutes later, as they drove away in Lizbet's car, Brooke watched the yellow house get smaller, and then disappear. She felt no regret for abandoning her childhood home, only relief from the massive burden that had been lifted from her shoulders.

As they crossed the Ashley River, Lizbet chatted about their plans for Labor Day. "Sean is having a cookout tomorrow. He's invited family and a few friends. We don't have to decide now. We'll play it by ear and see how you're feeling in the morning. It might be a good distraction for you, but if you're not up to it, we'll stay home and have our own cookout."

"We'll see." Brooke doubted she'd be in the mood for a cookout. She'd had enough of parties for one weekend.

She rested her head against the back of the seat and fell into a deep sleep. She'd taken the initial step toward a new life. With Sawyer out of the way, she could focus on protecting the two babies growing inside her, and mending her broken heart. She'd fallen hard for Grady, and she had no idea how she would ever get over losing him.

thirty-three
annie

Annie admired her reflection in the oversized mirror. The clam shell bikini top barely covered her small breasts, and the straw skirt rustled about her thighs when she swayed her hips. She added the finishing touches—three colorful leis around her neck and a pink hibiscus bloom tucked behind one ear. Tyler's eyes would pop out of his head when he saw her. She would win him back and never let him go again.

Turning out the bathroom light, she crossed through Tyler's bedroom. He was passed out on his stomach with his face buried in the pillow. She considered waking him. He would need to dress for the party soon. But he could use the extra sleep to sober up.

Downstairs, she found Cooper in the kitchen preparing the beans for the oven. He wore a tropical print shirt with khaki shorts, his auburn hair still wet from the shower. He let out a low whistle when he saw her. "You look fabulous."

His compliment pleased her more than it should have. "Thanks. I hope Tyler thinks so too."

When his smile faded, she wondered why she had said that to him. Probably to discourage his feelings for her. Cooper had declared his love for her last night, and she didn't want him to think there was anything more than friendship between them. Even though she was no longer sure what was going on between them. She'd been thinking about what he'd said all day. *You and I belong together. And one day we will. I'm willing to wait as long as it takes.*

"I checked on the pig a few minutes ago," he said. "I'm no expert, but it looks ready to me."

"I'd plan to let it cook for another hour, but if you think it's ready, we might as well bring it in. We can have all the food out when everyone arrives. The guests can eat whenever, and we won't have to worry about them."

"Good! Then you can take a break and enjoy the party. How are you serving the meat?"

"I'll slice some and mince up the rest for barbecue. I've got my special sauce all ready." She removed a Tupperware jug filled with dark red sauce from the refrigerator.

Slipping aprons over their clothing, they covered the counter with aluminum foil and brought the pig in from the smoker. Cooper was slicing and Annie mincing when a frazzled Lia entered the kitchen.

"That took some effort, but I finally got Tyler in the shower. He doesn't have a clue about the party. People will arrive soon. It's already six fifteen." Her gaze shifted from the clock to Annie. "What on earth are you wearing under that apron?"

Annie removed the apron and danced around in a circle, holding the grass skirt out beside her. "What do you think?"

"Cute. Tyler's own Hawaiian hula dancer. When are you planning to serve dinner?"

"Everything's ready. I'm going to put it out now, before the guests get here." Annie opened the refrigerator and removed two pitchers of watermelon punch.

Lia's lip curled at the sight of the pink liquid. "What's that gross-looking mixture?"

"Watermelon punch." Annie poured some into a stemless Champagne flute and slid it across the counter to Lia.

Lia took a tiny sip. "It's good. What's in it?"

"Watermelon juice, citrus vodka, lime juice, Midori, and wine. I didn't have time to go to the store, so I borrowed several bottles of rosé from your dad's wine cellar. I hope he doesn't mind."

Lia froze. "Please tell me you didn't use the Krug Brut Rosé."

The color drained from Annie's face as she opened the trash drawer. "Is this it?" she asked, holding up a black Champagne bottle with a pink label.

"You idiot! That rosé costs over three hundred dollars a bottle."

Annie's heart skipped a beat. "I'm so sorry. I'll replace it."

"You'd better," Lia said, draining her glass. "I'll greet the guests when they arrive. You can continue doing whatever it is you're doing to that beast." She refilled her glass and floated out of the kitchen, dramatically flipping her dark hair over her shoulder.

Annie and Cooper watched her leave. "She literally just instructed you to remain in the kitchen."

Annie stabbed her knife into the pig. "Whatever. I don't work for Lia."

Cooper grunted. "The way she treats you, she might as well be paying you."

"Shut up, Cooper." Annie put her apron back on and returned to work. She hustled to finish the barbecue and put the food on the table. When the first guests arrived at six twenty, she was standing beside Lia at the door with a basket of leis. She and Lia herded everyone into the dining room and closed the massive bifold doors, instructing everyone to get quiet.

Annie felt something off about the crowd. Maybe it was just her imagination, but she sensed the other girls were whispering about her. Were they making fun of her outfit? Or were they talking about what a great job she'd done with the party?

They heard Tyler's footfalls in the hallway, and when he threw open the doors, the crowd hollered, "Surprise!"

Tyler barked out a laugh. "Who did this? Lia, was this you?"

"It was my idea," Lia called out. "But Annie did all the work."

He sought her out in the crowd, and when their eyes met, Annie beamed.

"Come here, you." He pulled her in for a hug. "This is awesome. Thanks."

When she kissed his cheek, she noticed his red and swollen eye. "What happened to your eye? Did sand get in it?"

"Um, no." He dropped his arms from around her. "Your boyfriend punched me."

Annie furrowed her brow. "I don't understand. You're my boyfriend."

Silence settled over the room. "I'm talking about Cooper."

"Why would he do that?" Annie asked, her eyes on Cooper.

Tyler stroked his jaw. "I'm not sure, honestly. That part is a little fuzzy."

Kaylie emerged from the crowd, dressed in a white pantsuit that clung to her toned body. "I'm insulted, Ty," she said, wrapping herself around Tyler. "You don't remember what happened in the sand dunes?"

"I remember that part? I'm not sure what it has to do with Cooper though."

Kaylie walked her fingers up Tyler's chest. "He saw us in the sand dunes."

Every eye in the room fell on Annie. The walls began closing in, and panic rose in her chest. She inched closer to Cooper and whispered, "Please explain to me what's going on."

He pulled out his phone, his thumbs flying. "Check your phone. I just sent you a pic."

She stared down at her phone and clicked on the text. It took her brain a minute to register what she was seeing. Dread overcame her, followed immediately by anger. While she was working her butt off getting ready for his surprise party, Tyler had been screwing Kaylie in the sand dunes.

"Oh my god!" Lia exclaimed from somewhere in the room. Seconds later, she stepped out of the crowd toward Annie. "I knew you were hiding something. I just got a text from a friend in Prospect." She waved her phone in the air. "News flash, everyone! Cooper got Annie pregnant when she was sixteen."

The crowd murmured and gasped.

"It gets better. She lost the baby when she got shot in a gang war."

Cooper tensed. "Lia! You are way out of line. You don't know what you're talking about."

Annie placed a reassuring hand on his shoulder. "I've got this." She sucked in a lungful of air, her back stretched tall and shoulders squared. She would not let these people see her cry. "Not that it's any of your business, Lia, but I wasn't involved in a gang war. My friend's brother was messed up with some bad people, and I got caught in the crossfire. Not only did I lose my baby, I was nearly paralyzed. I'm lucky to be alive."

Tyler glared at her, his lip twisted in disgust. "You're a liar, Annie. You told me you and Cooper had never dated. Lia was right about you all along. You're a gold digger."

"And you're a self-absorbed punk." Cooper drew back his fist and punched Tyler in the other eye. "Now you have a matching set."

Annie heard the room erupt in laughter as she darted up the stairs. She changed into her cutoff shorts, packed all her belongings in her suitcase, and ran out of the house through the front door. As she rounded the corner of the house to the driveway, she heard the band playing Hawaiian music.

Tossing her bag into the back seat, she got behind the wheel and started the engine. She was backing out when Cooper came running up beside the car. She stopped the car and rolled down the window. "Why didn't you tell me? You had plenty of time.

We've been working together for hours. Instead, you let me find out like that, in front of a room full of people. I've never felt more humiliated. And it's all your fault."

Annie reversed the Mini out of the driveway and sped off down the road with the window still open and the wind whipping through her hair. Her anger was short-lived, and as she crossed over the Ben Sawyer Bridge, a profound sense of peace settled over her. She gulped in the salt air. There were few boats on the still water, and rays from the setting sun painted the sky blood orange. The sun would rise again tomorrow, and she would begin her life anew without Tyler. Autumn was upon them. The marsh grasses would yellow, and the water would turn muddy brown. A year would pass. And then another. She would forget all about Tyler. But she would always have her catering career.

Annie had never been in love with Tyler. In hindsight, she never really liked him that much. His shiny objects, the fancy cars and boats and houses, all the things girls from poor backgrounds always dreamed of having had blinded her. She'd spent a fortune on his party, but the price of the lesson she'd learned was priceless.

Cooper had been right about so many things. *Money makes life easier. But too much money corrupts people, makes them greedy for more money and strips away their code of honor. You, as the daughter of a fisherman, have had to work for everything all your life. Which makes you stronger in character than anyone at this party. You believe in yourself, Annie. You have an inner strength most people will never possess.*

She felt that strength now as she passed through Mount Pleasant and crossed over the Cooper River Bridge. She felt free for the first time in months. She could go back to being herself. Back to working all the time, in a career that fulfilled her and brought her joy. Back to wearing her cut-off denim shorts.

Annie could hardly wait to get home, to put on her pajamas and stare at her bald eagle painting. But a block away from her apartment, on a whim, she made a detour by her mom's house.

She hadn't shed a tear over Tyler, but the sight of Heidi sitting on the porch swing next to Hugh brought tears to her eyes. She'd come so close to ending their partnership and destroying their relationship.

Swiping at her eyes, she got out of the Mini and wandered up the sidewalk.

"Hey, sweetheart. You're home early. I didn't expect you back from Sullivan's until tomorrow."

Annie smiled. No matter what transpired between them, Annie could always count on her mother's love and support.

"Things didn't go so well," Annie said, leaning against a railing.

"Uh-oh." Hugh jumped to his feet. "I'll take that as my cue to leave." When he reached the door, he asked, "Can I get you anything to drink, Annie?"

"I'm fine. But thank you." She sat down in Hugh's vacated seat beside her mom.

"How did the party turn out?" Heidi asked.

"The party was great. Tyler, not so much. I was totally wrong about him. And you were right."

"Oh, honey." Heidi brushed a strand of hair off her face. "If being right means seeing you hurt, I'd rather be wrong."

"Surprisingly, I'm not that upset," Annie said.

"Do you want to talk about it?"

"Not really." Annie rested her head on Heidi's shoulder. "Let's just say I finally figured out I don't belong in his world. Why do I always have to learn things the hard way?"

Heidi chuckled. "You inherited that innate ability from me. The good news is, we rarely make the same mistake twice."

Shifting on the bench, Annie drew a leg beneath her. "I was wrong about a lot of things. If you'll still have me, I'd like to continue working at Tasty Provisions. I promise not to complain about being overworked ever again."

Heidi palmed her cheek. "I want you to complain when you

feel overworked. You deserved some much-needed time to clear your head."

"Despite everything else, I had fun decorating for Tyler's party. From now on, I'd love to help more with the decor side of catering."

"Honey, I'd be thrilled to share those responsibilities. We're closed for the holiday tomorrow. But on Tuesday morning, we'll have a long planning session and divvy up responsibilities for our upcoming events. The phone rang off the hook last week with clients booking for the holidays."

"Great! I look forward to diving in headfirst on Tuesday."

Mischief twinkled in Heidi's green eyes. "I understand Cooper was at the same house party. Did you two spend any time together?"

"How did you know Cooper was there? Oh, right." Annie rolled her eyes. "His mama told you."

"Charleston is a small town, sweetheart."

"Cooper's date didn't go so well either. He and I hung out a lot together. We connected. Or reconnected. But I just got out of a relationship with Tyler, and I need some time."

"If you ask me, you've already wasted enough time on Tyler. If you and Cooper are meant to be together, you shouldn't wait another second. Strike while the iron is hot, as the saying goes."

Annie burst out laughing. "We'll see."

She snickered to herself, thinking about Cooper giving Tyler two black eyes. How could she be mad at Cooper when he'd only been protecting her? She trusted him explicitly. He'd always had her best interests at heart, even back in high school when he'd gotten her pregnant. Truth be told, she'd been fighting her feelings for Cooper for weeks, and now she was finally free to explore them.

thirty-four
cooper

Cooper woke late Monday morning to the sound of barking dogs. Stumbling to the window, he spotted his twin in the driveway below with their five-month-old red lab puppies, Willa and Emmie.

Throwing on some clothes, he hurried down the stairs and out the door. He'd worried Willa wouldn't recognize him after being away at training for a month, but she ran straight over to him and covered his face in licks.

Cooper sat down in the middle of the driveway so the puppy could crawl onto his lap. "I missed you too, girl." He looked up at Sean. "Why didn't you tell me you were going to get them? I would've ridden with you to Virginia."

"Scooter called at the crack of dawn this morning. He was on his way down to Georgia for a hunt test, and he asked if I wanted to meet him at South of the Border. He says they're doing well. He wants them back at the end of October for formal training."

Cooper wrapped his arms around Willa, burying his face in her neck. "I'm not sure I can let her go away again."

Sean chuckled. "You will if you want her to learn to retrieve ducks."

"I guess you're right." Cooper got to his feet and scooped up his dog into his arms like a baby. "At least I have you for two months."

"Did you get my message about the cookout?" Sean asked, stroking Willa's ears.

"I did. I forgot to respond." He set the dog down. "Who's coming?"

"The whole family. Plus Winnie and maybe Brooke."

"Brooke? What's she doing in town?" Cooper asked, wondering how things ended with Sawyer.

"I'm not sure. She's staying with Jamie and Lizbet. Jamie called this morning and asked if they could bring her. Either Brooke is coming with them or none of them is coming."

Interesting, Cooper thought. He hoped they came to the cookout. He'd like to know more about Sawyer's fate.

The brothers moseyed over to the yard, watching as the dogs chased each other through the bushes. "What do we need to do to get ready for this cookout?" Cooper asked.

"Just clean up the yard. I got hamburgers and hot dogs from my supplier. The others are bringing the sides. Except Winnie, who can't cook. She's in charge of paper plates and club soda."

Cooper laughed. "She was smart to pick a chef for a boyfriend." He yawned. "I need some coffee. Want some?"

"Nah. I've already had more than my share."

"Watch Willa for me. I'll be right back," he said and jogged back toward the cottage.

While he waited for his Keurig to spew out his brew, he typed out a text to Annie. *Morning. I hope you're hanging in there okay. If you need a change of scenery, Sean and I are having a cookout for family and a few friends this afternoon to celebrate the holiday. Brooke is staying with Jamie and Lizbet. They may be coming as well. You don't have to let me know. Just show up. Starts around four. Hope to see you then.*

Cooper read his text several times before clicking send.

Stuffing his phone in his pocket, he went back outside to help his brother prepare for the cookout.

They spent much of the afternoon working in the yard. They mowed the grass, trimmed hedges, and sprayed down the furniture on the terrace.

Cooper didn't expect Annie, after everything she'd been through, to come to the cookout, nevertheless hoping she'd at least respond to his text. But with each passing hour and no word from her, his spirits tanked. Understandably, she was upset with him for not telling her the truth about Tyler and Kaylie. In time, he would make it up to her. Cooper would never give up on her. Not until he made her his bride.

Sean's girlfriend, Winnie, arrived at three thirty with a shopping bag filled with club soda, several bouquets of sunflowers, and two beef marrow dog bone treats for Emmie and Willa.

"One thing of club soda would've sufficed," Sean said, kissing her cheek as he relieved her of her burden.

Winnie was the quintessential girl next door, the perfect match for Sean, and Cooper wondered how she and Annie would get along.

Don't get ahead of yourself, Cooper, he warned himself. *Just because Annie is no longer with Tyler doesn't mean she will give you another chance. Even worse, what if she forgives Tyler?* She was really hung up on him. Would she be that stupid? His spirits tumbled toward rock bottom.

Sean and Cooper's parents, aunts, uncles, and cousins began arriving at four o'clock on the dot with side dishes—baked beans, macaroni and cheese, corn and basil salad, and a bowl of fresh melons and berries.

"You look wonderful, son." Cooper's mother turned his head from side to side. "Your haircut suits you. Is your healthy glow from the sun? Or is there a new special someone in your life?"

"The sun, I guess. I spent the weekend on Sullivan's Island."

"Did you see Annie? I heard she was down there too."

He smacked her hand away from his face. "How did you know that?"

Jackie inspected her manicured fingernails. "Heidi may have mentioned it to me. She's not very keen on this boy Annie's been seeing."

"Really? Did she say why?"

Mischief tugged at his mother's ruby-red lips. "We agree the two of you belong together."

"I wouldn't get your hopes up," Cooper said in a dejected tone as he glanced down at his phone. He was getting irritated. All weekend, he'd helped Annie cook and decorate and ice down drinks for her boyfriend's guests, while her boyfriend didn't lift a finger. And not once had she thanked Cooper for his help. Even if she was pissed off at him, she could at least respond to his text.

Jackie spotted her sisters heading inside the house. "Ooh. There's Faith and Sam. Excuse me a minute, while I go speak to them."

When his mom moved out of the way, Cooper saw Annie strolling up the driveway wearing an orange-and-white tie-dye print sundress with her honey hair dancing around her shoulders. His irritation vanished and his heart warmed.

He met her in the driveway. "Thanks for coming."

"Thanks for inviting me." She extended a casserole dish to him. "I made blueberry cobbler."

"My favorite," he said, taking the casserole.

"I remember." His puppy wandered over to greet Annie, and she knelt to pet her. "Who's this cutie-pie?"

"This is Willa. Sean and I got puppies from the same litter. There's her sister Emmie." He pointed at the second red lab puppy, who was sleeping curled up in a ball in the middle of the patio, oblivious to the commotion going on around her.

Annie straightened. "Is there somewhere we can talk? I have some things I need to get off my chest."

"Sure. Let's walk down to the dock." He retrieved two beers

from a nearby cooler and handed one to her. With Willa trotting along beside them, they cut across the lawn and walked out onto the dock.

"I owe you an apology, Coop. For a lot of things, actually. First of all, I never thanked you for all the help you gave me over the weekend. You went above and beyond the call of duty." She leaned against a piling. "I don't blame you for not telling me about Tyler and Kaylie. I probably wouldn't have believed you anyway. Even if you'd shown me the pictures. I've done a lot of thinking since I left Sullivan's Island, and I've come to some startling conclusions. I've had blinders on these past few months where Tyler is concerned."

"That happens when you're in love," Cooper said with a soft smile.

Annie sighed. "That's the thing though. I was never in love with him. I loved the idea of him. *Charleston's most eligible bachelor.* His big houses and fancy cars, the life I've always dreamed of." She shook her head in wonder. "And to think I was willing to give up my career for him."

"Heidi would never have let that happen."

"I'm not sure she could've stopped me. You know how I am when I set my mind to something."

"That staunch determination is one thing I admire most about you."

"A lot of blood, sweat, and tears went into developing that determination," she said with a reminiscent smile, as though thinking back to her childhood. "And that's the thing. At some point, my relationship with Tyler became less about the prize and more about the challenge. His mother telling me I wasn't in Tyler's league made me even more determined to prove her wrong."

Cooper's blue eyes grew wide. "Who would say such a thing to a young woman? That's downright cruel."

Annie laughed. "Yep. She said they had high standards, which

I didn't meet. And that I had nothing to offer their family. I should've taken her advice and saved myself a lot of heartache. Instead, I ran straight to Lia, thinking she'd be my ally. She's the one who came up with the idea for the surprise party. She really played me. They got a free party out of me. I'm sure it was out of control after I left."

"If it's any consolation, Lia fooled me too. I was never interested in her romantically, but I had no idea she was such a ruthless snob."

"What you said about them the other night on the dock is true. Their money has corrupted them." Annie closed the gap between them. "And that thing you said about my strong character really meant a lot to me. Even though we haven't been together for years, you have always understood me more than anyone else. Even better than I understand myself sometimes. In hindsight, I can pinpoint the exact moment I realized Tyler wasn't the right guy for me."

"Oh, yeah? When was that?"

"When I saw you across the room at the gallery opening. I knew then that my relationship with Tyler was going nowhere. I just wasn't ready to admit it yet."

Cooper's gaze shifted slightly left to where his mother was watching them from the patio. She blew him a kiss and wiggled her fingers.

When he chuckled, Annie asked, "What's so funny?"

"My mom. She's the president of your fan club."

"That's funny, because my mom is the president of yours. You realize they've been conspiring to get us together."

"I'm aware." Cooper smiled down at Annie. "I understand you need some time to get over Tyler, but when you're ready, I would love it if you'd give us another chance."

"Heidi gave me some solid advice last night. She told me I've wasted enough time. If you and I are meant to be together, we shouldn't wait another second. Do you think it's too soon after Tyler?"

Cooper's heart fluttered. "That's entirely up to you. I'm willing to wait as long as it takes for you to sort yourself out."

She pressed her finger to his lips. "I really wanted you to kiss me the other night on the dock. I wouldn't mind if you kissed me now."

Cooper hooked an arm around her, pulling her close and kissing her hard on the lips, not caring who saw them.

When the kiss ended, Annie whispered, "I don't remember the chemistry between us being so . . ."

"So strong?" he suggested.

"I was going to say *hot*," Annie said, her mouth close to his.

"Maybe that's because we've missed each other more than we realized, and we have a lot of kissing to do to make up for lost time." He covered her face in kisses—forehead, cheeks, and chin—before finally planting a peck on her lips. "I promise to make you happy, Annie. I'll buy you whatever you want. Big house, fancy car, you name it."

"My wish list has shortened dramatically. All I want is a loving home filled with children and a husband who supports my career."

"That goes without saying."

Her tone grew serious. "My career is in Charleston, Cooper. I know how much you enjoy your life down here."

"Funny you should mention that. I'm taking on a business partner. We're forming a web design firm that we hope will go national. We've agreed our headquarters should be in Charleston."

"Really?" Annie said, bouncing on her toes.

"Really. Moss Creek will always be here whenever I . . . whenever *we* need to get away. We're gonna have a beautiful life together, Annie."

"I can hardly wait." Placing a hand on his neck, Annie pulled him close, pressing her lips to his.

thirty-five
brooke

Brooke didn't argue when Jamie suggested they take his boat to the cookout. Being on the water gave her a sense of peace. As they approached the dock, they spotted Annie and Cooper kissing. Jamie finger-whistled while Brooke and Lizbet let out loud cheers.

Annie gave Brooke a hand off the boat and pulled her in for a hug. "You look great. How're you feeling?"

Brooke smiled, her blue eyes twinkling. "Much better today. Lizbet let me sleep until noon and then cooked me a fabulous brunch. The cramping and spotting have stopped." She pinched Annie's cheek. "Look at you all rosy-cheeked. What a difference a day makes for both of us. What happened with you and Tyler?"

"Turns out he was sleeping with Kaylie. You missed the fireworks. Cooper gave him two black eyes."

Brooke laughed out loud. "Good for him! I can't think of a more deserving jerk." She glanced over at Cooper as he helped Jamie tie up the boat. "Everyone knows you and Cooper belong together, anyway."

Annie beamed. "I hope so. Being with him certainly feels right."

The guys finished tying up the boat, and the five of them stood in a circle around the puppy, rubbing her belly and rolling the tennis ball for her. Annie looped her arms through Jamie's and Lizbet's. "I have a confession to make. I hope you're not mad, but I told Cooper about the babies. I had to tell him something after he overheard me rip into Grady for being a jerk to Brooke."

"That's fine." Lizbet wagged her finger at Cooper. "But it's top secret for now. Please don't say anything to anyone."

"I won't. I promise. Not even Sean. I'm super excited for all three of you." Cooper offered Jamie a high five and gave Lizbet and Brook hugs.

Brooke noticed Eli standing alone on the lawn. "Excuse me a minute. I need to speak to Eli about something," she said and strolled up the dock. When Eli had texted earlier with an update on Sawyer, they'd agreed to talk in person at the cookout.

Eli greeted her with a kiss on the cheek. "Your color has returned. Are you feeling better?"

"Much better. Thank you. Hopefully, we're out of the woods. Lizbet and Jamie have been taking excellent care of me."

Eli gave her a curt nod. "As they should." Taking her by the arm, he led Brooke out of earshot of the small group gathered on the patio. "I spoke with my detective friend in Charleston. Sawyer's father bailed her out of jail this morning. She's flying back to California with him. He's arranged for her to be admitted to a mental hospital where she'll receive a complete psychiatric evaluation."

Brooke's expression hardened. "Right. So he can use the insanity defense to get her off attempted murder charges."

"In this case, an insanity plea is justified. But I don't think you have anything to worry about, Brooke. According to the detective, her father was very concerned about your well-being. He was appalled by his daughter's behavior, and he personally guaranteed she would never bother you again."

Brooke let out a deep breath. "That makes me feel better. Her father is an honorable guy. He means what he says." She smiled at Eli. "I don't know how to thank you for all you've done."

Eli squeezed her arm. "I'm here for you, Brooke. If you need anything at all. Jamie's mother would never forgive me if I let something bad happen to her grandbabies."

Brooke rubbed her belly. "Don't worry. I will take excellent care of them."

They parted ways, and Brooke headed to a nearby cooler for a bottled water. When she heard someone calling her name, she looked around and spotted Grady waving at her from the driveway. She grabbed two waters and went to join him.

"What're you doing here?" she asked, handing him a water.

"I've been texting with Lizbet. She told me where to find you. I asked her not to say anything. I wanted to be the one to tell you."

Excitement flickered in her chest. "Tell me what? Is this about the house?"

"Yes! You won the bid, Brooke. You are now the proud owner of a pink house."

"Yippee! That's so awesome. I can't believe it." She victory-danced in a circle around him, chanting, "I own a pink house. I own a pink house."

Laughing, Grady asked, "Does this mean you're not mad at me anymore?"

Brooke froze. "Nope. I'm still furious with you. Correction, I'm disappointed in you. Thanks to you and Sawyer, I almost miscarried."

"What? I knew nothing about that." His eyes dropped to her stomach. "Is the baby okay?"

"Babies," she corrected him. "Lizbet and Jamie are having twins. They appear to be fine. For now. But I'm eliminating all the stress from my life. Which includes you. Thanks for telling me about the house." Spinning around, she stomped off across the yard toward the dock.

Grady caught up to her, taking her by the elbow to stop her. "Please, Brooke! Hear me out. I was wrong about so many things. You have to admit it's a lot—Sawyer stalking you and you being pregnant with your sister's baby. I felt overwhelmed, and I convinced myself I didn't need all the drama. But I've been miserable these last twenty-four hours. I've never felt so bad about myself, so *disappointed* in myself. I owe you a huge apology. I'm sorry, Brooke. Will you forgive me?"

His dejected face pulled at her heartstrings. "Eventually. This wasn't our first fight. And I doubt it will be our last."

Grady appeared relieved. "Does that mean we can start over?" he asked in a hopeful tone. "I'd love it if we could go back to being friends."

Brooke stared down at the ground. "I don't think I can be just friends, Grady. I'm in love with you. I realize my timing is rotten. Maybe it's too soon after Sawyer. Maybe you're my rebound person. Ugh. There are so many maybes in this situation."

He lifted her chin. "I told you on the beach, I'm in love with you too. I have been since the first day of our freshman year in high school."

She sniffled as tears blurred her vision. "The pregnancy complicates things. I'm gonna get fat and ugly."

Grady pulled her into his arms. "We'll work through those complications. And you could never be ugly. You're the most beautiful person I know, inside and out."

Brooke pushed him away. "But what will you tell your family and friends? This isn't a simple situation to explain."

Grady shrugged. "Who cares what my family and friends think?"

She swiped at her eyes. "Maybe we should put our feelings on hold until after the babies come in April. We'll have an Annie and Sam meeting on top of the Empire State Building like in *Sleepless in Seattle*," she smiled at him through her tears.

"I'm sorry, but there's no way I can put my feelings for you on hold for that long. Especially now that I know you feel the same about me." He flashed her a dimpled grin. "We'll think of this pregnancy as a warm-up for when we have our own kids."

Fresh tears streamed down her face. This was the old Grady, her Grady, the boy who had been her best friend throughout high school and the man she'd fallen in love with these past few weeks. She placed a hand on his cheek. "You realize I've never been with a man before."

He took her hand and kissed her palm. "I'm thrilled to have the honor. And I promise, when that time comes, I will make our lovemaking special. For you and for me."

———

Hours later, after all the parents had left, Brooke and Grady sat in a circle on the patio with Sean and Winnie, Annie and Cooper, and Jamie and Lizbet. Brooke couldn't stop talking about her pink house.

"I can't wait to see it," Annie said. "When do you close?"

"In three weeks. If Liz and Jamie will have me, I'll stay in Prospect with them and work remotely until then."

Lizbet smiled at her. "You may stay as long as you like."

"Thank you." Brooke's eyes fell to the dogs at their feet. "Lizbet and I are putting the Tradd Street house on the market soon. While we know it's the right decision for us, it will be a difficult move, both mentally and physically."

"I'm sure. Your family has lived there for three generations. But another couple with young children will snatch it right up." Annie rested her head on Cooper's shoulder. "They will love every minute of living in that house. And they'll make new memories to carry with them forever."

Lizbet locked eyes with Brooke. "Well said."

Brooke chuckled. "We'd better warn the new buyers . . . if they neglect Mama's roses, she'll come back to haunt them."

The small group burst into laughter, the sound warming her heart. She finally felt at peace. Sawyer was gone for good, and her path to the future was clear.

Leaving her mama's ghost behind would be bittersweet. While she still didn't believe in ghosts, there was no other practical explanation for the strange events she'd recently encountered in the house. The ones she couldn't attribute to Sawyer like the dumbbell she nearly tripped over and the For Sale sign in the window. She would be unburdened as she started fresh in her new home with the new man in her life. *Man*. Brooke Horne was entering a heterosexual relationship. Six months ago, she never would have thought it possible.

Brooke reached for Grady's hand. He wasn't any man. He was Grady, her person. Her soulmate. Her best friend.

I hope you've enjoyed *Weekend on Sullivan's Island*. Please consider leaving an honest review at your favorite online retailers and book-related social media platforms. Recommendations from like-minded readers helps other readers discover new authors and titles. If you're looking for more action-packed Southern family drama, you might consider my latest stand alone novel, *Scent of Magnolia* or my newest series. Virginia Vineyards is a family saga featuring the Love family with characters you'll love and those you'll love to hate.

acknowledgments

I'm forever indebted to the many people who help bring a project to fruition. My editor, Pat Peters. My cover designer, the hard-working folks at Damonza.com. My beta readers: Alison Fauls, Anne Wolters, Laura Glenn, Jan Klein, Lisa Hudson, Lori Walton, Kathy Sinclair, Jenelle Rodenbaugh, Rachel Story, Jennie Trovinger, and Amy Connolley. Last, but certainly not least, are my select group of advanced readers who are diligent about sharing their advanced reviews prior to releases.

I'm blessed to have many supportive people in my life who offer the encouragement I need to continue my pursuit of writing. Love and thanks to my family—my mother, Joanne; my husband, Ted; and my amazing children, Cameron and Ned.

Most of all, I'm grateful to my wonderful readers for their love of women's fiction. I love hearing from you. Feel free to shoot me an email at ashleyhfarley@gmail.com or stop by my website at ashleyfarley.com for more information about my characters and upcoming releases. Don't forget to sign up for my newsletter. Your subscription will grant you exclusive content, sneak previews, and special giveaways.

about the author

Ashley Farley writes books about women for women. Her characters are mothers, daughters, sisters, and wives facing real-life issues. Her bestselling Sweeney Sisters series has touched the lives of many.

Ashley is a wife and mother of two young adult children. While she's lived in Richmond, Virginia, for the past twenty-one years, a piece of her heart remains in the salty marshes of the South Carolina Lowcountry, where she still calls home. Through the eyes of her characters, she captures the moss-draped trees, delectable cuisine, and kindhearted folk with lazy drawls that make the area so unique.

Ashley loves to hear from her readers. Visit Ashley's website @ ashleyfarley.com

Get free exclusive content by signing up for her newsletter @ ashleyfarley.com/newsletter-signup/

Made in United States
North Haven, CT
04 May 2024

52104483R00159